To Raleigh
and John Boad
friends.
well best
wishes
Robert

THE LAST CALIFÓRNIO

ROBERT SANÁBRIA

ParaguasBooks

Published by Paraguas Books
www.paraguasbooks.com
© Robert Sanábria, 2011

This novel is a work of fiction. All characters and incidents are the author's fictional creations. Any resemblance to actual people, places, or events is strictly coincidental.

ISBN 978-0-9565786-5-5

Cover design: Nicole E. Kraft

All rights reserved. This book may not be reproduced, resold, or otherwise circulated without prior written consent from the publisher. No part of this book may be scanned, uploaded, or distributed electronically without the publisher's permission.

Acknowledgments

I owe a debt of gratitude to my writers group of many years, who helped me see more clearly where I thought I was going with the story: Iain Baird, Carlos Derr, Richard Haddock, Kathy Lyons, Val Patterson, and Claude Wilson. I owe an equally great debt to my friend and writer John Rolphe Gardiner, who guided me in clearing away the underbrush of my words.

Dedication

This book is dedicated to my wife, Sherry Zvares Sanábria, whose support and unfailing encouragement allowed me to complete what I so often was on the verge of abandoning.

1

Water lapped deceptively at the shore. Just steps from the bank it became a torrent, rushing and rain-swollen, roaring with terrifying life. Gar waded in with the others. Unseen flotsam slammed into his body. The relentless flow, chest high, pulled at him with an eager grip. His feet felt for purchase on the uneven trash-littered river bottom. Halfway across, where the channel ran deepest, he stumbled. Swamped by a wave, he had the sensation of being plunged into a black hole. A mouthful of foul river water left him choking and retching, spitting to get rid of the fetid taste.

Up ahead, Mercúrio, the *coyote*, heedless of Gar's desperate gagging, hissed "¡Silencio!" The seven other crossers, inky silhouettes in the black night, barely noticed Gar's agony. Each man, backpack held aloft, was immersed in his own struggle to navigate the 900 feet of the churning Rio Grande.

Gar had crossed this river before. Then, clothes and feet dry, it was over a bridge, smiling officials on both sides of the border, waving his passage through. That time, it wasn't survival on his mind, but life's professional and personal pleasures. He remembered that moment now, wondering whether he'd even live to make it to the other side.

They all feared it, even half expected it. Still, when it happened the shock was no less. Only minutes into the swirling waters, the shortest of the crossers, the man the others called Ignacio, became caught in the branches of a floating tree and was swept away like jetsam. His anguished cry, barely heard above the deafening furor of the water, sent a shudder through Gar. Some crossers registered the man's plight, but no one turned to help; every man fended for himself.

They strained onward, the silence occasionally broken by muttered curses after someone stepped in a hole or tripped over something. Afraid of losing the *coyote*, they stayed in a cluster, fighting to remain upright and trying not to stumble into each other.

After a seeming eternity, the group emerged on the opposite shore near Laredo, Texas, the twin of Nuevo Laredo on the Mexican side. Mercúrio hesitated a moment, found the path he was looking for and set off at a steady jog, with Gar and the others close behind.

They moved away from the river quickly, along one of the myriad trails through a tangle of mesquite, whitethorn, and cactus. The cool spring air intensified the chill from wearing soaked clothes, and the pelting rain reduced Gar's focus to the man in front of him. Despite the dampness, they found relief in the downpour, which muffled the shushing of sneakers through buffalo grass and the rasping of labored breathing. It would also wash away their footprints.

More curses and cries of pain punctuated their progress as unseen cactus spines penetrated trousers or tore at unprotected hands and arms. Once, when his ankle twisted, Gar unthinkingly grabbed for balance at what turned out to be a small cactus, and needles bristled his left hand. The new pain distracted him for only a moment.

Rain and darkness heightened fear and discomfort. Their cover also reduced the chances of being spotted by the border patrol's ground and helicopter missions with their low-light cameras, night-vision devices, and thermal-imaging scopes. Mercúrio warned that the riverbank was littered with seismic sensors and rushed the group into the brush to the north, with luck before patrols could respond. His zigzagging increased the distance but also avoided the network of raked sand traps the patrol used to track sneaker-sole markings.

Mercúrio's $2,000 fee seemed exorbitant, but Gar could see that without him they'd quickly have lost their way through the labyrinth of crisscrossing trails, the telltale evidence of the thousands who'd gone before them.

Jog-walking for what felt like hours without stopping, the fast pace at least warmed and kept his muscles from stiffening. The backpack chafed heavily on his shoulders, the dull ache vying for attention with the sharper pain of blisters, the penalty of new sneakers—his runner's endurance didn't matter much at all. Sitting at a desk for hours at a stretch while working at a city newspaper hadn't prepared him for this, either. Whatever his limitations, there could be no stopping or turning back. His Indian companions, though shorter, were better suited to the test.

On the brink of exhaustion, Gar finally saw the *coyote* raise a hand to halt the group. Mercúrio went on alone, leaving them crouched in place, steam from their overheated bodies and hot breath rising into an eerie cloud above them. Three of his companions, dark-skinned men from Oaxaca, eyed Gar as they whispered among themselves in Nahautl. Maybe it meant nothing, but he felt their interest at his back. Then Mercúrio was signaling for their advance. Gar's thought fled with their move to a large van hidden in the scrub-oak beside a rutted gravel road.

"Your ride," Mercúrio whispered, standing beside the van's open side door. "Now, *por favór*, the rest of my payment."

Each man counted out the *coyote*'s due and, throwing luggage and packs into the compartment behind the back seat, climbed in. After a few words with the man at the wheel, Mercúrio disappeared into the night. With the soft click of the side door as it closed, the driver started the engine. He pulled the van onto the narrow road and drove slowly for some distance with the headlights off.

On the way at last, Gar thought. The *coyote* had described the journey as effortless. Except for the physical strain, up to now it had been. Gar barely noticed the smell of wet hair and sweaty bodies filling the van. He leaned back in the seat feeling as if the last of his strength had drained away. His body begged for sleep, and he shifted to get comfortable even as he began to shiver in his soaked clothing. Others beside and behind him already snored softly, lulled by exhaustion and the *whap whap* of the windshield wipers.

To the distant east the first bands of light streaked the horizon. Reaching the main road, the driver steered onto it heading north, turned on the van's headlights and picked up speed. Once beyond Laredo, the van headed northwest on Route 83 to avoid the heavier traffic and highway patrols on the interstate.

Gar struggled to keep from dozing off, a premonition warning to make sure the driver made the turn. Moments later, alarm needled his scalp as the speeding vehicle flashed by Route 83's shield-shaped road sign, its bullet riddled numbers barely legible. The van blindly roared past it. Anxious now, Gar leaned toward the driver.

"*Oye*, didn't you see the sign? You missed the turnoff. Go back."

The driver said nothing, his eyes fixed on the roadway ahead. Gar waited, thinking the driver might be looking for a place to turn around. But he drove on at high speed, clearly with no intention of going back. Gar felt a shudder of panic as each minute ticked past, taking them farther away from the turnoff.

"Hey, driver," Gar tapped him on the shoulder, "didn't you hear? You passed..."

Before he could finish, the passenger in the front seat, a wiry man the others called Cordero, turned around to speak.

"*Hombre*, I been watching you. You're nobody special. You don't tell us where to go. Understand? We go through San Antonio to New York."

"No, no, wait, you can't do that. I paid to be taken..."

The man then turned to the driver.

"Pull off at the next exit." As he spoke, Cordero drew a pistol from under his jacket. Minutes later the van left the highway and pulled onto the shoulder of a deserted side road. A faded and battered sign advertised a cafe in the tiny village of Artesia Wells.

"Get out," Cordero ordered.

"Wait, you can't..."

"Get out, now!" His voice was a deadly calm. "You," he told the men beside Gar, "get out and watch him."

Disbelieving that this could be happening, Gar hesitated. As the gunman dismounted the others brusquely pushed him from the van.

"Put your hands on your head," Cordero growled. To the others, switching rapidly between Spanish and Nahuatl, he directed, "See what he's got."

It was common knowledge, and Gar should have remembered, that the border was full of people without scruples; hardly a day passed without someone getting robbed or killed. For a fleeting moment he thought how foolish he'd been to leave his father's pistol behind.

As they searched him, Gar realized that hiring the *coyote* at the border was an even bigger mistake. Time short and anxiety high, he'd failed to check him out first. As for the others in the group, he hadn't bothered to learn beforehand who they might be, concerned only that none of them be hampered with women or children. Now these failings had put him in a very bad spot. He saw, too, that his educated, university-honed speech, combined with an ingrained sense of superiority over whom he assumed were simple laborers or farmers, had only set him apart, marked him as a target.

"*Bueno, no hay problema.*" Gar shrugged and raised his hands higher as if giving in. "OK, I misunderstood the *coyote*. We'll go to San Antonio, like you say. San Antonio is no problem." His attempt to bargain was useless.

The men patted him down then took his money belt, passport, and watch, everything of value. Gar could only glare at Cordero and shake his head, incredulous. He cursed himself for not keeping some money in his shoes.

"*¡Pinche bastardos!*" Gar exploded. He'd often read of illegals turning on each other, even that something like this could've been planned. Had he been set up?

"Quiet!" Cordero looked hard at Gar for a moment as if debating about shooting him on the spot. "Get your stuff out of the van."

Seething, Gar opened the cargo door, rummaged around and pulled his backpack and belted canteen from the compartment.

"Drop them," Cordero ordered. To the others he said, "Open the pack and dump the contents on the ground. See what he's got."

With a foot, Cordero sifted through Gar's few belongings. Moments later, he shook his head, indicating there was nothing worth taking. With a jerk of his head toward the van, the gunman ordered the others to close the cargo door.

"You want to go to Carrizo Springs?" Cordero looked at Gar with a malicious grin. "It's that way," he motioned with the pistol. "Start walking."

Looking was Gar's next mistake. A blinding flash exploded in his head, the pain only slightly more acute than his surprise. A well-placed kick buckled his knees and in the next instant, he was face down in the dirt. The blows came more rapidly as the men—Gar couldn't tell how many—kicked repeatedly at his head, back, and midsection. He tasted blood. Helpless to defend himself, he curled into a fetal position, arms protecting his head. There was a last kick in the kidneys, but Gar was so far gone he barely felt it.

Fifteen minutes later, he opened his eyes.

The pain was a constant throb. Trembling from the receding adrenaline rush, shock began to wear off, replaced by permeating aching. He tried not to breathe too deeply, as every intake was excruciating. It took several minutes for him to find the strength to push himself up onto his knees. He made an examination of his torso and limbs, and then struggled to his feet to collect his canteen and the scattered contents of his backpack.

When he could think more clearly, he wasn't all that surprised that his *paisanos* attacked him. They were just desperate, desperate enough to turn on each other.

Aware of his surroundings for the first time, he surveyed the cluster of unpainted board and concrete-block houses. Windows from a few showed light, but most were dark, their occupants still sleeping. Maybe it was they whom the gunman had been afraid of rousing, why he hadn't been shot. Gar probably owed them his life.

At least the rain had stopped. Aching and stiff, he began a westward march.

Sleeping in culverts or makeshift brush shelters during daylight and walking at night, Gars reached Route 83 and the ragged little village of Caterina after two days. He guessed that Carrizo Springs was still another two night's walk away. Behind him, a veil of salmon-colored clouds bled across the sky, their streaks piercing the dark horizon of the desolate Texas prairie.

It was dawn, and in a few hours he'd have to find another place to hide for the day. The sparsely treed terrain left him vulnerable to discovery by police or border patrols and made capture or death the more likely outcomes of his misguided adventure. His hands and knees were raw from dropping to the ground each time a vehicle approached. His stomach growled from emptiness and he berated himself for not packing more food. He'd eaten everything, had almost no water and no money. It struck him that he couldn't even prove his identity.

Along with the pain of blistered feet and calves stabbed with cactus needles, Gar reflected on how quickly the good beginning had gone bad. The vast prairie stretched ahead, endless. With no landmarks anywhere, everything looked the same, the horizon unbroken in all directions. He could only guess at how far he had yet to go. As for getting to Los Angeles, the city might as well be on another planet.

The moon had set. The stars shone like pinpricks of light in a black bowl. It occurred to Gar that those stars in the inky sky were neither Mexican nor American. The division only existed in the minds of the men of their two countries who'd fought over controlling land.

Stumbling on rocks, fearful of snakes, he trudged on. Only the crunch of his shoes along the shoulder and the chirp of insects broke the stillness. Abruptly silent at his approach, they resumed their night song after he passed. At times it was so quiet his thoughts seemed to echo in his head. Then there was his own lurking fear. Drained and aching, Gar once again allowed the awareness that little in his life had prepared his mind or body for a journey like this.

The thought of dying in this foreign wasteland loomed large, made him shudder. He tried not to think about how he'd gotten into this madness.

It all came rushing back anyway.

2

Mexico City, five months earlier

Like a slap in the face the future caught up with Gar. In his five years as a reporter with *El Observador Diario,* he had seen his share of murders, fatal accidents, the whole range of annihilation and human folly.

Being summoned to the Metro editor's office by a colleague only mildly surprised him. On this ordinary late winter morning he found himself facing his harried somber-faced editor looking back at him over the top of his glasses.

"Montalvo, there's been a shooting. No details yet."

Gar frowned at him. "A shooting?"

"Yes, at your home. You'd better go."

"At my home? What are you saying?" But that was crazy. Had someone shot his parents? Had they shot each other? For a second or two he stood there, then reached for the phone on the editor's desk.

"No, just go," the editor said. "Carlos is on it." After a pause he added, "I... I'm sorry."

The simple "sorry" was all Gar could've expected, and he was grateful for the condolence. There was probably no good way to deliver that kind of news. Besides, his editor had a hard time expressing sympathy. Gar lost his concentration for the unfinished story he had been working on at his computer.

Bloody images flooded his mind. *¡Ándale! ¡Ándale!* He hurried the aged Volkswagen through the honking mid-morning crush of Mexico City traffic. The clogged road stretched interminably. When he finally turned onto his home's tree-shaded street, his terror became reality. A crowd of the curious, along with eager media crews, milled about the high-walled patio in front of the house, all craning for a glimpse inside.

Police vehicles and ambulances blocked the street, their flashing red and blue lights still twirling when Gar pulled up.

"*¡Ay diós!*" Gar muttered. A wave of nausea rose from his stomach to his throat. He swallowed hard to stop the burning. Policemen at the gate had their hands full holding back the crowd. With dread, he scanned for a parking space and, finding none, abandoned the Volkswagen front-first on the sidewalk in a gap between two cars. Breathless, he ran toward the crowd.

"Let me through!" He elbowed and pushed. "Let me through, damn you. This is my home."

Reporters converged on Gar, each trying to out-shout the other with questions. Gar saw and ignored his colleague Carlos, who called out to him. After a quick ID check, the police helped him make a path through the crowd. In the courtyard, Gar stared at the gaping front door of the white stucco building. He held back for a moment then dashed for the landing, taking the three steps to the threshold in one stride.

The devastation inside left him gasping. Police, who seemed to fll the room, picked through the litter of overturned furniture, the dumped contents of cabinet drawers, and knocked-over lamps. Paintings hanging askew or left on the floor leaning against the walls completed the picture of chaos.

"*¡Jesucristo!* My parents, where are they?" He blurted at everyone and no one as he took in the scene of destruction.

A short broad man turned to face him. "Who're you?" he demanded in a tobacco-beaten voice.

"Gar Montalvo," he managed, choking on his voice. "This is my home."

The man stared hard at him then flashed credentials. "Lieutenant Ramírez."

Gar ignored him and started toward the front door of the house.

"Wait." Ramírez raised a hand. "You'll see them soon enough.""

"Them?" At an even six feet, Gar looked down at the lieutenant.

Ramírez nodded, black narrowed eyes continuing an intense stare from under bushy brows. His lined face and receding hairline put him somewhere in his fifties. Powerfully built, he commanded the room, his shoulder holster showing under the unbuttoned jacket of his double-breasted pinstripe.

"Your parents I assume. And an older woman, a relative or a housekeeper?"

"Oh, God." Gar shook his head and put a hand to his face. "Her, too?"

"Your father—if that's who he is, wounded in here, managed to go in there," the lieutenant indicated the study with his chin, "where he died."

Gar saw the bloody trail splattered across the tile floor.

"The others are upstairs," the Lieutenant said, less officiously. "You'll have to identify all of them. Wait here until my men finish their work." Gar saw only weariness in his swarthy face.

"But who? Why...?" he murmured. His legs went rubbery, he dropped into a chair and buried his face in his hands. Ramírez put a hand on his back.

"Gun shots. This is a quiet neighborhood. Neighbors said your father's a professor at the university. We called."

Gar nodded.

"Where were you this morning?"

"At my office. I'm a reporter with *El Observador Diario*. Someone at the university must have called."

"You live here?"

Gar shook his head. "In an apartment near the

university, Colónia Obregón."

"Any of those items missing?" He pointed to the glass-enclosed wall system filled with pre-Columbian artifacts.

Gar looked at the gaps in the rows of figurines and pottery. "I, I don't know. It's hard to say. My father collected and traded all the time."

"With?"

"Other collectors, dealers. Who do you think?" His anger didn't seem to register.

"Any of that stuff valuable?"

"It's all valuable, some pieces more than others, but none worth killing for."

"He have an inventory? How about a list of the dealers and traders?"

"In his office." Gar waved a hand without looking up.

"That can wait."

"The neighbors," Gar raised his head, "did they see anything, anyone?"

"Witnesses? No one has stepped forward, if that's what you mean. People don't like to get involved, ¿sabes? They're afraid of gunfire, they take cover."

"This," Gar motioned at the destruction in the room, "makes no sense."

"It won't until we have a motive. Entry doesn't appear to have been forced."

"You're saying my father knew the killer?"

"It's the middle of the morning. Whoever they were— the footprints show more than one person—someone let them in."

Gar looked at the lieutenant, frowning. "They kept the entrances locked." He tried to sort out what the lieutenant implied.

"A buzzer from in here unlocks the gate, right?"

"There's an intercom." Gar nodded toward the wall phone near the door.

"Like I said, your parents knew who they were or

expected them."

"Which means what?"

"They weren't after the usual stuff."

"Money, jewelry, the art?"

"Yeah, like that. If they weren't here to deal artifacts, they came for something else, maybe information. Killed your father then trashed the place searching for it. As for your mother and the older woman, well... That's unfortunate."

There was no sorting through the lieutenant's logic.

"Any idea who might have done this?" The lieutenant extracted a pack of Marlboros from a shirt pocket, flicked a cigarette into his mouth, and cupped his hands to light it.

Gar shrugged. "Any number of people, if you consider everyone he's angered."

"Angered how?"

"His writings."

"What kind of stuff?"

"Editorials about corrupt officials, ambitious politicians."

"Yeah, I see what you mean." Ramírez blew a cloud of smoke at the ceiling as he nodded. "Though if that were the case, he could've been taken out anywhere, anytime. But it happened here, and that points to something else." He looked at Gar. "Your father involved in any illegal activity?"

"Of course not." Gar glared, as if he'd tell him anything, even if knew it.

"That you know of," the lieutenant said, staring at him deadpan.

Gar looked away, refusing to consider the possibility. "Wouldn't be the first time someone has been killed for exposing corruption. I can only guess whom my father might have been..."

Not letting him finish, the lieutenant said, "Come, I want you to identify the bodies." He stubbed out his cigarette with a toe.

3

They entered the study together, the lieutenant with a steadying grip on Gar's arm. The sight of his father brought a sudden intake of breath. He could bear only the briefest look before turning away. Then he seemed to go dead inside, as if his father were a mannequin. Out of journalistic habit? He steeled himself to look again, the reporter in him taking in details. In a browning pool of blood, his father lay face up on the tiles partly hidden behind his desk. The yellow silk tie he wore plastered to his bloodstained shirtfront made an exclamation mark below the ghastly look of surprise on his face. He'd died with his eyes open.

"Looks like he went for the pistol he had in one of the drawers, leaned here for support as he faced his attackers." The lieutenant pointed at a bloody handprint on the desktop. "Couldn't get off a shot before being gunned down."

Gar felt like he could barely breathe. He yanked his arm free of the lieutenant's grasp. He'd seen a fair number of corpses, in the flesh or in crime scene photos. The deceased's eyes always disturbed him. They indicate personality and therefore lingered in his memory.

"Couldn't your people at least have closed his eyelids?" The lieutenant's face hardened, his lips compressed to an annoyed line. Without a word and careful to avoid the blood, he knelt and closed the dead man's eyes. When he stood, his expression warned of something worse in store.

Gar stared at his father, whose face could now repose in peace. He was thinking how rarely he'd seen his family as people. Growing up he never really looked at his parents closely. As a child, they loomed large and their faces were vague, as if seen through a screen. He gazed at his father now as if seeing him at last without that partition. There was no explaining his lack of feeling; he could feel only guilt now. True, his father had been demanding, even aloof. Gar had often found it convenient to be freed from his father's attention. Their lack of closeness didn't mean an absence of love, though love was rarely demonstrated. What had he expected from a prominent academic who hobnobbed with populist politicians? From everything he'd heard others say about him, his father's adoring students were inspired by his daring exposés. Some of them had gone on to prominence themselves, following in his reformer's footsteps.

Still, Gar frequently resented the way his father had treated his mother and him. There'd been one or more mistresses, hardly unusual for Mexicans. Though it always made him uncomfortable to know about them, he'd long ago decided they were a problem for his mother to work out. Her deep involvement in her own academic career might well be responsible for his father's turning elsewhere for emotional comfort, to another outlet for his passionate nature. His parents were both attractive in their late fifties, young enough to need and want a loving companionship, even if not from each other. Their shortcomings saddened him, and he tried not to dwell on them. In his own way, he loved them both.

The lack of any deep feeling in the presence of his father's remains troubled him. Maybe it was the consequence of shock, with the full reaction to come later.

"Your father was shot twice trying to defend himself," the lieutenant said, hinting admiration.

"*Hombre*, he's dead, for God's sake. What does any of that matter?" Unable to stay longer with his father's remains, he left the room, the lieutenant following.

"Then you do identify him?" The lieutenant asked as if working through a checklist.

"Damn it, of course."

SANÁBRIA

A man wearing a white smock over street clothes came from upstairs and spoke to the lieutenant, who turned to Gar.

"They're finished. We'll go up now."

"You have any doubt about who they are?" Gar asked.

"I assume nothing. Until you identify them they're the bodies of two women." The lieutenant shrugged, his voice weary. "It has to be done. Let's go."

Resigned, Gar followed. The sight of his mother would be bad enough, but seeing his beloved Alma, the family's aged housekeeper, would be unbearable.

Through the years, his career-minded parents had often left to Alma his care and much of his upbringing. Present at his birth, she was the second to hold him and throughout childhood had showered him with the love his parents didn't seem to have the time to give. It was she who'd taught him his first words beyond *mami* and *papi*, to express his wants, the names of things, and how to amuse himself. Her gentle discipline guided him in learning right from wrong and to be responsible for his actions. For that, she'd become the one person in the world he truly loved and the one he knew loved him without reservation.

The sight of his mother and Alma stunned him as they entered the floodlit bedroom.

"Oh God! Oh God!" Gar's cries were so loud the technicians stopped work to stare. He was aware of the lieutenant holding his arm and a supporting hand on his back.

His mother, still dressed in a dark green silken robe, was face down, her thick auburn hair spilled into the white rug obscuring her face. Lying face up next to her, Alma, her hair a silvery crown, appeared to have flung an arm across his mother's body in a selfless protective gesture. Dressed in her usual white uniform, she'd perhaps tried to make a human shield of herself. Their mingled blood left a long crimson island on the rug beneath them. Her eyes shut tight, Alma's lined face in death was a distorted pale-gray. Images of her loving smile from his childhood flashed through his mind. Overcome, unable to hold back, he pressed his head against the wall and wept.

The lieutenant left him alone momentarily.

"OK, we have to get on now," he murmured, nudging Gar toward the door.

"*Pinche cabrones*," Gar yelled at him. "I'll find out who did this. There'll be justice."

"Better leave it to us." The lieutenant led the way down the stairs.

4

The "incident" was the only way Gar could speak of it. In the weeks after the murders, he struggled against the stark tableau of death. For a time, after he had the house cleaned and disposed of his family's belongings, he tried to live in it. But in the end he had to move out, haunted by the bloodstained grout between the floor tiles that could not be removed.

Sleeping brought nightmares. Growing up advantaged had made an optimist of him and his devastation surreal. The murders destroyed all confidence and dispelled any lingering innocence. His journalistic training might help him think like a detached observer, but no amount of objectivity could ease pain or erase the bitterness and sense of loss. The need to settle the score drove him crazy for lack of a target.

Work, Gar's editor at *El Diario* advised, was the quickest way to regain balance and salve his suffering. He accepted the sound advice.

Weeks later, another grisly story took his attention. With a deadline approaching, the reporter in the adjacent cubicle answered his ringing phone.

"Montalvo, for you."

Gar didn't welcome the interruption, but picked up anyway.

"Señor Montalvo?"

Lieutenant Ramírez's voice was one Gar would never fail to recognize.

"I'm in Cantina Ixtapa, just up from your place on the corner."

A few keystrokes later, Gar grabbed his coat.

"Where're you going?" the editor shouted at him.

"Copyeditor's got the story."

Inside the bar's darkened interior, Ramírez sat motionless in a corner booth with his back to the wall. He nodded as their eyes met.

"You have something on my family?" Gar slid in across from him and shook his extended hand.

For a moment he just looked at Gar, unsmiling. "I've just come from the prison hospital, where I took a man's statement. He'd been shot and died of his wounds shortly after."

"Come on, man, what about it?" Before Ramírez could answer, a waiter arrived to take their order. Ramírez waved him off.

"The man was one of a pair hired to rob your parents." He leaned closer.

"So, they didn't go there to kill?"

"They made an appointment under the pretense of being collectors. But inside they demanded something else. Your father refused. They shot to wound, to make him cooperate. Instead he went for the gun in his office."

"Who were they?"

"The man who died said his partner was the shooter."

"I don't care about that. Who sent them?" The detective's pedantic manner was maddening.

"He said they were acting for someone high up in the government."

"And did he say who?"

Ramírez nodded.

"A name. Did he give you a name?"

Ramírez waited a few beats. "Ever hear of Armando Salinas Gutiérrez?"

"Minister of finance?" Gar reared back in his seat, the force of it shaking the booth. All he'd thought about for months was finding the responsible *hijo de puta*. His eyes bore into the faux woodgrain on the table.

"The same."

Gar looked up to see Ramírez studying him through half-closed eyes.

"What were they after that was so important?"

"His partner had that information." The lieutenant sat back in his seat. "A document. They didn't find it."

Gar shook his head and pounded the table. "So you'll have this Salinas bastard arrested, right?"

"I don't think so." Ramírez looked away, almost as if ashamed.

Gar gawked at him. "But you've got the evidence, or didn't you believe the man's story?"

Ramírez shook his head. "What I've got is hearsay—from a dead man, a criminal. How far do you think we'd get with that? If I even try to arrest someone like Salinas, with aspirations to be president? He'd buy off the judge. There'd be a cover-up. He'd have *me* arrested or killed."

Gar, aware that this kind of corruption wasn't new to the country's political elite, stared helplessly at the detective.

"Sorry. I can't do more." Ramírez shrugged. "At least now you know. What you do next is up to you." He paused and looked at Gar. "Be careful."

Gar's impulse was to hunt down Salinas with his father's pistol. The gun, which he set about getting trained to use, was the easy part, but did nothing to get him closer to Salinas. He knew the minister, like others in positions of power, went nowhere without bodyguards. And as time passed, Gar could not see himself as a killer.

But avenging his family's deaths remained an obsession. He could no longer sleep through the night. Awakening he knew the pain in his jaw meant he'd been grinding his teeth. He lost his appetite. Dark circles appeared around his eyes.

There might be other ways. Salinas had long been rumored to be involved with organized rackets. Gar probed for crimes involving the minister. The work paid off. Salinas was laundering money for a Mexico City drug cartel. With this information and a persistence born of pent anger, Gar gathered what should have been enough evidence to at least send Salinas to prison.

"Good work, Montalvo," his editor told him.

The compliment gave him a short boost. Before he could thank him, the editor continued.

"What you don't realize is that if the publisher and I were to allow this story to hit the street, tomorrow we'd each receive a funeral wreath. And the next day, all three of us would be dead."

Gar knew he was right. Since 2000, the number of journalists murdered in Mexico had been second only to those killed in Iraq. Yet there was no way Gar could just bury the story. If his newspaper wouldn't publish it, *The New York Times* might, under another byline.

Jorge O'Leary was the *Times*'s Mexico City bureau chief, an American Gar had known vaguely as an exchange student at university. O'Leary was almost gleeful about filing the piece as his own.

Gar was mistaken, however, in believing that exposing Salinas would lead to his arrest. The administration did nothing. Salinas remained in office and the brief scandal died a quick death, with the *Times'* story denounced as American propaganda. Gar never supposed that Salinas would strike back, and so he never learned how Salinas unearthed his authorship of the exposé. That had become clear, though, when Salinas's goons came after him. He was frightened away from work and wore out his welcome hiding out at friends' homes as they were automatically jeopardized by having him there.

Options diminishing, he sought out O'Leary.

"Jorge, you've got to help me."

"What's up?"

"The story. I don't know how he found out, but Salinas

is after me."

"No shit. So what can I do?"

"I'll have to leave the country."

"Tell me what you need. Airfare, money, or what?"

"I can't go that way. The minister's narco agents will be watching for me at the airports and borders."

"So where does that leave you?"

"What I'm saying is, I need you to help me find a *coyote*."

Dangerous as it sounded, he meant to join the thousands of illegals who crossed daily to the other side. That would make him just another *mojado*, a "wetback." It was ironic and humbling.

After helping Gar collect money and supplies for the crossing, a guilt-ridden O'Leary drove him to Nuevo Laredo on the northern border. Though farther removed from California, Gar's wanted destination, the area was without a fence and had less border patrol activity than other possible sections. Leading illegals across the Rio Grande was a thriving business there. Contacting a *coyote* was easy enough, but placing his future in the hands of one was risky.

Even once across, there would be a host of uncertainties waiting. And his plans for the other side were vague at best. The only person he knew in *el Norte* was a boyhood friend of his father's in Los Angeles. Getting there would be daunting enough. Finding him, if he was still there, a desperate hope.

5

Texas

The distant sound of an approaching motor vehicle this time raised more hope than fear, clearing his mind. Any car or truck meant potential danger but this one was a relief. He was no mechanic, but even he could tell that its engine was laboring. The border patrol wouldn't have a vehicle that sounded so ailing.

The *coyote* had warned about rednecks: "Doesn't matter who you are or where you come from. To them you're all Mexicans and they don't like you. They think it's a sport chasing down *mojados* like you. If they catch you, you'll be lucky if you're only beaten and robbed." Should he chance trying for a ride? After walking nights, hiding in culverts and ditches during the day, he was exhausted. Now without food or water, did he have a choice? If he didn't risk catching a ride he might never make it.

Bearing down on him through the darkness like Cyclops, the light of a single headlamp grew larger, the vehicle rattling its parts, engine complaining.

With the distance narrowing, he had to decide: should he stand his ground and pray that it wasn't police or the border patrol? Or worse, what if they were rednecks? He had only a flashlight for a weapon; no telling what they might have. He gritted his teeth and ran to the road's edge, waving the flashlight and afraid the driver would pass him by.

In a small cloud of dust, a rusted-green Toyota pickup clanked to a stop on the shoulder.

SANÁBRIA

"Where you headed, buddy?" The driver leaned across to the open passenger-side window. His English had the accented hint of Spanish.

"Los Angeles," Gar said in the best accent he could muster. It didn't fool the driver, whose face split with a smile.

"Ah, a *paisano*. You're a long way from there, buddy. Throw your stuff in back and hop aboard."

Gar threw his backpack into the truck bed and climbed in. Underway, the driver glanced at him sidelong.

"The hell you doing alone way out here, man? This ain't no place to be traveling solo any time, especially on foot."

Gar parked his hat on a knee and ran a hand through his hair, looking for an answer.

"So, where you from?"

"Uh, Laredo."

"Yeah?" The driver grinned, his shiny teeth reflecting the greenish glow of the dashboard instruments. His tone, both amused and accusing, hung in the air for a moment. "Hey, look man, relax. I don't give a shit who you are or where you come from, OK? It's hard enough just getting along with the *gabachos* here without us hassling each other, too."

The truck's clamor made talking difficult. Gar preferred silence, but the driver seemed starved for conversation.

"Name's Fausto, what's yours?"

"Gar."

"That short for somethin'?"

"That's all. Just Gar. You have water?"

"Behind the seat."

Gar unscrewed the cap on a large plastic bottle and, with both hands holding it, tilted back his head and gulped. Water spilled from the corners of his mouth and dribbled down his shirt. Finished, he gasped.

"On the road awhile, huh?" Fausto grinned, amused by the desperate display of thirst.

"Thanks." Still panting, Gar replaced the bottle.

Fausto, on the lean side, looked about the same age and height as Gar. Both had shoulder-length hair, full droopy Zapata mustaches, and a week's growth of beard. There the resemblance stopped. Fausto's dark, bushy-browed face wasn't unlike the moon's surface—pockmarked with scars. His black hair was stiff from going unwashed for too long. Surprisingly, he didn't smell like someone with bad hygiene. Or did Gar's own ripeness leave him unable to notice? A rosary with crucifix hung from the stem of the rear-view mirror, swinging over a statuette of the Virgin of Guadalupe anchored to the dashboard. To protect the driver, he wondered, or to keep the old pickup rolling? In the truck bed, Gar had seen a jumble of tools and bundles.

"How far are you going?" Gar asked, staring ahead at the oval of pavement lit by the lone headlamp.

"Got a job pickin' at an irrigation farm a few miles up the road beyond Del Rio."

Mierda, Gar thought, another town near the border river, well within patrol territory. If they were stopped he'd be in trouble.

"Is that what you do?" Gar asked, keeping the focus off him. The man's large, gnarled hands marked him as a farm hand or a laborer of some kind.

"Off and on. Picking's seasonal. Off-season I'm a mechanic." He waited a beat, and then brightened. "Hey man, you lookin' for work? I know the crew chief at this farm up ahead, I could talk to him."

"Uh, what's there to pick now?"

"Onions. After that cabbage, and then something else. Anyway, you could work steady into the summer, if you wanted."

"Stoop labor?" The thought of crop picking made him cringe.

"Man, you got that right. It ain't easy and the pay ain't much either. To make out you got to work like hell. Can't even stop to piss. Men and women do it right where they stand. No offense, buddy, "he said, glancing at Gar's hands, "you don't look the type for heavy labor. But if you wanna work..."

Fausto's words suddenly broke off. He looked up at the rear-view mirror. "Oh shit! Someone's on our ass!"

"What?" Gar reacted to the alarm in his voice.

"Truck right behind us, riding our tail. Could be fucking rednecks out looking to have a little fun. No way to outrun them in this pile of junk."

As he spoke, a red pickup with an extended cab roared alongside, keeping pace. Menacing faces leered. In the gray morning light Gar counted four men, two of them in back, asleep.

"Probably on the way home from partying. Maybe still drunk." Fausto spoke without turning, a quaver in his voice.

At that moment the man on the passenger side of the front seat, teeth bared, leaned from the window and motioned at them.

"Hey, you fuckin' Beaners, pull over." A voice distorted in the wind. "Pull over!" The man yelled again, a finger jabbing the air, pointing to the shoulder of the road. Fausto held his speed, looking straight ahead.

Gar's adrenaline pumped. *¡Chinga!* They're as bad as *ladrones*, highway robbers in Mexico, he thought.

Fausto refused to give ground, but the driver in the other vehicle was swerving towards them and forcing them over, closer with each pass. His scalp popping sweat, Gar took in the red pickup's roll bar, chrome rims, and running lights. The driver wouldn't want to damage it by ramming them. Wishful thinking.

"Just playing games," Fausto said, talking from the corner of his mouth, sounding confident. But as he spoke his right hand went from his lips to the dashboard, a fingertip touching the Virgin. A religious cynic, Gar held back an impulse to do the same.

After another feint at them, the other truck roared off ahead. As it pulled away Gar shuddered at the sight of two baseball bats hanging in its gun rack.

"Told you they were jes' playin' games." Fausto exhaled in relief. "Happens all the time."

"Does it?" The encounter left Gar breathless and trembling.

"They really like to go after illegals—the wets, they call them." He looked at Gar for a reaction.

"Why?"

"They think the country's bein' overrun with Mexicans."

"It's not only Mexicans who cross." Gar tried not to sound defensive. He thought of the men who'd beaten and robbed him.

"Doesn't matter. To them all Latinos are Mexicans. Anyway, they think Latinos are taking over in some parts of the country. Word's out illegals gotta be stopped. They're building towers, miles of border walls, and fences. Around here some of these assholes think it's open season, like they've got a license to go after them. No telling how many are killed or die along the way."

"It's that bad?"

"Bet your ass. Bad enough the country's gone nuts over terrorists."

"Since the attacks on the World Trade Center?"

"Starting with that. But none of them were Latino. If they had been, we'd really be up shit creek, us along with the Arabs."

They rode in silence for a few minutes. Fausto picked up where he left off.

"Strange thing is, the poor bastards who cross on foot only do it to work and send money back. People here need them to work and still hate them for being here. You figure it out. Now for a lot of reasons hate crimes against Latinos are way up. There's a lot of confusion about the whole mess."

Still uneasy, Gar settled back in the seat, his breathing

back to normal. In the graying light the landscape had changed, the truck laboring harder as it made its way through a series of low-lying hills. For a while they seemed to have exhausted conversation, for which Gar was grateful. The drone of the engine made him drowsy and he gave up trying to stay awake. Cresting a promontory, they began a descent. A yell from Fausto pulled Gar awake.

"What the fuck? Where did those assholes come from?"

The red truck reappeared as if from nowhere, again keeping pace alongside them. Gar felt the dull knot of dread return to his gut.

"Sonsabitches must've been backed into a fire break waiting for us to catch up!" Fausto's eyes bulged.

Gar didn't need to understand his words to know that this time they meant to force them off the road. The big truck pressed so close, Fausto could almost touch it.

The shoulders on either side of the road were narrow, with the one on the left bordered by a cut in the hillside, the rocky outcroppings making a sharp jagged wall. The slender shoulder on the right, with no guardrail, dropped steeply.

¡Ay, Chihuahua! They'll force us into the ditch, Gar thought. Fausto, leaning white-knuckled over the steering wheel, must have been thinking the same. If they veered into the ditch, Gar's side of the truck would likely hit first and he'd be crushed between Fausto and the door. His thought was to jump clear before the truck went over the edge.

The driver of the pickup continued to press them, mindless now of any damage to his vehicle.

"Get over there next to the door. You might have to jump." Fausto's eyes darted from one shoulder to the other as if calculating which threatened the lesser danger, or whether to stop.

Gar had already moved, wondering how they'd survive if they stopped. He saw now that the rednecks were determined to have at them one way or another.

With a shuddering thump, the larger truck's bumper hit

the Toyota's front fender, which was followed in an instant by a grinding screech of metal on metal. The Toyota's front end bounced away at impact, the back side panel slamming against the larger truck's body, righting theirs. But in the next instant they hit the shoulder. The Toyota's front wheels dug into the sand and twisted crazily, leaving Fausto fighting for control.

Gar's shoulder slammed into the door and he was launched into the void. He pulled his knees to his chest and covered his head with his arms, tensing for impact. His balled form crashed through the brush lining the ditch. He scarcely noticed the tangle pulling at his hair, lashing his face and hands before he hit bottom. Beyond him the careening Toyota plunged into the deeper trench. With a dull crunch it came to rest in a swirl of dust.

On the roadway above, the throaty roar of the rednecks' pickup faded away in the morning calm.

Gar was badly bruised and covered with dirt and brambles, but the brush had broken his fall. For a few moments, he lay stunned. He began to tremble and hurt all over. There was a bloody gash on his left calf but it would have to wait. His fingers came away blood-red after touching his face. Otherwise he seemed to be intact.

He scrambled to solid ground and struggled through the clinging bushy snarl to Fausto. The truck was upright, but the jammed driver's door was stuck fast. Forcing his way back through the tangle he came precious minutes later to the passenger side. A foot braced on the truck's body and pulling with both hands, he managed to yank open the door—but too late to help Fausto. His head had traveled through the shattered windshield, and his neck had twisted at a grotesque angle. His blood had made an abstract pattern of rivulets on the truck's hood. Gar felt for a pulse.

"You poor bastard," he muttered as if Fausto could hear him. "Even if you'd survived the crash, you'd have bled to death." He pulled the body back into the seat. Blood was everywhere. He stared at it and began to shake, nauseated. Eyes raised to a presumed heaven he pounded the dash and screamed hatred at the people who killed his friend. "What kind of godforsaken country is this?" he asked aloud. Overcome, he slumped back in the seat, still trembling. Calming, he realized he had to get moving.

6

The sun had risen above the nearby hills. The gulch and collection of brush hid the pickup from the few vehicles passing on the highway above, their drivers unaware of the tragedy below them.

If he hadn't seen it firsthand, Gar wouldn't have believed this deliberate attempt to murder out of hatred and malicious enjoyment. His mind still reeled from the encounter.

He'd survived once again, and, though he hated to think it, Fausto's dying had saved him considerable trouble. If he were faced with getting help for Fausto, he was certain police would have detained him, ending his odyssey.

Shock, injury, and two days without food left him sapped. His impulse was to scavenge what he could from Fausto's supplies, climb out of the gulch, and be on his way. But leaving Fausto in the truck would be an act of cowardice; he owed him a decent burial.

Though he craved rest, Gar aimed to finish the burial as quickly as possible and set about clearing a large enough area. Tumbleweed spines and rough mesquite bark bloodied his glove-free hands. With the clearing complete, he dragged Fausto's body from the cab and laid it face-up on the ground. Then he stopped to catch his breath. In recent years he'd seen a lot of death up close, most of it impersonal, the stuff of a reporter's life. Knowing the deceased, though, was still a phenomenon for him.

Fausto's pockets contained little of interest. Gar kept the loose change, a book of matches, and his dirty comb. Rolling him over to get his wallet, Gar saw a bulge under his shirt at the small of his back. Even before he pulled out the shirttail, he knew there was a pistol stuck in the trouser waistband. A 9mm Beretta. Like his father's, the type he'd trained with in Mexico. He wondered why Fausto hadn't used it. Maybe he thought the odds were too high. And who knew what else besides baseball bats those rednecks might've had?

He stared at the pistol for a few moments before touching it. What should he do? Being caught with it would for certain mean arrest. But this was hostile territory and he had no real means of protection. Assessing his vulnerability erased further hesitation. Picking up the weapon he removed the magazine and saw that it was loaded. Pulling back the slide ejected the chambered round, which he replaced in the magazine and shoved it back into the handle. He released the slide to re-chamber a round. He felt a measure of relief as he set the safety and put the weapon in his backpack.

Without looking further at it, he removed Fausto's wallet and shoved it into his own back pocket. There'd be time to look through it later. Only the act of taking Fausto's watch, a Seiko, made him feel like a thief. It still worked. Telling himself Fausto wouldn't need it, he shrugged and put it on. Being able to tell the time—then almost ten o'clock—made him feel connected to society again, and that was good.

The sun and temperature rose together. He welcomed neither. He scrambled up into the truck bed and went through the assorted tools, among them a machete, shovel, and hoe. Everything was so well tied down it appeared nothing had been thrown from the crash. Not even his backpack. With the machete he cleared more brush. Then with the shovel pressed to the hard ground, he shimmied the blade into it and sent the first scoopful of dirt aside. The packed earth made the going slow, the hot heavy work draining his strength. He craved water. Afraid of drinking too much, he forced himself to save what remained.

When the grave looked deep enough, Gar dragged

Fausto's body into the hole and stood gazing at it while he rested. Then, shovelful by shovelful the body disappeared. Gar shaped the mound over the body and stepped back to look at his work. Using mesquite branches and strips torn from Fausto's shirt, he made a cross and pushed it into the soil at the head of the grave. As an afterthought he retrieved the statuette of the Virgin, its suction cup still holding tight to the dashboard, and placed it at the foot of the cross, draping Fausto's rosary on the crossbar.

"The Virgin didn't protect you this time," he muttered. He hadn't been to Mass since his mother stopped forcing him to go as a boy. Much later as an adult, he'd given up on religion as a divisive and antiquated institution. But now as he stood with bowed head looking at the mound where Fausto lay, he felt compelled to cross himself and utter his idea of a last rite. "He was good and simple, this Fausto," he said into the air. "He didn't deserve to die this way. For hate. For nothing."

Guilt washed over him. Why had he been spared? His fury at the rednecks returned. "God damn the miserable whoring mothers who gave you birth!" He picked up the machete and with both hands swung it wildly in every direction. Then, rage spent, dropped to the ground.

For some time afterward he sat panting, sweat drying on his clothes. Head cleared, he replayed the tragedy, trying to rationalize and make some sense of it. He told himself that, even if Fausto hadn't stopped to pick him up, crossing paths with the rednecks was inevitable. In that event, he might be lying here dead anyway, with no one to bury him. At least he'd done that for him. The thought gave little consolation. He turned back to the matter of his own survival.

In a wooden crate leashed to the truck bed was Fausto's bedroll, a backpack with spare clothes, a shaving kit, and a container with a few first-aid supplies. Fausto had traveled well-prepared, which was more than Gar could say for himself. He found a box of 9mm bullets in a sealed plastic container, instant coffee, packets of jerky, and dried fruit and nuts. He tried but couldn't get down a piece of the jerky, his mouth too dry to moisten it. He did better with the fruit, little as it did to allay the hollowness of hunger.

Salvaging what he might need and could carry from the truck, Gar attached the bedroll to his backpack. Reclaiming his hat, he refilled his canteen and, with the near-empty water jug and food container in hand, he picked his way up and out of the ravine to the roadway.

A large concrete culvert about a mile up the road from the crash site was as far as he got. After checking for snakes and other varmints, he spent the rest of the day there. Forcing down some jerky and dried fruit, he nursed his bruises and took stock.

Though Gar went easy on his leg when he walked, the gash on his calf proved superficial and no longer throbbed. Hoping the wound had bled enough to prevent infection, he applied antiseptic ointment from Fausto's first-aid kit and bandaged it. He slept.

Hours later, he woke startled. He sat up on the bedroll drenched in sweat. He'd had a nightmare. Even with his eyes open to the dim light, its images remained fixed on his retinas.

He dreamed, as he often did, about the three classmates who used to back him against a stone wall behind the school and shake him down for money. But in the dream this time, even knowing he could be beaten up, Gar refused and stood his ground. As the largest boy advanced on him, Gar put his weight behind a fist and smashed it into the boy's face, bloodying his nose and knocking him down, the blow surprising him as much as his assailants. Seeing their leader on the ground, the others fled. Gar could have walked away. Instead, he jumped on the boy and with his knees, pinned the boy's arms. Flailing as if crazed, Gar punched him into near unconsciousness. Then, picking up a rock he raised it two-handed over his head. Terror in the boy's eyes must have kept him from using it. And then the boy's eyes turned to those of Fausto, who was the one pinned under Gar with unblinking, accusing eyes staring up at him. The reoccurring dream never failed to horrify Gar even after he'd awakened, and this version had no less effect.

Sweating and disoriented as much from the troubled sleep as the heat, he lay dozing, from time to time waking with a new jolt. His mind turned a kaleidoscope of images, flashbacks of his murdered family and his recent brush with death.

There was little day left when he finally roused himself. In the fading light of early evening, he looked through Fausto's wallet. The picture on the driver's license showed a frowning Fausto. His age was 32, a year older than Gar. He'd guessed right about them being the same height.

Nothing in the wallet hinted at whether Fausto was single or married. There were no pictures of family or even a girlfriend. Just as well. He couldn't imagine notifying survivors of Fausto's death, much less explaining it.

There were close to three hundred dollars in the wallet. Among the bills was a pay slip from the corporate farm where Fausto had worked. There was a variety of business cards, some from bars or restaurants that had women's names and phone numbers scrawled on the back.

After going through everything, he studied the pay receipt again. In one block there were the letters SSN and a series of numbers. Sorting trough the cards in the wallet, he'd seen one labeled Social Security Administration. The numbers on it matched those on the pay slip. He'd heard about this card and knew its importance for Americans. He studied the picture on the driver's license. Clean-shaven, he'd have trouble passing for Fausto. But with the beard now thickening on his face he might just get away with it, despite Fausto's visible scars. With these two cards he could become Fausto Vásquez.

He stripped off the clothes he'd been wearing for more

than a week. Blue-black bruises covered his ribcage, shoulders, and arms, souvenirs of the beating near Laredo. He imagined a similar array on his back. He craved a shower. But there was no water for that. Clean underwear would have to suffice. He exchanged his bloody shirt and trousers for a clean pair of Fausto's jeans, a plaid work shirt, and a jacket. Wrinkled, but with an ID and money, he already felt like a new man, with new possibilities.

Armed with the Berretta and with enough provisions for a few more days, his confidence was returning. Survival depended on catching a ride, which meant dangerous exposure to police and vigilantes. Despite two brushes with death, his luck had held.

7

It was dark when Gar awoke. He rose shivering in the night to prepare for the next—and what he hoped would be an uneventful—leg of his journey. By the time he packed the bedroll and had eaten some dried fruit and jerky, the glow of dawn began to streak the eastern sky. He drank the remaining water in the plastic jug and crammed the rest of the food into his pack, which he hoisted on his shoulder before climbing up to the roadway.

For a change, no morning mist lingered. Blue sky stretched to the horizon. The visibility was sharp and free. Gar kicked up gravel and dust as he walked along the highway's shoulder, turning to stick out his thumb at approaching vehicles. For the next several hours few passed, their intense drivers scarcely noticing him. It struck him that they might be as afraid of him as he was of them. He remembered what Fausto said about rednecks' hatred of Latinos. Yet he knew that to reach Los Angeles meant catching a ride, even a series of rides. There was nothing to do but walk and thumb.

Light breezes carried the fragrance of plants. Gar began to sweat in the rising heat. Full daylight brought increased traffic. Still, none stopped or even slowed to offer him a ride. An hour or so later, a large pickup approached, roaring as though missing its muffler. Gar stuck out his thumb even though something about the vehicle seemed off: the right side wheels rode the shoulder, trailing a plume of dust. He wondered if the driver had full control and backed further from the side of the road.

Still the vehicle was bearing down on him, the truck's tires hanging on the shoulder, the driver making no effort to steer back on the roadway. Was the driver trying to hit him? Just in time Gar jumped aside. Unbalanced, he stumbled and landed sprawling in the dirt. The pickup continued beyond him for a ways, its locked brakes bringing it to a skidding halt in the gravel.

Now fully alert, Gar struggled to his knees, watching as two men jumped from the vehicle and came running towards him. Briefly, he wondered if they might think he was injured and were coming to help. But then he saw the baseball bat. No doubt now they'd meant to hit him with the truck. And having missed, they came on at a dead run to finish the job, screaming words he couldn't make out but whose meaning were all too clear.

Still on hands and knees, Gar wriggled out of the backpack and fumbled in it for the Beretta. The men were almost on him as he pulled out the gun and aimed, stopping his attackers in their tracks. One of the men raised his hands. Then, as fast as they'd run at him, they fled to their truck. Gar watched them speed away.

Trembling, he stayed on his knees aiming at the retreating truck. Dusting himself off, he replaced the pistol in the pack and squatted on it for a while longer. Fausto hadn't exaggerated the dangers Latinos faced in the border areas. Gar hadn't believed that being Latino was reason enough to provoke an attack. Until now.

The sound of another approaching vehicle put him on alert again. But this time, what he saw brought relief. Emerging from the highway's shimmering heat waves, the silver form of a bus hurtled toward him with such speed he was surprised when it stopped to wait for him.

The driver looked at Gar askance, telling him the bus was going only as far as Del Rio. Gar nodded and handed over the fare asked for. He expected a similar reception from the passengers, but they, some bored, others dozing, barely glanced at him. Shoving his pack into the overhead rack, he settled with a grateful sense of reprieve into an empty seat next to a heavyset older woman, who reminded him of his late grandmother. She wrinkled her nose and leaned away.

He tilted back the seat, pulled his hat down over his eyes, and tried to relax. He'd been right to take the Beretta, though he wondered if he could have pulled the trigger. He was glad it hadn't been necessary to find out.

What seemed like only minutes later, the bus pulled into the Del Rio station. Now there was probably no way to avoid meeting border patrol officers face-to-face. From what he could see, the clusters of outbound passengers waiting to board were mostly Latinos. But that did little to ease his anxiety. There was trouble in the very name Del Rio, it being so close to the river.

Pack in hand, he stepped off the bus and headed for the men's room. If he looked anything like he felt, he figured he must come across as a derelict, maybe worse. The image in the mirror, red-eyed and wild-haired, stared back at him and he saw that his face had turned red-brown from the wind and sun and that hunger had given his cheeks a hollow appearance. To his mind, he was the very picture of a fugitive.

His stomach was rumbling but would have to wait a little longer to be satisfied. He spent most of the hour-long layover cleaning himself up, hoping to attract less attention. Washing his face raised his spirits and restored his optimism. He was desperate for a shower but could only pull off his shirt and splash his chest and arms with cold water. "*Orale hombre*, watch it," a man at the next sink warned him. Others in the crowded washroom gave him a wide berth, staring at the bruises on his back, arms, and chest. Ignoring them, Gar doused his head and dragged nettles from his hair with Fausto's dirty comb. Still dripping, he put on his shirt, did a quick comb of his beard and mustache, and stepped back for a critical look in the mirror. Except for his long wavy hair and the scabbed scratches on his face and hands, he looked pretty much like other men milling about the station, though noticeably taller.

Fausto's money had covered the fare to Del Rio and would buy Gar's way to L.A. as well as leaving enough to eat on for a while. When the boarding call came for the overnight leg to El Paso, he was still in the snack shop trying to fill his stomach.

The queue stretched from the gate to the bus and inched along under the scrutiny of a pair of uniformed border patrolmen. There was no way to avoid them. From where they stood near the boarding area gate, the patrolmen had a clear view of the loading island. Even as Gar watched, one of them moved to challenge a stony-faced man at the head of the line. Startled, the man fumbled his documents, dropping one or two. No sooner had the first patrolman led the man away than the other took his place. He began randomly checking passengers' documents.

Gar thought of the pistol in his backpack, reminding himself that his name was Fausto Vásquez. He mouthed it silently, repeating the name to himself. Instinct urged him to leave the line, but his head warned that doing so would certainly invite arrest.

The patrolman's voice asked for his name.

He looked at Gar, expressionless, alert for a reaction.

"Fausto Vásquez." To Gar's surprise, saying the name aloud for the first time came easily. "You checking documents?" He reached for his hip pocket.

For a moment, the patrolman stared hard at him, his eyes narrowing. "Please keep it moving, sir."

Gar's luck during spot-checks continued to hold at each of the next terminals. But there was nothing certain about it. Disaster could strike at any time.

At the El Paso station, the mass of humanity teemed like maggots on a moldering carcass. Though larger than any of the previous stations, air conditioning in this one did little to ease the choking diesel exhaust and heat well above 100 degrees. The stifling temperature only added to the sense of looming menace. The people appeared to be mostly Mexican, but this did little to calm him. Any one of them could be an undercover lawman or a Mexican agent. El Paso, merely a river's width from his homeland, was just another hostile place for him.

A year ago, while reporting on the many unsolved murders of young women in Juarez, he'd came across the Rio Grande to this very city. He liked what he found, especially the nightly jazz at a lounge called Aceitunas, the Spanish word for olives, and the woman he met there. He enjoyed using his English with her, and a couple of days later they'd passed a wonderful night as lovers. He wondered what had become of her and was sorry he hadn't kept his promise to see her again. The proper papers, money, and the freedom to move about had made El Paso a pleasure. But in his present circumstances, it was just a city filled with unknown eyes searching for him.

El Paso had long been a major entry along the border for Latinos, legal and otherwise. He hadn't dared to cross here. Now, with the threat of terrorism and such strong anti-immigration sentiment rampant in the country, there was increased surveillance. And Salinas' agents, if they were searching for him, would have this place well covered.

Gar scanned the crowd for police or other lawmen. Though none stood out, he knew they were present and in force. At the same time, he had to control his paranoid fear that anyone who looked at him twice must be one of Salinas' agents.

His fear seemed to materialize in the form of a swarthy mustachioed man leaning against the wall near the ticket window. He was pretending to read a newspaper while actually watching the queue. As Gar came closer, the man looked away. The man was so obviously an agent. When their eyes met, Gar stared him down.

Anxious for the departure of his bus, Gar sat in the waiting room reading a newspaper. This time, he saw no law enforcement types watching the loading queues. Settling into his seat while passengers filled the bus, Gar resumed reading. The loading was complete and the scheduled departure time had passed. Still the vehicle remained parked.

He checked his watch again. Then he became aware of a palpable tension in the bus that hadn't been there before. The passengers had all fallen silent. Some turned in their seats to look for a reason. Resisting a similar impulse, Gar shifted his gaze from the newspaper to a movement in the aisle. There was a man standing beside his seat. Looking up he saw it was the same man who'd been watching him in the station. He swallowed and felt sweat moisten his scalp.

"Border Patrol." The man showed a badge. "Your identification, please, sir." The voice was flat and menacing.

Mierda, Gar muttered under his breath, as he realized for the first time that the newspaper in his hands was a copy of *El Diario*, Juarez's major daily. But was that incriminating? The seat was suddenly hot against his back and beads of sweat formed on his upper lip, but he kept his breathing slow and even. At best, he'd be detained. Being caught with the Beretta could mean an indefinite stay in an American prison. Any arrest could also mean being thrown back across the border into the arms of his enemies.

As he reached for the wallet in his hip pocket he peered up again and realized the agent was focused on the man sitting next to him, who appeared confused.

"He doesn't understand." Gar looked up just past the brim of his hat at the agent.

The agent repeated his demand, again in English.

Ah, a *pocho*, Gar said to himself, a Latino who can't speak English. He turned again to his seatmate. "*Tus papeles.*"

The man nodded and reached for his wallet.

The patrolman, a grim look on his face, inspected the

photo on the man's driver's license then looked back at its owner. Without a word, he shoved the license into a shirt pocket and motioned with his head for the man to come along. As Gar stepped into the aisle to let him pass, the agent, holding the man's arm, hesitated and glanced at the folded newspaper in his hand.

"What's that you're reading?"

"A newspaper." Gar answered evenly.

The patrolman glanced at it, and then looked at him.

"Let's see some identification."

"Right." Gar tried to sound confident. As he reached for Fausto's wallet, the prisoner with a sudden jerk pulled free and bolted for the door.

The patrolman wheeled around. "Stop! Stop him!" he shouted. "You, driver, shut the door!"

No one moved. If the bus driver heard, he didn't show it. His head partially out of a side window, he continued to talk to another driver standing outside. Cursing, the patrolman ran down the aisle and jumped from the vehicle in pursuit. The driver closed the door and backed the bus from its dock. They drove onto the main roadway, picking up speed. Gar blessed him with the breath he'd been holding.

"Close call, huh?" A *gringo* from across the aisle leaned toward him.

Gar shrugged and looked away. His thoughts centered on the rest of the trip, the ordeal to be repeated at the remaining stops in New Mexico, Arizona, and on to Los Angeles.

"Goin' all the way to L.A.?" The passenger across the aisle persisted.

Gar ignored him, hoping he would take the hint and shut up. He was obviously enjoying himself.

"What do you play?" he said, studying Gar's hands.

"What?" Gar turned to look at him.

"Your hands. What instrument do you play?"

"I sing."

"Yeah? The passenger brightened. "Rock, huh?"
"*Conjunto.*"
"Oh," the man mumbled, losing interest.
Gar had meant to have his hair cut in Los Angeles. Now he thought it might not be such a good idea.

8

The crowd could easily pass for one in Mexico City. But for Gar it only meant more agents prowling. He tried to reassure himself that a beard made him less recognizable and, once away from this Latino multitude, his height would make him less conspicuous.

That he'd made it to Los Angeles at all struck him as miraculous. Almost broke and homeless, he'd braved dangers to get here on the slim hope of finding his father's friend, Hernán Gárza Cortés. There was no way to know whether he might live in the city or even be alive.

Though it was still too early to call, Gar paged through a number of thick directories at the phone bank for Hernán's name. But the listings for Cortés and Cortéz numbered in the hundreds. American Latinos often dropped the second surname, so it was possible Hernán used only the name Gárza. He was stymied until he remembered that Hernán headed an organization that helped Latino immigrants get documentation and represented them in court.

He waited impatiently for a man at the adjacent stall to finish using the business directory. The vast number of listed lawyers also defeated him. The organizations dealing with immigration were also legion and left him equally perplexed. He gave up the search and settled for a breakfast of fried eggs and toast in the neighboring coffee shop. He sat with a second coffee, hoping the caffeine would help him sort out his predicament.

Contemplating the next move, his eyes wandered to the cluster of storefronts and buildings across the street. His gaze rested on an entryway leading into an old stone-faced building with classical columns of carefully carved whimsical flowers and birds. Much of the weathered façade had been pasted over with signs and posters. A young man stood outside, considering the diverse offerings. Above his head, centered in the old archway, a sign advertised the New Life Immigration Service.

It wasn't the promise of a new life that caught his eye, but the word "immigration." Though it was still early morning, he checked the Seiko. After eight o'clock. Business hours might have begun.

Leaving the coffee half finished, he shouldered his pack and crossed the street. He inspected the signs—nearly all in Spanish—for the businesses inside: passport applications, legal aid, work permit advice, insurance sales, instant photos, jewelry stores, weddings, but none for the immigration office.

He entered the building through a dim trash-strewn passageway, checking doors as he went. The acrid stench of urine in the dank coolness made him breathe through his mouth. At the hall's far end he found the door he wanted. He wasn't surprised to find it locked. A button at the base of a small speaker box in the doorframe brought a voice.

"*Diga*," a woman commanded in mispronounced Spanish and followed immediately with, "Yes, who is it?" in an accent even Gar could tell wasn't American.

He hesitated. Though he'd spoken his name as Fausto, he was now unsure how to identify himself.

"Uh, Fausto Vásquez. I've just arrived here and need your help," he said in English.

"Are you legal?"

"Yes."

"What kind of help do you need? Our assistance is only with legal matters, we don't provide food or shelter."

"I'm looking for a friend, a lawyer who's in the same business as you."

Silence followed as the woman at the other end

apparently considered his reply.

"The office is upstairs."

Hearing a buzzer, he pushed through the door and climbed the staircase to the second floor. He had an eerie feeling once again of stepping into the unknown.

Her nameplate read *Riona Welch, Director*. She spoke with an Irish lilt.

"Who is this attorney you're looking for?" Riona was petite and attractive, with arresting green eyes. She might be even prettier if she smiled.

She was cool to him. Another older woman in the cramped office made no attempt to hide her disdain, fixing him with a distrustful eye as Riona answered her phone. Hanging up, she offered him a chair. He tossed his backpack on it.

"I'm not sure which variation of Cortés he uses," he told her. "Or he might only use Gárza."

Riona was impeccably dressed for such a shabby office. Her pale freckled cheeks flushed when her eyes met his, but her gaze never wavered. She touched her red hair as if reassuring herself of its condition, her fingers trembling slightly. As he was a total stranger in her office, her reticence would be understandable. Yet her flushed reaction surprised him. The macho in him wanted to respond, but involvement with a woman had no place in his plans.

"You say he represents immigrants in residency cases?"

"That's how I understand what he does." Gar really didn't know that, but it sounded plausible and kept her attention.

"Well, it's not what we do here." She was impatient again as she wrote the name he spelled. "I'll have someone try to locate your friend. It could take a few days."

When a woman interested him, he could sometimes read her the way a salesman knows a buyer. Behind Riona's coolness, he thought he saw loneliness and vulnerability. And he saw the way she'd appraised him, taking in his dress, haircut, voice, and even his ring hand. This had often happened and, when it did, he knew he could make use of the insight. He needed her help, and if he played it right she might provide the break he needed.

"Traveling here, I'm nearly out of money and I need work and a place to stay." He tried to say this without sounding pleading, expecting her to remind him of the limited assistance her office provided.

"Well, if you're short on cash, there are cheap hotels a few streets over and even cheaper ones in skid row, just beyond Main Street and up from Seventh."

"Skid row?"

"Where the down and out end up when there's no place lower to fall. Every large city has one."

"Sounds pretty grim." His own country didn't lack for such bleak places.

"It's not anywhere you'd want to stay unless you're desperate." She looked at him steadily. "But one does what one must."

"Thanks for the warning." He rubbed his chin, wondering just how far he could push her for help. What she said next told him he'd read her correctly.

"What work do you do?"

"I'm a writer, a journalist." His appearance hardly made him look the part, but his speech didn't brand him as a day laborer, either.

"Is your Spanish fluent?"

He almost smiled—she must've heard his accent. He wondered if she might be joking. He nodded. "And I use a computer." That last bit brought the briefest smile to her face for the first time. He reacted with one of his own. There was no coquettishness now, so he wasn't imagining the attraction. Their exchange was evolving into a game he knew only too well. He felt a tremor of excitement. He reminded himself that he needed this woman's good will. This was no time for moves that could be misinterpreted. Even so, he regretted being unable to follow through.

"Have you tried a newspaper?" Her face displayed skepticism. "There are a number in the city. The *Los Angeles Times*'s office isn't far."

"Where would that be?"

"A few blocks from here, up on First Street."

"Right now I'm hardly dressed for it, but I'll try there eventually." He suspected he'd just been tested and had failed. She probably already had him pegged as illegal and he waited to see what she'd do about it. It would be easy for her to pick up the phone and it would be all over. Instead she surprised him again.

"If you need something immediate, with your Spanish the Universal Relief can probably use you. I know the director. I'll call ahead, if you're interested."

"I am and I would appreciate that very much. Is it far?"

"Up on Main Street about 15 minutes from here, just beyond Olvera Street."

"Good." He nodded. "But I don't know this Olvera Street."

"It's what's left of the original Main Plaza of the Old Pueblo of Los Angeles. It's a national monument. Known around here as La Placita. It's just across from Union Station. When you're near it look for tourists. Ask anyone."

"Thanks for your help. Should I contact you again in a few days about my friend?"

"Do that." This time her smile seemed more genuine. While Riona wrote down directions and handed them to him, her companion continued to stare at him. Probably sees herself as Riona's guardian, he thought. In this seedy part of town who could blame her?

Once on Los Angeles Street, Gar knew he'd entered the edge of what Riona called skid row. The air was heavy with loss and defeat. A swarm of ragged humanity shuffled along the sidewalks like a slow-moving lava flow with no place to go but down. Laden with their worldly goods in overstuffed plastic bags or stolen shopping carts, many were obviously homeless. In places, a parade of large graffiti-scrawled cardboard boxes lined the sidewalk. Gar wondered about their purpose until he bumped into one. Like a prairie dog popping from its hole, an ancient wild-haired woman growled at him out of one side of the box.

In the back seat of a rusting car, a man and woman had set up housekeeping. Just beyond them, a man lying on newspapers slept under a tarp tied to a shopping cart. Across the street, people, without so much as a glance, shuffled past a man lying in the gutter and who was wearing what looked like a hospital gown. For half a block, Gar found himself following a ragged man of indeterminate age waving his arms and talking to the wind and then disappeared into a dilapidated storefront. Inside the building, a crowd of derelict men and women were being served a meal. For a moment, Gar considered joining them. But he hadn't yet fallen that far. He walked on.

Progressing uptown, he noted that most of the heads bobbing in front of him had dark hair and brown faces. As far as he could see in either direction, the signs above and on the windows of storefronts were all in Spanish. He'd heard that Latinos from everywhere collected here, giving L.A. the largest concentration of Mexicans outside of Mexico City. Their vast numbers here made it certain that *la migra* prowled these streets.

9

The Plaza of Old Los Angeles was unimpressive with no garden. Instead, a bandstand stood at its center and eight large planters dotted its periphery. Neither the bricks paving the plaza floor and forming the bandstand nor the planters looked old enough to be original. Otherwise, the circular plaza featured a bronze statue of Don Francisco Ávila. The plaque bolted to the plinth proclaimed that he'd staked out the site in 1818 and in the process founded the city that had now grown to mammoth proportions.

Near the bandstand at the plaza's center, a passable mariachi quartet of overweight musicians played intermittently for the applause and gratuities of passersby. He stopped for their rendition of "La Malagueña," the woman from Malaga, a favorite Mexican tune. If Gar could've spared it, he'd gladly have dropped one of his few remaining dollars into the open guitar case at their feet. A nod and a smile of approval had to suffice.

Olvera Street was little more than a pedestrian mall, a jumble of cheap souvenir stalls. A few cafes offered alleged Mexican fare. The odors emanating from them set his stomach churning again.

A couple of small museums caught his attention. As he walked by one of the latter, his eye was drawn to a long glass-enclosed display of pre-Colombian ornaments, pottery, and figurines. He stopped to look them over and wondered if they were authentic. A sign in the window's lower corner invited tourists inside. Intrigued, he entered. Enlarged historical texts and photographs depicting Los Angeles in the early stages of development hung from the museum walls. Well-worn kitchen utensils and other tools of the time were displayed on tables and didn't interest Gar.

The extensive collection of pre-Columbian antiquities did, however. Most of the pieces were from Mexican cultures, though many were of Central and South American origin. He doubted the authenticity of the clay figures and pottery, the kinds of objects most readily forged.

Standing in the semi-dark interior pondering the collection, he became aware of someone looking over his shoulder.

"Nice stuff, isn't it?" The voice behind him said.

Gar turned to confront a man of about his height. He stepped back, repelled by an odor of beer and garlic. His first thought was that the man might be a *maricón* trolling for a pick-up, or an undercover policeman.

"It's all right," he answered.

The man, pale-faced with pleading eyes, grinned broadly, baring yellow teeth. A gold loop earring glinted on one ear, and he wore his stringy blond hair in a ponytail. Tall and heavy, he looked to be in his forties and came across as a person looking for someone to attach himself to. Though dressed in a suit without a tie, his rumpled clothes and slouchy demeanor gave him the aspect of a mangy dog.

"If you'd like to see more, I mean some really fine collector's items, I can arrange it." The man patted what appeared to be a display case. He extended a hand as he spoke. "My name is..."

"Not interested." Gar cut him off. He took another step back, turned abruptly, and left the museum. He continued down the street, sensing the man's eyes on his back. He didn't look back until he reached the end of the line of souvenir stalls. When he did, the man was indeed standing outside the museum watching him.

The gaudy stalls offered all the usual junk tourists buy to document their travels: florid pottery, dolls in peasant costume, plastic flowers, fake leather products from China, velvet paintings of bullfight scenes.

Especially repellent were the ashtrays and mugs depicting a drunken *peón* propped asleep against a Saguaro cactus. They perpetuated the false stereotypical myth of the lazy Mexican. Gar felt like smashing it all. The glass blower and juggler at least looked professional and, for a few moments, he stopped to watch them work the crowd. Passing another café, the odors wafting from it promising the traditional fare of peasant Mexico, food he loved. But even knowing that it might be authentic did little to make the diorama-like display agreeable.

The street, probably intended to portray a California of a bygone romantic era, came across as a *gringo*'s theme park idea, a caricature of what it might have been like three hundred years ago. The spectacle disgusted him.

Likewise, the Universal Relief Office did little to raise his spirits. But its director, a large disheveled dark-roots blonde, who showed a flushed quixotic cheerfulness, seemed eager to put him to work interviewing applicants. He was grateful for the opportunity. Inside the office, he found the sickly, destitute, and dispirited. A rattling air conditioner did little against the stifling heat and the smells of unwashed supplicants. They were a mix of Blacks, Latinos, Whites, a few Asians, and a few others whose ethnicity he could only guess. By early afternoon the line of people seeking help clogged the sidewalk outside.

The men, the most beaten, were careless in their dress and manner. After a while the men's faces began to look alike. Occasionally, one or two stood out because they were clean-shaven and held defiance in their eyes. These few, embarrassed to be there, were quick to say their need was only temporary. Gar wondered about their stories, what had brought them to their present misfortune. He wasn't that far from being in such a line himself. Some men came with families, though the majority of those standing in line were single women with kids in tow. Above the din of voices, the occasional high-pitched whines and cries of the children could be heard.

Time passed quickly. The relief office had been full to overflowing all day and remained that way when Gar finally left. The director seemed pleased with him, professing her gratitude, and he promised to return. She gave him directions to the YMCA.

Fortified with nearly a full day's pay, he stopped at a café for beer and a meal before heading to the Y. He paid for a night's lodging, telling the clerk he intended to stay the three nights allowed.

A steaming shower washed away days of travel grime and anxiety. Clean at last, he collapsed on the bed in exhaustion, still too worked up with nervous energy to sleep. He tried to imagine his next moves, but contented himself with the thought that tomorrow would bring its own problems. With any luck, it would bring solutions too.

10

In the late afternoon a day later, Gar headed to Riona's office. A large crowd had collected outside the bus station and the mass of people flowed onto the street, blocking the entrance to her building. Crowds meant trouble and, though he stopped to watch for a moment, his impulse was to leave.

The commotion centered around three men in plain clothes, patting down an elderly Latina. A tray of cigarettes, chewing gum, and sundries hung from a strap around her neck. Two ragged children pressed close to her, one crying, both clutching her skirt. While one man looked over the woman's documents another searched through her merchandise. The third man faced the burgeoning crowd. Probably immigration or narcotics agents, Gar thought, and wanted nothing to do with them, whoever they were.

The woman seemed well-known to the people as some shook raised fists, protesting the way the men were treating her. "Leave her alone, she's not hurting anyone," someone yelled. "She's only trying to support her children."

The crowd grew, splaying into the street and halting traffic. Blaring horns added to the roar of angry voices and attracted still more passersby. Then, as one of the agents handcuffed the vendor and tried to lead her away, the jeering throng pressed in to block their path. One of the men flipped open his cell phone. The police would be on the scene within minutes.

As he turned to leave, he saw Riona's red hair in the sea of dark heads. She was being forced against the building, trapped by the crowd. Jabbing his elbows, he plowed through to her.

"Thank God it's you," she said.

With one arm around her shoulders, he used the other to clear a path out of the melee.

"Are you all right?" he asked.

"Fine." She nodded, her face drained of color. She was still clutching her purse and briefcase to her chest.

"The crowd doesn't like what the police are doing to that old woman. Mobs like that can easily get..."

"I know," she said, "it happens all the time around here. This area crawls with pimps, pushers, the undocumented, or what have you, and the bus station is where they're usually arrested."

"Would you like coffee? Something stronger? There's a restaurant a few doors from here." Gar was holding her arm, and she made no move to pull free.

"I...I don't, but thank you for getting me out of there."

"This isn't the safest place for you to be working."

She shrugged. Couldn't be helped.

"Do you live near here?"

"I was on the way to my car. It's in a lot one street over."

"I'll walk you to it."

They walked a short distance before she spoke again.

"Did the Universal Relief job work out?"

"Very well, thanks." He wanted to say they were even now, but didn't. Instead he said, "Riona is an interesting name."

"You think so?" She looked up at him with a trace of a smile.

"Very close to *reina*, Spanish for queen."

When they reached the parking lot, she stopped at her car's door and faced him.

"Stop by the office sometime tomorrow. My co-worker has been calling around trying to find your Mr. Gárza. Perhaps she's had some luck."

"I'll do that. And I appreciate the effort."

"By the way," she paused by the open door of her car, "Riona is Irish for queen, too."

"We haven't found your Mr. Gárza yet," Riona told Gar in her office the next day. Her co-worker still eyed him warily, but without the obvious distaste of his first visit. He felt sure she'd heard about the rescue.

"Where are you staying?" Riona's amiability seemed genuine.

"The YMCA, up on Hope, near 4th." He wondered why it mattered, but didn't ask. "I have to check out later this afternoon—they only allow three days. I'll have to find something else. If you know of another place I could stay I'd appreciate the tip."

Eyebrows arched, Riona glanced at the other woman, whose shrug seemed to say, go ahead. She wrote on a slip of paper and handed it to him.

"Any reputable place in town is bound to be expensive. Try this address. It's a little farther out of the city center. I believe there's a room available at a fair price." She flashed a smile again. "You get there by bus, the number's there, too. Catch it on Main Street, going north."

In Mexico City only the poor, students, and tourists ride the bus. In Los Angeles, Gar was among those who had to rely on public transportation. It was late afternoon before he arrived at the Culver City address.

The house, on a quiet tree-shaded side street off Venice Boulevard, sat in an odd conglomeration of courtyard apartments and single-family ramblers. Ordinary by any standard, the houses, skirted by lawns and lush plantings of decorative trees and shrubs, sat back from the street with little space between them. Strangely, no people could be seen on the sidewalks or in their yards. The only sign of life was the yapping of a few dogs. He supposed he could be anonymous here.

The old two-story house stood out for being larger than the smaller ones lining the block. Otherwise it seemed unimpressive. Gar's knock on the front door brought no response. He knocked again. Still no one answered.

As he walked away, heading next door to inquire about the address, the door opened behind him. Turning, he saw an athletic looking woman in the doorway. With hair piled high on top of her head, she appeared to fill the entire frame of the open door.

"Keep your pants on, will ya? Don't be in such a damned rush. Jeezus, nobody can wait for anything anymore." After focusing on Gar, she quickly softened and a smile lit her face.

"Well, well, who've we got here?" Her voice dropped a notch deeper, reminding Gar of a husky torch singer. Barefoot, she wore cut-off shorts and a halter that barely contained her chest. She crossed her arms under her ample breasts, relaxed against the doorframe, and unabashedly looked him over. Her streaked blonde hair highlighted a tanned complexion. Gar guessed her to be in her mid-forties.

"I was told you might have a furnished room available."

"Yeah?" She waited a beat. "Might." Taking a step back, she motioned him into the foyer and leaned on the banister leading upstairs. "How long you plan to stay?"

"Indefinitely."

"OK, come in, take a look. Rent's a hundred a week, due in advance. You miss, you're out."

She led the way to the interior, through a hall of stale cooking odors. He followed her, taking in her narrow waist, tight buttocks, and the long muscular legs of a runner. A curt woman of that size, easily as tall as he was, made him wonder what her criteria were for lovers.

"You get your own sink here." She pushed open the door to a room at the end of the dim passageway. "You share the toilet, tub, and shower across the hall." She pointed. "Comes with kitchen privileges, provided you clean up after yourself and label all your stuff in the fridge." Moving a few paces into the room, she made a sweeping motion with her arm. "Come in, take a look. You want it, take it now, 'cuz it'll be gone tomorrow."

He didn't ask but felt sure Riona had called ahead to hold it for him.

The room had been created by a partition dividing a much larger space. A pea green sink hung on the added yellow wall. An ample double bed, a worn overstuffed chair, and a veneered armoire with a scuffed bureau next to it occupied most of the rest of the space.

Except for a faded oriental rug, threadbare in places and covering most of the floor, the room was devoid of decoration. A bare lightbulb dangled from the center of the ceiling. The open Venetian blinds allowed daylight to seep into the room, saving it from all-out depressing darkness. While the room could hardly offer the sort of living Gar was used to, it was an unlikely place for *la migra* to come looking for him.

"I'll take it." He reached for his wallet and started to withdraw some bills.

"Whoa, hold on there. Who'm I talking to?" She fixed him with a steady look, one hand on a hip, the other holding her chin.

"Gar, uh." He said it before catching himself.

"That short for something?"

"No."

"That it? Just one name? Need the whole thing," she said, a look of suspicion growing on her face. "I have to keep records, you know."

Damn, too late to change now. "Of course. I understand. Montalvo, Gar Montalvo." He spelled it for her.

"OK, I think I got that. One more thing, Mr. M. Two actually: the room comes with towels and bedclothes that get washed once a week, and make sure you get them to the laundry or otherwise..."

"I understand." He moved to the bed and dropped his backpack.

"Where you from, Gar? You don't mind if I call you that, do you?"

"Not at all. Texas, Laredo," he said, careful to use the American pronunciation.

"No offense, never been there, never want to go there, either, all I've ever heard of Texas. You can call me Gisela, hard *g*, accent on the *i*, pronounced like a long *e*. It's German," she added as he handed her the first week's rent.

Before leaving, she stopped and leaned against the frame of the open door. "Oh, nearly forgot. A college girl, Annie, lives upstairs. Mine's the room next to this one, other side of that wall." She pointed to the partition with her chin. "You need anything," she paused, smiling, "you know where to find me. You wanna watch TV any time I'm in, you're welcome. Just knock first. OK? You can park your car in back, too. Keep it off the street. Safer that way."

"I don't have a car yet."

"Bummer. Can't live in L.A. without a car. How you gettin' around? Or don't you work?"

"I work downtown near the Civic Center. I have to take the bus."

"Oh yeah? Work there myself. You get up early enough you can ride with me, if you like."

"Great, and thanks, Gisela." He returned the steady gaze she fixed on him. A half-smile still lit her face as she closed the door. He thought her expression, though flattering, was a little too hungry and eager. He hoped she wouldn't be a problem.

11

Traffic on the Santa Monica Freeway surged like two rivers running across multiple lanes in both directions, sometimes at high speed but just as often at a crawl. The congestion took some getting used to, though it had an orderliness that traffic in Mexico City lacked.

"This ever let up?" Gar asked.

Gisela wore a suit and blouse for her receptionist's position at City Hall. Her hair, gathered in a twist on top of her head, gave an impression of power. Even without a horned helmet, the image of a Valkyrie crossed his mind. That aside, she had a direct, unaffected way about her that made her likable.

"Nah, 'fraid not." She shot him a quick glance. "When I was a kid, there used to be a rush for a couple hours in the morning and then again in the evening. But now it's pretty much non-stop. Real drag, and so is this friggin' smog. It's 'specially bad this morning."

They rode in silence for a few minutes.

"Look, why don't you drop me off and take the car? Where you're going there should be plenty of parking. Save me the expense. Getting back on the freeway from the Civic Center's no problem."

"That'd help. What time should I pick you up?"

Alone in Gisela's aged Ford for the first time, Gar managed to get back onto the freeway with little trouble. The bumper-to-bumper traffic hadn't let up, but he soon caught the rhythm. He dialed the radio through talk, hip-hop, and rock until he found a station devoted to jazz. Lost in the music, he nearly missed the exit onto the 5, taking him into East L.A., where he got off. A few daily trips with Gisela had helped him develop a mental map of the drive to the Civic Center, but anywhere beyond remained a mystery. For a while, he was lost and, though the actual driving distance was short, an hour passed before he found the Mexican American Institute on Indiana Avenue.

Housed in a squat building, it sat on the edge of the East L.A. barrio in a trash-strewn neighborhood. Like others around it, the building sported its own colorful graffiti. Bolt-anchored metal grills shielded the door and windows. A small brass plate affixed to the wall near the door bore the institute's name and logo, the metal dulled to a green-brown patina.

In either direction and on both sides of the street, dozens of small businesses operated out of houses, garages, and commercial buildings. Bold, colorful decorations and lettering both advertised and provided cultural identification. Their owners wasted no time making their businesses comfortably Mexican, Nicaraguan, Salvadoran, or Asian. The light traffic belied the throngs swarming the shops, the cacophony of humanity competing with blaring music, hip-hop and Latin beats. The air, redolent of roasting chiles and the steaming masa of tortillas, mingled with the exhaust of delivery trucks, reminding Gar of home.

The buzzer was answered by another unlocking of the front door. The fluorescents in the reception area sapped color from the drab walls. An older man in shirtsleeves, cuffs upturned, his tie loosely knotted, leaned against the office doorway. He eyed Gar over his reading glasses, a thumb hooked into one of his suspenders. Despite what his seventy or so years had done to him, the man bore a strong resemblance to the impressive man Gar remembered as Hernán Gárza Cortés. His face revealed the same intense expression and alert aggressiveness.

"Fausto Vásquez." The man spoke first, his gravelly

voice seeming to state a fact more than a question.

"And you are Mr. Hernán Gárza Cortés?" Gar asked.

Hernán's protruding ears framed a slightly hooked nose. His complexion had yellowed, his face topped by thinning white hair. Gar wondered if alcohol still plagued Hernán's life, as it had in the past.

Hernán ignored Gar's opening question and continued to eye him with the cynical look of someone who expects little from mankind.

"You seem familiar." He paused and pursed his lips. "You're Mexican, no?"

"Well, yes."

"I mean from Mexico."

Surprised, Gar hesitated. "What makes you think that?"

"Your manner more than your accent. Something about your English. It's too careful, too precise." The man paused, studying Gar with his gaze. "So tell me, did your father sell his soul to the devil? Or maybe promise him yours?"

Gar was puzzled for a moment. "Ah, you refer to my name."

"Precisely."

"I can't speak for any trade my father made, but so far the devil hasn't contacted me. I admit to some knowledge, but as for power, I have little, as you can see." He indicated the condition of his clothes with a downward sweep of his hands.

Verbal sparring seemed to animate Hernán. He straightened, his eyes widening.

"Well, well, a literate man. A rarity these days, I assure you." He extended a hand in greeting. "Don't just stand there, come in, come in. Yes, I'm Hernán Gárza. Dropped the Cortés years ago. It only confused people. Some thought it clever to ask if the Conquistador was my ancestor. Fools didn't realize he's ancestor to us all." Coaxing Gar by the arm, Hernán led him through the outer office. "What is it you think I can do for you?"

On their way into Hernán's office, they passed an attractive young woman sitting in front of a computer monitor. Gar caught her eye and smiled. Inside, Hernán offered him a chair, while he remained standing.

"Suppose you begin by telling me how you got my name." Gar saw no reason not to tell him the truth.

"A woman at immigration services near the 7th Street bus station gave it to me."

"Is that a fact?" He stroked his chin, eyebrows raised. "Didn't think they'd heard of me." He turned grim. "If you're here illegally you have my sympathy. Nothing more. I've been out of the immigration business for years. The clients can't pay their way. They're up against a maze of tough laws. Besides that, everybody's scared shitless of terrorism."

Gar looked up at the older man; the fan framed his head like a slow turning halo.

"You've described my circumstance exactly."

"As I suspected." He fixed Gar with an intense look. "As pleasant as it might be to chat with you about literature or Mexico, our conversation is at an end." He turned away, showing Gar his back.

Gar could hear the ticking of the clock on the wall behind him. Hernán had removed his glasses to check their cleanliness. When he put them back on, he saw that Gar hadn't moved and grew irritated at his remaining seated.

"There's no ashtray on your desk," Gar said.

"Ashtray? You want to smoke before you leave?"

"I don't smoke, but you used to. As I recall, you also drank a lot—or at least that's how you impressed me when my parents and I visited you back in the '80s."

These details altered Hernán's stance, and he no longer wanted to evict Gar from his office.

12

Hernán's eyes narrowed, his face clouding. "All right," he said, "you have me at a disadvantage. Who the hell are you?"

Gar rose and extended his hand. "Gar Montalvo, *a sus órdenes*, at your service."

"What?" Hernán was mystified.

"You and my father were boyhood friends in Mexico City, before your family emigrated."

Hernán peered over his glasses and leaned closer to study his face.

"Well, sonuvabitch!" He smiled and took Gar's outstretched hand in both of his. "I knew there was something familiar about you. I'm usually pretty good with faces. That beard and rock-star hairdo and the passage of years threw me off."

They stood with hands clasped for a few moments, Hernán shaking his head, still marveling.

"Something to drink? Coffee OK? Bonita..." He called the order to his secretary.

"Don't feel bad. You couldn't have recognized me even without this hair. After all I was just a boy. Father and I never resembled each other. He was taller than I am now, his eyes gray and his hair lighter. I took after my mother's *mestizo* looks, her features. She was more typically Mexican."

Hernán returned his hand to his pocket and looked away. "My condolences on your parents."

"Thanks." Gar bowed his head. "How did you know?"

"*La Opinión*, the newspaper here, used to publish Francisco's op-ed pieces. It carried his obituary."

"Those articles of his made him enemies. When I was growing up, I didn't always understand why people were so upset by his writings. But he had friends in important places. His students thought him courageous."

"So you remember visiting me when you were a boy, do you? That's remarkable."

"As I said, your office smelled of cigars and you..."

"I've given up booze," Hernán said before Gar could finish. "Tobacco, too, for that matter. My only vice now is eating well."

"As for the visit," Gar said, resisting the impulse to look at Hernán's belly, "I was so young. I have no recollection of why we came or what we did here."

Hernán looked at Gar as if he were about to explain something. "We can talk about that later, if you wish," he said. "It's been what, 23, 24 years?"

"About that."

"What have you been doing all that time?"

"The usual. University, then journalism. By the way, you aren't the easiest person to find."

Bonita set two steaming coffee mugs on the desk. Gar nodded thanks.

"That's the way I intend it." He let the statement hang in the air.

"There's much around here that reminds me of Mexico, including the building armor on the windows and doors." Gar waved an encompassing hand. "It's a little ominous."

"You get used to it. This isn't the most hospitable place for an office, but the rent's fair. It's not as bad as it appears out there." His tone changed as he pursed his lips. "A man like you, a professional, doesn't come here illegally unless he's running from something."

Gar said nothing.

"So what can I do for you—no, we can discuss that in due time." Hernán moved to the chair behind his desk and reached for his coffee. He waved Gar to a chair. "Bring me up to date. Tell me about the assumed name."

Gar, cradling the cup, began to relax. Slowly and deliberately, he told of his illegal crossing—the shakedown and beating by his companions, the thirst and hunger.

Hernán listened without interrupting, sipping his coffee from time to time. Only when Gar described Fausto Vásquez's death, did Hernán begin to ask questions, about Fausto's identity.

When Gar fnished, Hernán sat rubbing his chin thoughtfully.

"Tell me, you ever find out what your parents' killers were after?"

"Not with any certainty. Months later, the investigating detective interviewed one of the hired killers. They were acting for a government minister. But the man died shortly after the interview. He told me we couldn't make a case."

"What were they after that was so important?"

"The man seemed sure it was a document but knew nothing about its content. Anyway, it's hard to say if they found what they were after. Later, I searched the house and father's office at the university, but found nothing useful. There were a few pieces missing from his collection of pre-Columbian artifacts, but they could have been sold or traded away. As far as I know, none of the pieces had that kind of value. Archeologists at the university where he taught thought the killers might have been after information about a new archeological site he was privy to."

"Why'd they think that?"

"I found a letter with a map about a dig in his safe deposit box. Though I intended to follow up later, I was too upset to study them or take them to someone who might know something about their significance. I do know the artifacts market is large and insatiable. Tomb robbers can strip even a large site in a night. Word of a new location has to be kept closely guarded."

"Your father wasn't an archeologist, or am I mistaken?"

"His interest was in collecting, but he was passionate about preserving Mexico's archeological heritage. I've since come to doubt it had anything to do with that. There must have been something else that made them want to kill him."

"Like incriminating evidence?"

"Father was about to reveal the president's deposits in a Swiss bank account."

Hernán nodded, but changed the subject.

"Your situation is no worse than others who come here illegally. But two, three, brushes with death and still unscathed?" He shook his head. "Sure you haven't made a deal with the Great Horned One?"

Gar looked down at his clasped hands. "I might have considered it."

"The first thing we have to do is find out about the real Fausto Vásquez. You can't be using the identity of someone who was in trouble with the law."

Hernán's use of "we" was reassuring. "I wondered, but had no choice." If he mentioned the Beretta, Hernán would've advised him to get rid of it. He wasn't yet ready to do that.

"Let me see the driver's license and Social Security card," Hernán stretched out his hand." Bonita can run down the information while we have lunch." Hernán looked at his watch. "I don't know about you. For me it's lunchtime. I know a little place near here that won't offend your Mexican palate. Great burritos. If you can believe it, some of them weigh as much as two kilos."

"You don't mean it?"

"I do. That's American. All-you-can-eat. My treat. Sound OK?"

13

A lunch crowd jammed El Tepeyác, where the odors of cooking meats, onions, spices, and toasting tortillas floated in the air. Hernán, a favored customer in the little restaurant, was shown to a table in a small patio at the rear. There, he and Gar could talk without shouting.

"I've been coming here since the place opened in the mid-50s, before everybody and his uncle discovered it."

The owner came over to greet Hernán with an *abrazo*, promising to send a waitress to their table before he rushed off. While they waited for service, Hernán explained why he'd gotten out of the immigration business. He also confessed to being *persona non grata* with U.S. Immigration for one too many court appearances defending dubious clients. He settled back in his seat and studied the menu.

"What do you do now?" Gar Asked.

"Some legal work involving Latinos, a kind of fundraiser and part-time lobbyist. Works for me." He waved a dismissive hand and would say no more about it.

The waitress set down two glasses of water. Hernán ordered the daily special for both of them.

"Just because I don't drink doesn't mean you can't have something." He looked at Gar over his glasses.

Gar declined, reaching into the newly arrived basket of warm tortilla chips and dipping one into the salsa.

Hernán surveyed the private courtyard for a moment, and picked up the conversation.

"You didn't come here to interview me. You need a job, right?"

"That's right. In fact I came to Los Angeles because I remembered you, hoping to find a familiar face, someone who knows the territory."

"I'd do the same in your position. I'm right about your needing a job?"

"I have one of sorts, working at the Relief Office downtown. It isn't steady and doesn't pay much, but they don't ask questions. We, uh, appreciate each other, you might say. In my situation, there's not much else I can do."

"I wouldn't say that. You could probably work as a stringer. I have contacts at the *Los Angeles Times* and *La Opinión*. They might want to see a résumé, though, and that might create problems. I can check it out, if you like. Meanwhile, you could work with me. I could use your help."

"You're not concerned about my status?"

"I am, but yours is a special situation. You're a refugee. Besides, your father was more than a good friend. I couldn't turn you away."

"Thank you, Don Hernán. I appreciate your loyalty to my family. I hope I'm worthy of your trust."

Hernán brushed the sentiment aside.

"What would I be doing?" Gar asked.

"It's quite legitimate." Hernán removed his glasses and put them in a shirt pocket, his eyes widening as he looked at Gar. "Research, grant proposals, newsletter copy, that sort of thing. But what I need most is someone who can translate English to Spanish, and vice versa, correctly. I'm not much good at Spanish any more."

"I could do that. I accept if I can really be useful. But I didn't come looking for charity."

"Charity? Shit, don't worry, I'll work your butt off." He looked at Gar like he meant it.

The special wasn't the five-pound burrito Hernán had mentioned, for which Gar was glad. The meal's tastiness also came as a welcome surprise.

Over coffee, Hernán became serious.

"If we're going to work together," he said, "I need to know the details of why you left Mexico in such a hurry. You can understand that, I'm sure."

"Of course."

"Don't like surprises."

Gar nodded and took a deep breath. It pained him to tell the story. "My parents were assassinated at the orders of someone high up in the government, the minister of finance."

"Right, you discovered that from the same detective who investigated the murders. I thought death-bed confessions only happened in the movies."

"If it weren't for him, I might never have found out."

"You intended to ferret out the contractor and do him?"

"If that means kill him, I did give it serious thought. But I soon discovered he went nowhere without his bodyguards, and trying to shoot him would've been foolish." Gar paused. "I realized that arming myself and going after him was not only irrational but not my way."

"Agree with the first part, I'll take your word on the second."

"I decided I'd rather see him tried and jailed for life."

Hernán nodded. "What did you do about it?"

Gar sipped from his glass of water.

"You got to him in some other way?" Hernán asked, as if impatient for the punch line.

"I did." Gar told him about the minister's laundering money for a drug cartel, his newspaper's refusal to run the exposé, and asking the Mexico City bureau chief of *The New York Times* to publish it as his own.

"And that got him?" Hernán asked.

Gar shook his head. "On the contrary. The administration did nothing. The minister traced the story to me and put a contract on my head."

Hernán said he remembered that story in the *Times*. "Good work for which someone else got the credit."

"Writing it was the least I could do. I'm not sorry. One way or another I'll get that *pendejo*."

"I can appreciate your frustration. His people made an attempt on your life?"

"They came close to capturing me. Probably to find out what I knew, if not to kill me. I went into hiding. I was warned his people were closing in. That's when I crossed."

"You think they're still looking for you?"

"I don't doubt it."

"No resolution in sight?"

"In time, the regime will change. The minister would be vulnerable to prosecution. Eventually they'll figure out I've left Mexico, but won't know I'm here. This is a big country."

"And this is a big city. But you know they'd expect you to come here."

"Could be, though there are Latino populations in Chicago, New York, other places."

"No matter, the work you do with me should keep your visibility low. In your private life, you're on your own."

Gar noticed other diners at the nearest tables.

"Fair number of non-Latinos here."

"A popular place even with Anglos," Hernán said.

"Is that what you're calling *gringos* these days?" Hernán shrugged. "We're suffering under something called political correctness. We use terminology that offends no one. In the process, we offend everyone."

"Everywhere in L.A. I've seen mostly Latinos," Gar said. "Is it satisfying to have a Latino as mayor after so many years?"

"Last time was in 1872. Cristobál Águilar. We've allowed ourselves to be outmaneuvered and outsmarted for 160 years, since Mexico lost California."

"What kind of man is he, your *alcalde?*"

"A Democrat, no worse or better than others we've had. In a way, they're all alike. Regardless of race or affiliation. Our mayor's no different."

"Meaning what?"

"That a position of power in a society like ours requires compromises."

"It's like that in any democracy."

"True. But when those compromises are too great, you're no longer acting for the public benefit."

"Are you saying your mayor is in the pocket of his backers?"

"He and the whole ass-kissing bunch of them."

"What can you do about it?"

"I'm part of a group trying to answer that. We're raising money and developing strategy. If you're interested you can sit in the next time we meet."

"I'd like that."

Hernán changed the subject. "I've been waiting for you to ask me why your family came to see me all those years ago."

"Of course, I'd forgotten."

"Did you know you had ancestors who were *Califórnios*, the Spaniards and Mexicans who settled California?"

"I recall that being mentioned when I was growing up."

"Your parents came here hoping to reclaim land the Mexican government gave your father's people."

"Did they have proof?"

"They brought documentation and sent more later, but that wasn't the crux of the matter. I did some preliminary inquiries into the disposition of the grant and decided the outcome of a suit could only be inconclusive—and too expensive. It discouraged your father."

"There was no case?"

"Most of the evidence he sent me was anecdotal. I've got the file somewhere in my office, and some documents in a safe deposit box. You're welcome to go through it all."

Talk of his parents left Gar pensive and staring into his coffee cup.

"This woman in whose house you're staying, you tell her

your real identity?"

"It slipped out. She didn't question me."

"How about the woman at the immigration services?"

"She knows me as Fausto Vásquez. I think she knows I'm not legal. She's an Irish immigrant herself. Probably legal, since she has a job with a non-profit."

"Where's the house?"

"Culver City. A livable neighborhood."

"You got to my office without difficulty?"

"Your highway system is frightening, but efficient. I have no problem using it. I'll have to ride the bus or with my landlady until I get a car of my own. She let me use hers today." Gar looked at his watch. "I have to leave here in time to pick her up. I'm not sure what she's expecting in return."

Hernán shifted the conversation again. "Okay, are we agreed on your working with me?"

"With gratitude. But I should give the woman at the Relief office some notice. She's got her hands full."

"Yeah, sure, do that. You could use an advance on your salary, right?" Hernán removed a checkbook and billfold from inside his coat. "You won't get rich working for me. A little cash and check for the rest of your first month's pay are all I can afford. Use the bank named on the check. I keep an account there. It's near here, and the manager is a friend."

Hernán handed Gar a business card on which he'd written a Pasadena address. "For account purposes, you may use my address and phone number until you find a place of your own, if that's what you have in mind. Don't open an account until we find out whether Fausto was clean."

14

In the weeks that followed, Gar's life settled into a routine. But the comforting regularity didn't last.

"He's not happy," Bonita told Gar when he entered Hernán's office on a late June morning.

"What about?" Cryptic, she said nothing and returned to her work. He stopped at the coffee pot and poured himself a cup before continuing inside.

Hernán was facing the wall behind his desk as if studying the map of Los Angeles County hanging there. He spun around when Gar walked in.

"Is there a problem, Don Hernán?" Gar asked.

"Shit, yes, I guess so!" Hernán smacked the top of his desk. "Read that." He practically threw a copy of that day's *Los Angeles Times* across the desk.

Gar put his coffee cup down on the desk and sat in the nearest chair. His eye immediately caught the picture near the bottom of the page. ¡*Ay mierda!* Fausto's mustached face accompanied a news story:

> **Body of Missing Border Patrol Agent Found**
> Laredo, TX (AP)—The whereabouts of U.S. Border Patrol Agent Fausto Vásquez, missing since early April, was discovered today with the recovery of his body, which had been buried in a shallow grave near the wreckage of a pickup truck determined to be his. Both the wreckage and his remains were found by the highway maintenance workers in a ravine adjacent to U.S. Route 227, 40 miles from Carrizo Springs, Texas.

The vehicle, a 1989 four-wheel drive Toyota pickup, appeared to have been heading towards Del Rio, Texas, when it crashed.

Officials from the Del Rio office of the U.S. Border Patrol suspect foul play. One official, who asked to remain anonymous because the case is still under investigation, believes a passenger may have been with Agent Vásquez at the time of the incident and was responsible for burying him. The official, also the agent who investigated the scene, stated that the driver may have fallen asleep at the wheel or otherwise been rendered unconscious before the vehicle went into the ravine.

Judging from the damage sustained by the truck and paint on the fender, the pickup may have been forced off the highway by another vehicle. Ownership of the truck was determined by its license plate registration. Dental records were used to identify the body.

Law enforcement agencies across the country have been alerted to be on the lookout for anyone using Agent Vásquez's identification, which was taken along with his personal effects—most likely by the person who buried him. Anyone with information about the incident is asked to contact the nearest law enforcement office.

Gar sat shaking his head.

"You get it, right?" Hernán stared at him. "Cops really hate it when one of their own goes down."

"His picture might as well be one of me." Gar read the article twice more.

Hernán stood up and leaned across the desk.

"Look, I need to know, to be absolutely certain *you* didn't kill this guy."

Hernán's uncertainty stunned Gar. What could he say? A denial would be expected, so what was left? For a few silent moments he simply looked back at Hernán. He took a deep breath and spoke as calmly as he could.

"Don Hernán, I am not a killer. What I told you about Fausto and me is true—in every detail. I nearly died with him. His death was unfortunate, but you must believe me."

Hernán sat back in his chair and removed his reading glasses. As he rubbed his eyes, he said, "The way trouble seems to come to you reminds me of Tar Baby."

"What?"

"Nothing, something from a child's story. Forget it." He returned his glasses to his eyes.

"*Increíble.* I just can't believe it." The paper was shaking in Gar's hands. He looked up again at Hernán. "It's hard to accept that Fausto's beat-up truck, his tools, his clothes, all of it was just a cover to catch people like me. He played the part too well. I was completely taken in."

"That's the way it looks. But it's not that surprising." Hands behind his head, Hernán leaned back and gazed up at the ceiling.

"What do you mean?"

"The Immigration and Customs Enforcement, what we call ICE, and its border patrol have taken so much criticism in recent years, they've had to get tougher, be more clever, try out all sorts of things."

Gar shook his head in amazement again. "It still seems incredible. Vásquez had no border patrol identification, no radio. His hands were rough like a field worker's."

"Fits the role he played. Picking crops would be a likely place for large numbers of illegals to earn some fast money, get food and water, wouldn't you think? No questions asked by farmers happy to get the cheap labor without paying benefits and pocketing the deductions. Vásquez probably checked out the large farms in his region, labored alongside other migrants 'til he found out how many illegals worked the place. Then if there were enough to justify a raid..."

"His damn friendliness made me feel that he really cared about helping me. It was us against them, the *gringos*—

rednecks, he called them. He offered to help me get work. He was interested in my English. He noticed my hands. He played the role perfectly and I fell right into the trap."

"Don't beat yourself up. There's no way you could've known. Without food and water you were in a tough spot. Be grateful that, for whatever else, Vásquez was compassionate. Still, it's strange we didn't find a connection with the border patrol when Bonita checked Fausto's documents."

Gar replayed the whole scenario. "You see what this means? What if he and I hadn't met those *pinche* rednecks? Fausto would have arrested me and driven me straight to jail in Del Rio to be deported. Or what if we'd stopped, instead of going off the road?" He paused again. "They'd probably have killed us. Some choice."

"Either way, you wouldn't be here now."

"If you were still a smoker, Don Hernán, I'd be puffing on one of your cigarettes."

"And if I weren't a recovering alcoholic, I'd be offering you a shot."

"So I'll have to be satisfied with coffee." Gar raised the mug with both hands to keep it from shaking, and drained the cold dregs.

"There's something else you have to be concerned about." Hernán pointed at him, barely able to keep from wagging his fnger. "The border patrol and other law enforcement agencies are looking for Fausto Vásquez, which is not the most common name."

"You think I should leave? The last thing I want is to compromise you."

"That's not what I mean. But you have to think about whom you've met since you got here, the people who'd remember you as Fausto Vásquez."

"There can't be many. The woman I rent from knows me as Gar Montalvo. Those other two women, the one at the immigration services office and the one at the Universal Relief know me as Vásquez."

"She pay you with checks?"

"I cashed them at one of those check-cashing places."

"How about at the Y? Didn't you use his name there?"

"Yes, but the clerk seemed indifferent, like he could barely tolerate his job."

"You'll have to hope those people don't see the article, or keep their mouths shut if they do."

"Exactly what I'm hoping for." Following up with Riona was now out of the question.

"Good thing you didn't apply for a new driver's license." He pointed a finger at Gar again. "You know, you're taking a helluva risk driving around the city using that license in your landlady's car. If you're stopped..."

"I know, I know."

"The important thing now is to get you some new documentation."

"How?""Gar spread his hands.

"Not that difficult. Like everything else, all it takes is money. Fifty to a hundred bucks for a Social Security Card. With that you can get a driver's license. You'll have to take the tests, though."

"You know where to go?"

"Over on Alvarado Street, across from MacArthur Park. You'll see a couple of guys, Mexicans or Salvadorans, who look like they're loitering. Drive up and down the street a few times. You'll see them. Once you make contact, they'll take it from there—photo ID, Social Security number, everything."

"But that's illegal, too."

"Bet your ass it is. You've got no other option. I suggest you buy a car as soon as you've got the documents."

"You really think there's no other way?"

"Well, you could turn yourself in to immigration," he said, deadpan. "If they don't deport you on the spot, you'll land in jail while you wait for an asylum hearing. That could take months while you try to prove there is a real danger to your life in Mexico."

"And expose my whereabouts to those looking for me."

"Yeah, there's that." Hernán paused. "Then there's the matter of how Fausto Vásquez died. Think of the mess that would entail."

They sat silent for a moment, Hernán watching Gar.

"You OK? You look awful."

"I'll be all right." Gar took couple of deep breaths, and picked up the newspaper again. "You know what's strange? I've been feeling guilty about what happened to Fausto, because I survived and he didn't."

"You feel like he got what he deserved, even though he was just doing his job?"

"He didn't deserve what happened. I had the idea that somehow Latinos on this side would naturally do what they could to help a *paisano*."

"You kidding? We have a Latino from El Paso in the U.S. Congress, who got there by being the meanest sonuvabitch border patrol agent. The border patrol is full of Latinos. They need the work, and the patrols need people who can talk to the illegals."

"I wonder that they don't suffer a confusion of loyalty."

Hernán let the comment pass. "Anyway, I've told you what I think your next step should be, and I wouldn't waste any time making it."

"Right away. Should I use my real name or pick another?"

"Your landlady already knows you by Gar. You might as well continue with it. No point raising her suspicion."

15

Fausto's secret life was still playing in Gar's head the next morning. A pounding on his door interrupted his thinking. Barefoot and wearing jeans, he opened the door to his panic-stricken and wild-eyed housemate, Annie, whose hand was poised to knock again.

"It's Gisela," Annie said, chest heaving. "Can you help me with her?"

"What happened?"

"I don't know. I'd just finished up in the kitchen and thought I heard someone moaning. When I went to check it out and opened her door, she fell across the threshold, blood all over her head. If I hadn't been late on my way out, she might still be lying there."

He followed Annie, who was already halfway down the hall. With the door ajar, Gisela was face down, unconscious.

There was so much blood! For a moment, he had to shut his eyes and fight back a spurt of anxiety and a wave of revulsion. He knelt beside her, pressing a finger to her neck, feeling for a pulse.

"She's alive."

"Thank God," Annie whispered, a hand to her mouth.

"Gisela? Gisela?" He shook her shoulder but got no response. "Come on Gisela, speak to me." He shook her a little harder.

"Oh Gawd, my head," she groaned.

"Can you sit up?"

"Gimme me a minute. Yeah, I guess so." She started to push herself up.

"Let us help you." They grabbed her by the arms and propped her against the doorframe. Her torn halter fell away, exposing her blood-spattered breasts. Annie stared with him.

"Cover her," he said.

Annie pulled up the ends of the torn strap and held them together behind Gisela's neck.

Gisela touched her scalp and looked at her hand. "Christ, I'm bleeding like a stuck hog. Must've passed out."

"Did you fall?" Gar asked.

"Hell, no. A couple of assholes attacked me at the end of the bike path. Tried to rape me. I bashed one of them. You should've seen the bastard spit blood."

"Did they say anything to you?" Gar asked.

"Yeah, but nothing I understood. The big one just grunted. Couldn't fgure out what the fuck that was all about." She sucked in a breath and let it out. "But grabbing my tits was clear enough. I smacked him in the face. He hit me back and I fell. That's when the other one clobbered me. When I got back up and started screaming they ran. After that, I don't remember much."

Annie, mouth still agape, was trying without success to tie the ends of the halter strap.

"How bad is it?" Gisela mumbled.

"Lower your chin and I'll take a look. This might hurt." He pulled apart the hair at the source of the blood. "It's hard to say how long or deep the wound is. Cuts on the head bleed like a spigot. It's stopped, but you've got an egg-sized lump. You should have it stitched. Think you can walk?"

"Yeah, sure."

He motioned for Annie to help him get Gisela back to her room.

"Is there a clinic or hospital nearby where we can take her?" he asked.

"A clinic's up on Santa Monica Boulevard," Annie said. "I'd go with you, but this is exam week and I've got a biggie this morning."

"Do you know where the clinic is?" he asked Gisela. She nodded. Then to Annie he said, "Have you got time to help her out of that…"

"Sports bra, it's called a sports bra," Annie said.

"OK, that, and clean the rest of the blood off her so she can get into something clean. While you're doing that, I'll get dressed myself. Then I'll take her to see a doctor."

Annie left the room and then returned to Gisela with a damp washcloth. "You really shouldn't let this attack go by without reporting it to the police," she said.

At the clinic, Gar worried about bringing the police into the picture, even though Gisela said she didn't want to report the incident.

"It's a waste of time," she told him. "Just a lot of questions, paperwork, and who knows what else. No use."

"Up to you," he said, relieved but worried about her.

"First time I've been attacked, but you read that it happens all the time."

"You think the police don't care?"

"Probably do. But they treat these cases with the same attention they give to littering. They never catch the jerks that do it. Oh, they'd question *me* all right. Then they'd throw the report in the circular file. I mean, what is there to investigate? But those assholes didn't get away clean. I gave one a good punch in the kisser. Worth it to see the look on his face. One of them was spittin' teeth. They won't be bothering anyone for a while."

Jesucristo. "So you fought them off."

"Bet your sweet ass. I raked the smaller guy's face and tore him a few gashes. He'll be marked for a while, too."

"The nurse thought I'd beaten you up."

"What? You're kidding."

"Asked me about it right there in the waiting room. Didn't bother to keep her voice down, either, and had everybody looking at us like she should call the police."

"You know what they say about good deeds..."

He didn't know, didn't ask. Instead he told her, "Lucky you wear your hair up the way you do. The nurse said it saved you from worse injury. Whatever he hit you with might otherwise have given you a concussion, cracked your skull, or maybe killed you."

"Then the bastard would've gotten laid by a corpse." She chuckled. "Probably wouldn't have mattered to him."

They drove the rest of the way to the house in silence, Gisela resting her head on her hand against the window.

When they were back in her room and she was propped up in bed, Gar realized they'd missed breakfast.

"We haven't eaten, Gisela. What can I get for you?"

"Toast and coffee'll be fine, maybe some juice. Not really hungry. The pain killers took away my appetite."

"Are you sure? You've lost a lot of blood, not to mention the emotional shock. You really should eat more."

"Don't worry about it. I'll fix something later, if I feel like it."

"I've been thinking. Maybe I should start running with you in the morning. I could use the exercise and I'd be there in case your admirers come back for an encore."

"Hey, I'd really like that, with or without the admirers."

When they'd finished eating, Gisela gazed at him, her eyes drug-shiny.

"I appreciate what you did for me today, Gar. You're a sweet guy."

"Anyone would have done the same." He waved off the remark.

"No, you really cared."

He steered her to another subject. "I hope you don't plan to go to work today."

"Nah, I'm a mess. Besides nobody wants to see a receptionist with her head bandaged. Annie called in sick for me. Take the car and go on with your day."

"I'll call you around noon to see how you're doing. If

you need anything..."

"Don't sweat it. All I need's rest. The pain killers are making me sleepy. Annie'll be home in the early afternoon."

"Ok, I'll look in on you after work."

"I'd like that. Maybe we can watch some TV together again tonight." As he picked up the tray of dishes and moved to leave the room she called.

"Hey."

He stopped and looked back at her.

"I won't forget this."

"I certainly hope not." He tried to make a joke of it.

Her eyes continued to hold his until he turned away and closed the door.

He tried to deny that he felt anything for her. But that body...and he'd been so long without sex. In spite of his intentions, matters between them might take a turn he'd neither expected nor wanted.

Thinking again over Gisela's attack, he wondered about the language her attackers spoke. Could they possibly have been trying to get to him? No, how could that be possible? He dismissed the thought, returning to the more immediate concern. As much as he hated doing so, he began to think seriously that maybe he should find another place.

Gisela's head ached and her hands still weren't healed, but, showing her mettle, she was back at work the following Monday. She waved off Gar's suggestion to take a full week to recover. As she told Annie, she just couldn't stand to be home alone all day.

Gisela began offering to cook for him. He declined repeated invitations to watch TV with her in the evenings, claiming a need to study the motor vehicle department pamphlet to get a California license. Her attentions were disconcerting. He wished she'd stop laying it on.

Maybe she'd taken his offer to run with her as more than concern for her safety. As each day passed she seemed to become more insistent that she show her gratitude in some manner. By week's end, her attitude made things in the house increasingly uncomfortable for Annie. Over the weekend, he found reasons to spend as much time as he could away from the house.

The following Monday morning, he padded to the shower, hoping to avoid her. He had no intention of getting involved with any woman, much less his landlady. What he needed was a cold shower to quell arousal and clear his head.

When he entered the kitchen a while later, Gisela and Annie were already preparing breakfast for themselves.

"Morning, Gar," Gisela said without looking at him.

Annie was silent. He returned a greeting meant for both of them. He hadn't yet figured out how to clear the air and was thankful for Annie's presence. Gisela avoided making eye contact and the three of them ate in silence.

"Running late. Better get moving." Gisela rose from the table, pretending nothing was amiss. That suited him fine—he preferred not to discuss their situation.

She remained detached on the drive into the city, waiting for him to make the next move. But he'd already decided to change the arrangement, to end his dependence on her and stop further involvement. He would get his own transportation first and then move to another place. He hoped she wouldn't feel insulted.

Gisela made no comment when he called to say he'd bought a car and left hers in the city garage. She did acknowledge the old Volkswagen Golf parked behind the house that evening.

"Like I told you before, you gotta have a car in L.A." she said.

<u>16</u>

The Golf put needed distance between Gar and Gisela, but he did miss their daily commute. Though she showed no resentment about the car, he knew she felt rejected. Within a week, he felt life in the house was back to normal and he put off looking for another place to live.

Hernán applauded the car purchase. He'd been wanting to get Gar out to his home to meet his wife. Gar took the invitation as a sign that Hernán had no lingering questions about Fausto's death.

Despite heavy Sunday traffic, the trip to Pasadena took less time than he thought it would. With time to spare, he drove through the tree-lined neighborhoods for a look around. The city had more than its share of beautiful gardens and stately homes, the kind that show up in decorator magazines. He wondered how Hernán could afford to live there. His white stucco rambler looked expensive. Gar wouldn't mind living there himself.

Hernán's petite and attractive wife answered the door.

"You must be Gar, the mystery man Hernán's been talking about. I'm Aurélia." She flashed a sincere smile.

"You're kind to invite me to your home," he replied.

"*Holá*, Gar, hope you got here with no trouble?" Hernán strode into the foyer. They exchanged *abrazos*.

"May I offer you wine?" Aurélia asked.

Hernán led him into the well-appointed living room. Gar's eyes settled on a pair of glass-fronted cabinets filled with pre-Columbian artifacts. The collection took up a whole wall. Even from across the room, it appeared to be as extensive as his father's had been. Gar wondered how Hernán could afford it. Or if he might have trafficked in plundered art. He knew that technically it was all stolen. The origins of pre-Columbian art were usually impossible to verify. It gave collectors the excuse they needed to justify their acquisitions.

"Hernán tells me that you were a journalist for a Mexico City newspaper," Aurélia said as she entered the room with wine and two stemmed glasses. She poured one for him, another for herself, then sat on an adjacent sofa. "Do you plan to work for a newspaper here?"

"That's a possibility, but Don Hernán made me a generous offer I couldn't turn down." He glanced at Hernán, wondering why he hadn't told her the whole story about him.

"Both your parents taught at a university? May I ask your mother's field?"

"Sociology. At the same university as my father's. They met as students before they were married."

"Romantic." She appeared delighted. "Do you have brothers or sisters?"

"My parents always explained that being academics didn't leave much time for raising a large family." He looked for a way to end family questions, but she went on.

"You must have been lonely growing up."

"I had playmates," Gar answered a bit too quickly. Before Aurélia could get around to asking why he'd left Mexico, he was saying, "Pasadena is quite a beautiful city. When I first heard of it, I thought the name was Spanish."

"You mean it's not?" Aurélia looked surprised.

"According to the City of Pasadena's website, the name is Native American."

"You can blame a group of Indiana farmers for that," Hernán joined in. "When they came in the late nineteenth century, they named it after the Chippewa word for valley. Funny, since Chippewas had never set foot in California."

"Apart from its charm, I'm wondering how you chose to live in Pasadena."

Hernán and Aurélia looked at each other.

"Tell him, Hernán." Hernán, nodding, pursed his lips and seemed to decide on an answer. Gar looked at one and then the other and back again, wondering if his question embarrassed them.

"Yes, this is quite a city but we're not here just because it's a nice place to live. Like a lot of Mexican immigrants, we lived first in East L.A. My dad had a job there teaching high school. Living among *paisanos* did have its good side. But the barrio was—still is—ignored by the city. It's a dangerous place to live and grossly rundown." He paused for a moment and stared at the floor. "Those were rough times."

"Dad always hoped to save enough to move the family to a neighborhood like this," Hernán continued, "but when he could afford to and tried to buy a house here, there were covenants that kept Mexicans out. Even renters. Of course they applied to Asians and Negroes, too."

"What did your father do?"

"He moved us to central L.A., which was an improvement."

"There's more." Aurélia said, looking at Gar.

"Fair housing became law in the '60s," Hernán picked up the story, "and I decided to do what Dad couldn't, and thumb my nose at the bastards who'd kept us out before."

"You've done that very nicely," Gar said.

"He makes it sound a lot easier than it was." Aurélia rose to pour more wine. "We had problems buying here. The covenants were gone, but the conspiracy to keep us out was still in place."

"Then how...?"

"A little conspiracy of our own," Hernán said. "An Anglo buddy I served with in Korea bought this place and sold it to us."

"You should have seen the hell the neighbors raised," Aurélia smiled at the memory. "After nearly forty years, the climate has changed. We get along."

"When we had lunch, Don Hernán, I meant to ask why your family left Mexico in the first place."

"Same reason lots of people of my parent's age did: The Mexican Revolution. In ten years, more than two million people died. When it ended in 1921, they hung on for another dozen years. I was born and arrived here along with the Depression. Not very good timing."

"Lunch is ready. You must be hungry." Aurélia stood and led the way to the dining room. While they ate, she gave an entertaining description of their neighbors' eccentricities.

Later as they sat drinking coffee, Gar told her, "Your home is very attractive. Much in it reminds me of Mexico. Especially your collection of pre-Columbian artifacts."

"Hernán's pride and joy." Aurélia's sarcasm hinted at discord, but Hernán took no notice.

"Come on, let me show you," he said.

Gar could tell immediately that Hernán had invested seriously in his collection. Gar's father had owned some exquisite pieces, and many in this display were their equal: delicate figurines of silver and turquoise, intricate nose and ear ornaments, a gold face mask. Some of the fragile clay pieces, their polychrome symbols still distinct, were also like those in his father's collection.

"These are quite extraordinary," Gar said, meaning it, while recalling his father's crusading attitude about protecting Mexico's heritage. His father's viewpoint had rubbed off on him. Looking at the beautiful ancient pieces stirred some resentment. He had to remind himself that they were also part of Hernán's heritage, and he could appreciate the man's affection for them.

"Are they all from Mexican cultures?" Gar recognized Aztec and Olmec pieces.

"Most are, but this one," Hernán opened the class door and gently picked up a golden goblet, "is Peruvian, from the Moche culture."

Gar saw its tissue-like delicacy. He supposed it could

easily be worth thousands.

"These gold beads and discs," Hernán went on, "they're Moche, too. The crown there is Inca. In fact, everything on this shelf is from Peru."

"I keep telling him," Aurélia said, joining them, "that buying this stuff only encourages the looting, not to mention that it might also be illegal to own it. Honestly, it wouldn't surprise me if one day the FBI raided us."

"*Mi amor*," he turned to look at her, a weary expression on his face, "I've told you I have provenance documents for every piece." He spoke gently but with a trace of annoyance.

"Somehow I don't find that reassuring," she replied. "What about the people you have to deal with? Like that man who insists on showing you his wares. You know who I mean, the one with the silly grin."

"In any realm there are unattractive people." Hernán shrugged. "It can't be helped."

Aurélia raised her eyes skyward.

Watching and listening to them, Gar could see how much they cared for each other, despite their disagreement. In a similar circumstance his father would have snapped at his mother, leaving her hurt and both of them angry.

"Didn't you tell me your father collected?" Hernán turned to Gar.

"He did, but he never had to worry about being raided or having his collection confiscated."

"Why was that?" Maybe Aurélia hoped his answer would score a point for her side.

"He had everything registered with the antiquities authorities. And he kept the collection in the country. He believed he was rescuing the artifacts from destruction or loss. And he had a point." Gar thought the argument was self-serving.

"Of course he was right," Hernán said. "That's exactly how I feel about these pieces." He appeared grateful for Gar's rationale.

"How is this stuff smuggled into the country?" Aurélia's question brought Gar out of a reverie.

"Many ways, some more creative than others." Hernán didn't seem to care that he might be stoking suspicions. "Some dealers bribe customs officials and airline employees. Think of the influx of drugs. Needless to say, there are other ways."

"Just like that?" Aurélia shook her head.

"You must be concerned that you might be trading with shady people." Gar regretted the comment as soon as it left his mouth.

"I admit I can't be sure, which is why, though they contact me all the time, I rarely buy from individuals. I deal with reputable galleries that belong to the dealers' association. And I make sure I have documents for every piece showing where and from whom I purchased it. My exposure to prosecution is minimal to nonexistent."

The lawyerly reply still left Gar wondering how Hernán had acquired a collection of such quality. All together, it was worth a small fortune.

17

Aurélia was still thinking about Gar long after he'd gone. Her overall impressions of him were positive. She liked that he came from a family of educators. Her husband's relationship with Gar left her wondering, though. His boyhood friendship with Gar's father happened so long ago.

Her husband was more animated when they talked about Gar, which was often. Hernán's liveliness was even more noticeable during the visit. Maybe he liked having a younger colleague in the office. She thought, too, he might be looking at Gar as a surrogate son, the child they'd wanted but couldn't have. Sessions with a therapist hadn't gotten them to closure. Even though the medical tests proved inconclusive, she blamed herself.

Hernán, in the study watching the L.A. Dodgers going down in defeat again, failed to hear the doorbell. Startled out of her pensiveness, Aurélia waited a moment to see if he would answer it then went to the door herself. She hadn't invited anyone else and was annoyed that someone would call so late on a Sunday afternoon without at least phoning.

The chime sounded a third time. Was it a neighbor in an emergency? Though the thought alarmed her, she mainly felt irritated as she reached the foyer. She didn't take time to look through the peephole before opening the door. She soured as she recognized the oversized briefcase and the man who carried it.

"You again." She'd asked Hernán repeatedly not to deal with him, but here he was again.

"Good to see you, too, Mrs. Gárza." he said, exposing a

mouth full of yellow teeth as he grinned.

Aurélia, repulsed, couldn't look him in the face. Why would a middle-aged man wear a ponytail and an earring? Good Lord! She'd been surprised to see Gar wearing one. What was that all about, anyway? She wanted to tell the man to stand up straight, clean himself up, show some self-respect. Instead, she sighed and let her manner convey her feelings.

"Wait here," she said, refusing to look the man in the eye as she closed the door and headed for the den.

"He's back again, Hernán."

"You mean Gar?" Hernán rose.

"I wish. No, it's that man you insist on dealing with." She turned on her heel. From the kitchen she heard Hernán allow the man to enter.

"I don't think your wife likes me, Mr. Gárza," the man said as he stood in the foyer.

Hernán said nothing, leading him back to the den. He switched off the TV and faced his visitor.

"Barney, I think you'd get a friendlier greeting if you'd call first, especially on a Sunday."

"I should know better. I apologize." He looked sheepish. "But I've really got some good stuff here. I wanted to give you first chance at it. With all the appointments I've got tomorrow there might be nothing left for you."

"I understand, but I've told you before I still prefer going to that office of yours. You see my wife's reaction when you come here."

"I know, I know. I'm sorry." Barney was whining. "Like I said, I have other calls to make. I wanted you to have first crack this time."

"OK, you're here. Let's have a look." Hernán set to clearing the desktop.

Barney's eyes were gleaming as he laid the case on one end of the desk and opened it. He took each piece from the case, carefully unwrapped it, and set it on the desktop for

Hernán's inspection.

"That's quite a haul," Hernán said, looking over the array. "You've got documentation for this stuff? I've told you before, I can't afford to take anything that doesn't have a clear provenance."

"I assure you," Barney said, sobering, "everything here is documented the way you like. But as you know, I can't tell how I come by any of it. That I can't do."

"I don't want to know about your sources. What I do care about are authenticity and value. The last things you showed me were poor quality. And I'm afraid that's true of these pieces."

"Yeah, well I don't have any control over that, Mr. Gárza."

"No, I suppose not. Well, thanks anyway for showing me. After this, let's set up an appointment at your office."

"Whatever you say."

"And by the way, aren't you afraid of getting mugged? Anyone can see that you're carrying a display case. And they could assume there's something valuable in it."

"Don't worry about me, Mr. Gárza. I'm not alone." He pulled aside the left flap of his jacket to show the .38 pistol in his shoulder holster.

"You have a permit to carry that?"

"You bet I do. And I know how to use it."

"I'll take you at your word," Hernán said.

"I signed up for instruction and target practice at a gun club," Barney continued, warming to his subject. "I don't mean to brag, but I'm a good shot. Steady as a rock, not like most beginners, who flinch even with earplugs." Indeed, Barney never flinched. He could hit a silhouette at 50 feet, the club's maximum indoor range. That fact alone, he thought to himself, makes me one of the guys.

Hernán listened impatiently.

"Single or double-handed," Barney said, smiling, "I always to go for the head. Never miss." He was full of self-admiration.

In the kitchen, Aurélia was fuming at the conversation in the den. Hernán's collection was every bit as obsessive as an addict's to drugs, she thought. Even if he wasn't using their retirement money to pay for it, she considered it wrong.

Half an hour later, when she heard the front door close and Hernán return to the den, she waited a few minutes to calm herself before following him there.

"You aren't showing much respect for my feelings."

He looked up at her. "What do you mean?"

"Allowing that revolting man in our home." She crossed her arms, but Hernán was focused on the ballgame. He couldn't ignore her. He switched off the TV.

"If it makes you feel any better, *mi amor*, I told him not to come here again. He had a lot of pieces, most of it disappointing. I didn't buy anything."

"Well, I'm grateful for that. Was that because you thought the stuff was hot?"

"*Ay, mi amor,* I'm an old man, won't you allow me one of my few pleasures?"

"Don't you play on my sympathy." She sat on the sofa next to him. "I'm not trying to deprive you of anything. But I don't like that man! You know I worry about the legal side of it. If he's dealing contraband, he may drag you down with him."

Hernán leaned over and kissed his wife on the cheek. This was a talk they'd had before and would most likely have again.

18

The front door slammed.

"You're late again, Barney." Mrs. Spokes turned off the faucet and dried her hands, waiting for the response. "Barney?" She called out, louder. "I've been holding dinner so long it's nearly ruined."

Barney shuffled to his room at the back of the bungalow.

"Be there in a minute."

He set his display case on the desk, removed his coat and threw it on the bed. Shrugging out of the shoulder holster, he hung it on the back of a chair. In the bathroom he splashed water on his face, toweled off, combed his hair and retied his ponytail. He didn't like his reflection in the mirror. If she's sulking, he thought, we'll spend the rest of the evening arguing about what to watch on TV.

My fault, he told himself. Shouldn't have hung out at the club so long. But it was only there that he had what passed for friends. Even so, he didn't fool himself that he was really liked by any of them. Still, when they gathered around to watch him shoot, it gave him a charge. He'd won more than one trophy for the club.

Why did he have such a hard time making friends? People pushed him away. Like the man he met at Olvera Street by the museum with pre-Columbian stuff a few weeks ago. With a shared interest in ancient art, why couldn't they be friends? Such a nice looking fellow, and he wore an earring too. Why was he hanging around the museum for hours with that backpack, Barney wondered.

His mother called again.

"Barney, you gonna keep me waiting all night, too? I'm starting without ya, hear?"

At forty-five, Barney still lived at home. He knew his widowed mother was disappointed in him. She wanted him married. She wanted grandkids. He'd tried to live on his own, to be ready in case he met someone. But that hadn't worked. He'd met no one. Meanwhile, he and his mother had both been miserable apart. She was a fearful woman who needed help to get by.

Barney was a good provider, despite his mother's complaining, and she was keenly tuned to his moods. On this night, as he took his place at the table, she knew he was angry. She knew better than to disturb him at the dinner table, however. By mutual agreement they left their troubles somewhere else, at least while they ate.

She disliked having a gun in the house, but had better sense than try to make him get rid of it. She worried about her son being robbed. He was licensed to carry, to protect himself and his wares. She'd heard all about his marksmanship and knew the pistol was one of Barney's few pleasures. She admitted pride in the trophies he won.

She was happy he took pleasure in his work. As he liked to tell her, the people he dealt with had class. Even in a down economy the money was good, though it came with the constant threat of trouble. She tried not to think about the fact that the stuff he sold was smuggled. That bothered her. He told her not to worry. Only in the beginning was he afraid of being caught. Then he'd discovered that buyers were more concerned with their collections than provenance. Over time, he'd become something of an expert at valuing artifacts. Experience and market savvy had turned him into a shrewd bargainer. His income had moved steadily upward.

He kept a sales relationship with that real estate agency to avoid scrutiny from the IRS. To account for his income, Barney paid the agency's principal broker what amounted to a monthly bribe, since he sold no real estate. The job's unstructured hours fit neatly with the time he spent selling artifacts. He marveled that there were always buyers for contraband, even at steep prices.

But that was before the new regime. He flushed at the thought: He should've known business was too good to last. The decline began when the new man arrived. He turned out to be a hard ass, an arrogant bastard who wanted a higher percentage.

When the goods started to dry up, Barney wasn't too concerned. There'd been dry spells before, but even then there'd been at least a trickle. For a time now, there'd been next to nothing. And even when the flow resumed, both his commission and the quality of the pieces declined. Sales were more difficult to make. His income had fallen.

When repeated attempts to renegotiate his deal failed, he decided he could be a hard ass, too. His threat to expose the smuggling operation brought no improvement in either the number or quality of the artifacts he was allowed to sell. The new man reacted by lowering Barney's take again.

With each slight, his anger grew. He was tired of the disrespect. He'd deal with this latest insult and put an end to the poor treatment.

"Everything go OK today?" His mother didn't usually ask, but working on a Sunday seemed like overdoing it.

"Yeah, I guess you could say that."

"Well, you don't look like it."

19

Visiting the Gárzas eased Gar's anxiety about Hernán's trust. Before he left, the old attorney had suggested they collect the Montalvo land grant documentation from the safe deposit the next day. The prospect made him anxious and elated at the same time.

Gar was about to discover what his father hadn't shared with him, what he'd gone to some lengths to hide. Gar had already decided to take the documents, whatever they were, back to the office, rather than sorting through them at the bank.

On the way to the bank, Hernán told Gar why he had an account and kept his valuables in such a downtrodden neighborhood. Banks have little interest in serving the working poor. He'd lobbied hard to have the branch put there. Part of the deal was finding a manager who could relate to the locals the branch would serve. The man, a Latino who got the job, seemed made for the position. After all that effort, Hernán felt obliged to use the bank too.

A one-story building, it squatted on a corner lot at the fringe of the East L.A. barrio not far from Hernán's office. The street teemed with traffic and Monday morning shoppers. It was the same bank Hernán sent Gar to cash his first check. Like other nearby buildings, graffiti sprayed most of the exterior. Gar admired one piece that stretched along the bank's windowless wall.

The young woman at the reception desk smiled at them.

"Joe Mendoza still running things here?" Hernán showed her a safe-deposit box key.

She nodded and spoke into the intercom on her desk. While they waited, Gar looked around the near-empty lobby. A murmured discussion between a customer and a teller at the far end and the air conditioning unit in the ceiling produced the only sounds. The quiet reminded Gar of being in an empty church, and here the presence of money created its own kind of hushed awe.

A sharp clicking of heels on the terrazzo floor broke the silence and indicated the manager's approach.

"Mr. Gárza, it's a pleasure to see you again."

"Likewise, Joe." They shook hands. "My associate, Gar Montalvo."

"I seem to recall that you were in here a few weeks ago. To cash a check, wasn't it?" Hernán interrupted before Gar could answer.

"When did you commission the mural outside?" Hernán inclined his head in that direction.

"You kidding?" Joe turned to Hernán. "I left here one night about a week ago with the usual scribbling on the walls. Next morning, *voilá*. Imagine doing that freehand with spray cans and working by streetlight. He must've used a whole case of spray paint."

"It's well done. Very impressive," Gar said.

"So well done no one else has touched it, no one wanting to contest the territory. That's not only amazing, but also fine with me."

"Too bad a kid like that doesn't go legit and make some money at it," Hernán said.

Joe nodded. "I ever meet him, I'll suggest it." He led the way to the vault at the rear of the room.

Hernán signed the log and handed over his key. He followed the manager into the vault and emerged moments later with a large metal box. Gar carried it to the viewing cubicle.

"You need anything else, just ask." Joe paused and addressed Gar again. "Now I recall. You're one of our new accounts."

"That's right." Gar nodded and waved as the manager left, heels click-clacking back to his office.

"I never opened an account," Gar told Hernán, "but I was still afraid he'd remember my using Fausto's name to endorse your check.'"

"I thought of that, too. Don't sweat it. He's not likely to be involved in that kind of detail. Even if he's figured it out, Joe's a very discreet man."

Hernán might be right about Joe, but the encounter left him unnerved.

The large metal container weighed much less than its size suggested. Gar placed it on the table in the small enclosure and stepped back for Hernán to open it. When Hernán hesitated, Gar moved toward the door.

"I'll wait outside."

"No need. All the stuff in here was your father's." Hernán lifted the lid and removed a sealed foot-long, black plastic tube and handed it to Gar. He took it and slowly let out the breath he'd been holding. He shook it. No sound. It must contain a document, he told himself. He laid it on a nearby chair. He watched Hernán remove one large envelope after another and put them on the narrow table next to the container.

Then Gar saw it—a wooden chest from his boyhood.

"Go ahead, take it out." Hernán encouraged.

Gar lifted the chest. Cradling it in one arm, he ran his fingers lovingly over the cover. The scuffed dented surfaces had once been polished. The chest had belonged to some relative, the reason he supposed his father had forbidden him to play with it. He remembered trying to secretly pry open the mysterious box. Over the years, he'd forgotten all about it. Now, here it was in his hands, to do with as he wished.

"Strange, I remember it being much bigger." He held it at arms length the better to see it.

"It's big enough," Hernán said. "It took Joe's largest safe

box to hold it."

Gar studied the lid again. "When I was a boy, I found the carving on the cover interesting but never realized it was the family's coat of arms."

"It's the Montalvo name that's entitled on the crest. It may or may not have been awarded to your ancestors."

Still readable and carved in high relief, the crest retained much of the original deep blue background in the crevasses. Gar wondered about the meaning of the white, three-turreted castle dominating the center of the shield and the silver crescent moon hovering above the castle. The Montalvo name floated beneath the coat of arms, in an extravagant florid script on an unfurled banner.

"The mahogany, or whatever it is, has held up well," Hernán observed.

"T'zalam. It's T'zalam," Gar repeated, "a hardwood from the Mexican rain forest. It's like mahogany, but with a unique grain and more colors. The copper and purple tinting the brown are hard to see, dulled after so many years." He rapped the wood with a knuckle. "But as you say, it's still solid. As a boy I used to carve figures out of it."

"Well, go ahead and open it," Hernán said. "It's not locked."

"I'd rather wait," Gar said, "until we get back to the office, where I can spread everything out on my desk. Do you plan on keeping the safe deposit a while longer? I don't have a place to keep any of this."

"The box is paid for the rest of the year. We can decide whether to keep it later," Hernán told him.

Gar stuffed the chest and the other items from the safe deposit into the carrier they'd brought along. Hernán was suddenly somber. Gar didn't ask why.

20

The contents of the canvas bag made a satisfying pile on Gar's desk. He doubted that anything they might contain would reveal a motive for his family's murders.

He hesitated opening the black plastic cylinder until he knew more about what was in it, but couldn't wait to examine the envelopes and chest.

He raised the lid to a musty odor of old paper and leather. Among the documents on top was an envelope, addressed to Hernán, which he set aside. Beneath the envelope Gar found a small leather-bound diary, held shut by a fraying band of blue satin ribbon. On the inside cover of the diary, his grandmother, Josefina Montalvo, had written her name. The same tight neat Spanish script covered the diary's brittle yellowed pages. Gar leafed through a few of them and then retied the ribbon.

Under the diary, bound with more of the same faded ribbon, lay a thick packet of hand-written letters. He lifted it and felt its heft. The top-most envelope, in an ink that had faded to a pale brown, bore a Mexico City address and the surname Zavala. At first look, Gar was let down by the contents, though the stuff must have been pretty important for his father and Hernán to have taken such pains with it.

In English, the letter addressed to Hernán was from Gar's father, who had used his office stationery from the National Autonomous University of Mexico. The letter was dated January 31, 1982.

Estimado Hernán,

THE LAST CALIFÓRNIO

If you have been following events here, you are doubtless aware that the economic crisis has created an unstable political situation. I have always been outspoken about government policy and, now falsely, I have been accused of inciting my students to insurrection. As you may know, recent demonstrations have resulted in outrageous countermeasures. While my blunt response has made me unpopular in some circles, I never thought it a cause to fear for my life. Yet, friends in and outside of the administration have warned me of my danger.

I am getting my affairs in order, and am especially concerned for my wife and son. To that end, I am sending the attached documents, which will supplement those I earlier gave you dealing with our family's legacy.

There is more here about the grant of land made to our ancestor, Capitán José Montalvo y Mejía, by the Government of Mexico. The black plastic tube contains the original land grant document for the Rancho Santa Anita, which I have had restored by a conservator. It is sealed in the cylinder to protect it from humidity and ultraviolet light. When you look at it, do so in a low light or preferably an infrared environment. Photocopies of the grant document I previously left with you should suffice for most purposes.

The letters were written by my great-great grandmother, Enriqueta Montalvo (nee Zavala). The earlier ones are addressed to her grandparents in Mexico City, and the last to her husband's parents, who were then living in Chihuahua.

The diary is the work of my mother, Josefina Montalvo, based on oral histories and the letters of other family members. In the diary, note the repeated attempts to reclaim the rancho. Enriqueta, on her deathbed, charged her son, Ricardo, with returning to California to reclaim it. Ricardo, unable to carry out the obligation, in turn passed the charge on to his son, Emiliano. To escape the revolution in Mexico, Emiliano immigrated to Texas in 1916. During the Great Depression, he was arrested while leading a copper miners' strike in Arizona. He escaped and returned to Mexico without making any claim on the rancho.

I knew little of this until shortly before my mother died. She preserved the letters and the land grant document as well as her diary. When near death, she asked me to look into reclaiming our family patrimony. After my first visit with you, I never had the time. Financing further effort remains another major question. I shouldn't have let so much time pass without pursuing this matter more aggressively.

I don't know what can be done about it now. If you think the matter is worth pursuing, please let me know and we'll decide how to proceed.

With great affection and gratitude, my wife joins me in wishing you good luck and the blessings of God.

Francisco Montalvo

Gar's eyes welled as he stared at his father's signature. It was hard to believe that his father, fearing for his life, would have written this letter without a word to his son, even if Gar had only been a schoolboy. He'd never taken the time to tell Gar the family history. Here were the written words he should have heard from his father when he was alive. Gar thought, too, about his mother, who had rarely hugged or kissed him, even as a child. He pushed the papers away.

Still, he could see that a window on his past had opened. With the exception of his grandmother, he couldn't conjure the images of any of the people mentioned in his father's letter. Yet he felt as if he'd closed a circuit, fulfilled part of an important task. Had his ancestors wanted him to come here to reclaim the rancho, land not far from where he now sat? He'd never believed in a supernatural ordering of events, though he figured that his being here was more than a coincidence.

He pushed aside self-pity and regret and began to sort through the envelopes. *GRANT*, he read in large scrawled letters and, *Photocopy*. Written in Spanish, it granted *La Merced Rancho Santa Anita,* to *José Montalvo y Mejía,* Captain of the National Army of Mexico, posted to the garrison at the village of *Nuestra Señora Santa Bárbara, Alta California.* The acreage totaled 8,100 hectares. He couldn't make out the signature, which was most likely that of the Governor of Alta Califórnia, written in a showy hand on behalf of the President of Mexico and by the grace of God, dated June 2, 1837.

"This come as a surprise?" Hernán stood in the doorway, arms folded.

"All of it," Gar said, "and in more ways than one. My parents never told me about any of this."

"When we first talked I could tell you didn't know that's what they'd been to see me about. Did you run across anything I can explain?"

"It all begs explanation."

"Like what happened to the land?"

"For one."

"What your father wanted me to find out."

"You didn't because of the cost?"

"That was part of it."

"Well, there's no way I can finance it. Besides, I'm here for another reason entirely." Gar sat and studied the document. "There's one thing you might tell me," he said. "8,100 hectares. That's a lot of land, right?"

"At two and one half acres per, 8,100 of them work out to something over 20,000. That's a good-sized spread anywhere." The old attorney spoke over his shoulder as he left the room.

Gar picked up the grant facsimile and followed Hernán to the large map of Los Angeles County behind his desk.

"Any idea where the Rancho Santa Anita was located?"

Hernán studied the map through his half glasses.

"An area around Arcadia. Right here." He pointed to a spot northeast of Los Angeles.

"Did you ever go look at it yourself?"

"Been to Arcadia, but not for that. Your parents didn't want to take the time. We didn't know where the boundaries were."

"Anything remarkable about it?"

"Good orchard and farmland in times past. Santa Anita Race Track's there, and it's infamous for the Japanese internment camps during World War II."

"Otherwise you never explored it?"

"Never. But there's no reason you can't. It's not that far from here."

"I'd like to at least see the land, stand where my ancestors once did. How would I go about finding the landmarks?"

"That might not be so easy after so much time. There's no specific description in the grant. Besides, there've been more people eager to obliterate than preserve them."

"No doubt."

"Look, I have a good friend, a retired professor of ethnic studies. He might help you. At the very least I'm sure he'd like to get his hands on the letters and diary, might even get them translated and typed."

"I'd like to meet him, but..."

"But what?"

"Can he be trusted?"

"About your status? I'd trust him with my life. In fact I once did. I'll see what I can set up."

"All right, fine."

Back in his office, Gar re-read the grant photocopy. Having his hands on these papers gave him a sense of duty to the family's lost legacy. Who knew where it might lead?

21

Two weeks later, Hernán welcomed UCLA Professor Emeritus, Dr. Felipe Villareal, into his home. The old academic set down his briefcase to greet Aurélia, who smiled her own welcome.

"Felipe, my friend," Hernán swept a hand toward Gar, "meet Gar Montalvo. Gar, meet the man I owe my life to."

"*Mucho gusto, señor profesór.*" The men shook hands.

Felipe, with his shaggy gray head, and the resonating voice of an old lecturer, could still command a room.

"You saved his life?" Gar asked.

"He makes too much of it."

"So he says." Hernán eyed his old friend. "We were in the same infantry platoon in Korea and about to be overrun when I got shot. My friend here, himself wounded, dragged me to safety. Then, until reinforcements arrived, he called in artillery on top of us while manning a machine gun, holding off a swarm of Chinese. That won him a Silver Star."

"A high honor, no doubt."

"Only two higher for heroism," Hernán said.

"You were volunteers? Or am I being impertinent?"

"Not at all." Hernán shook his head. "The Korean War didn't inspire volunteers. The U.S. Army had financed my education and I had to go when called." He turned to Felipe. "You can tell your own story."

Felipe shrugged. "You might say I volunteered. In 1950 I'd been convicted of robbery and assault, and the judge let me choose between going to Korea or going to jail."

"That choice was mainly offered to Blacks and Latinos,"

Hernán added.

"You obviously made the right one." The professor's long, arresting face reminded Gar of a Goya painting.

"Come, sit and take a load off," Hernán said. As they did so, Aurélia joined them. The professor, declining her offer of coffee, began withdrawing documents from his briefcase.

"The letters and diary your grandmother saved tell quite a story. How many letters have you read?"

"I got as far as the ones describing José Montalvo's arrival in Santa Barbara and his marriage to my great-great-great-Grandmother, Enriqueta. The handwriting soon defeated me."

"I've had all the letters copied and some translated." He took a manila folder from his briefcase. "Her writings are charming and poignant." Holding up a document he said to Aurélia and Hernán, "Later, you might want to read this letter to her grandparents in Mexico City, which she wrote in 1827, when she was only eight, telling them of her idyllic life on her parents' rancho."

"That was six years after Mexico won its independence from Spain," Gar said.

Felipe nodded. "The first of these next two letters, written respectively eight and ten years later, tells of your ancestor, José, coming on the scene and leading a small contingent of soldiers. Then Enriqueta's life really gets interesting when she and José marry, as she writes in the second letter. It's obvious they were unaware of American settlers agitating for independence in Mexico's Texas region, the beginning of the end in many respects."

"Great research material for a graduate student interested in U.S. and California history," Aurélia said.

"You're right," Felipe agreed. "This next letter, dated November 1846, gives real insight into the approaching war and American settlers making inroads in the Alta Califórnia territory. The outnumbered *Califórnios*, fearful of what would happen if Mexico lost the war, could only watch when the settlers rebelled against the Mexican governor."

Gar shook his head. "I can imagine how they felt as they saw their world crumbling."

"The Montalvos hung on for a while," the professor continued, "but things went downhill as this letter, five years later, shows."

> January 31, 1851
> Rancho Santa Anita, California
>
> Beloved Grandmother,
>
> I hope this letter finds you in good health, and I include the best wishes of the entire family.
>
> Since the war ended three years ago, many changes continue to take place here. We have become citizens of the United States, by virtue of our having chosen to remain in California, and California itself has become a state of the American nation. But the change has not augured well for us. Every day is a struggle to survive in a climate in which most of the people who surround us do not speak a language we fully understand. José and I are learning English to better comprehend what is happening to us.
>
> Our professed friend, Don Perfecto, whose native tongue is English, has been of some help but, as we know he covets our rancho, I don't trust him. When it became clear that Mexico had lost the war, he reverted to his original name, believing anyone with a Spanish surname would be at a disadvantage. And right he was. For reasons I don't understand, we Mexicans, rich and poor alike, are referred to as "greasers" by the gringos. (Please forgive the pejorative, but it is so richly deserved.) I don't know what they mean by that epithet, but it is one of the many ways they let us know they despise us. The antagonism is mainly due to the recent war, of course, but in California

it is also due to the fighting over land and gold, the latter discovered in quantity two years ago by Sonoran miners. Our main problem is with prospectors of any nationality. They refuse to recognize any boundaries in their frenzied quest for gold. José and his loyal vaqueros spend much of their time chasing them from the land and protecting our herds from ending up being slaughtered and eaten. I fear for his life. Everyone is armed. There's no hesitation to use weapons, particularly if they think they won't be brought to account.

For us Mexicans, justice is far less likely to be upheld. To illustrate just how true this is, one need only consider how even our former Governor, General Mariano Vallejo, who earlier had conspired with the Americans to revolt and make California an independent republic, was subsequently imprisoned by those same Americans during the war. What then can the ordinary Mexican expect? Punishment is more often graduated by the color of the skin than the nature or severity of the crime.

Dearest Grandmother, I must apologize for adding our worries to yours. But since you asked for a truthful account of what is transpiring here, I've taken you at your word. I am grateful, at least, that our letters continue to get through. Is that not miraculous? I pray our next exchange is more hopeful. Until then, I am,
Your obedient and loving Granddaughter,

Sra. Enriqueta Montalvo de Zavala

"And things only got worse," Gar said.

"Right," Felipe confirmed. "All the letters are worth reading, but I'll just read this next one. It brings to an end this part of the Montalvo saga. Written five years later, it's addressed to Enriqueta's in-laws."

June 8, 1856

THE LAST CALIFÓRNIO

Rancho Santa Anita, California

Esteemed Señor and Señora Montalvo,

I have written to you only sparingly in the past, that pleasure having been previously undertaken more consistently by my beloved José. I so fervently wish that I were simply writing another letter of greeting. Instead, I have the sad duty to inform you of the death of your magnificent son, who was killed while protecting our home and family. We and our remaining friends are in shock at the tragic and senseless loss of a fine man, who tried his best to be a citizen of his new country.

I know José had from time to time kept you apprised of the worsening conditions we Mexicans had been suffering since the war ended eight years ago. But I fear he never told you the extent of it, undoubtedly to spare you anxiety. Since then, we have watched nearly helpless as the lands and fortunes of our friends and associates have been taken away. My own parents, as it happens, were correct in anticipating such developments and sold their lands some time ago, albeit at prices below their worth. They, together with my brother and his family, returned to Mexico, urging us to do likewise.

José was determined to remain in California and to be the American that fate had destined him to be. From this statement, however, I infer no blame on José. We both decided to remain here and hold on to the lands granted to us. The Lord knows well the efforts José expended, while attempting to defend them. It was that same stand that has now resulted in his death at the hands of gold prospectors and squatters.

Like the rest of the former Californios, who stayed here, I am without any protection whatsoever; our properties are being claimed by those who are no better than thieves. They have the support and collusion of the authorities.

Permitting me the barest period of mourning, I was summoned to an American court to prove the ownership of the lands granted to José, God rest his soul. When I presented the grant documents in court, the judge told me the description of the property was too general, that I had to prove the boundaries. This despite the fact it had been re-done using an American surveyor.

I understood little of this. The judge and lawyers refused to speak in Spanish. I was at the mercy of a neighbor who has long coveted our lands. He was but one of a number of such Americans, who came to California in the years before the war, settled with us, and who have now abandoned and turned against us. Although I lack proof, I believe this person is responsible for José's murder. I had to suffer the outrage of having him represent me in court, where I knew not what he offered to the American judge. Still, I refused to relinquish any right to the Rancho Santa Anita. Instead, and in spite of my misgivings, I left the Rancho in the care of this so-called friend, with the understanding I would later send instructions as to its disposition.

The other purpose of this letter is to accept, most gratefully, your kind and generous offer of refuge for your grandchildren and me. Within days I will begin our journey to Chihuahua, trusting you will accept us upon our arrival. Hoping this letter reaches you before we do, and I pray it finds you well. May God see us through to your side. Until then, I am
Gratefully and Faithfully yours,

Sra. Enriqueta Montalvo de Zavala

The room remained silent after Professor Villareal finished reading the last letter. Gar could not erase the image of Enriqueta and her children making their own desperate crossing of the Rio Grande, in the direction opposite to his.

22

Felipe told them, "Enriqueta's losing the rancho after the U.S.-Mexico war wasn't an unusual story."

"Did she actually lose it?" Gar asked.

"That's hard to say. You'd have to check court, tax, and land sale records to find out what California and federal authorities did. Its loss came long after the war and in violation of the Treaty of Guadalupe Hidalgo, which ended the war. Like those made with Native Americans, it was for the most part worthless."

It struck Gar that regaining the rancho could be another way of avenging his family's murders, something he could work at until his return to Mexico to deal with their killer.

"History is written by the winners," Felipe reminded them. "That's why our texts only describe Mexico as an obstacle to America's Manifest Destiny."

"Destiny," Aurélia muttered. "The only thing Manifest about it was the quantity of land stolen."

Felipe looked at her and nodded.

"Yeah," Hernán said, "the books are written as if God gave the United States the right to rule this land. Including those parts already occupied."

Aurélia sighed, "So long ago. It's over."

"You kidding, *mi amor*?" Hernán sat up. "The world's full of places where people are still fighting over lost land. Have the Arabs and Israelis forgotten? How about the Kurds, the Armenians, the Greeks, the Turks? It's what the Balkan wars were about. Why should this be any different?"

"OK, calm down, my love." Aurélia fanned her hands at her husband. "I'm only saying that the situation here didn't strike me as analogous."

"Just like the Balkan wars, the territorial battle with Mexico masked racial and cultural conflicts," Felipe said.

"Please explain what you mean," Gar requested.

"Stephen Austin, leader of American settlers in Texas, called the struggle *a war between a mongrel race against civilization*. Once the war got underway, some writers described it as *a battle of the pure white Caucasian and Anglo-Saxon blood, against that so-called mongrel race.*"

"How nice," Aurélia grumbled.

"It's an important characterization," Felipe continued. "The war was a brutal affair. It drove home Manifest Destiny's darkest notion that racial and national supremacy were inseparable. That bigoted attitude has left us with a legacy of lost property and tenuous civil rights. Add to that the assumed racial superiority of white Americans and you understand how so much underlying hatred exists today."

"With so many Latino immigrants streaming into the country in recent years, I can understand the antagonisms," Hernán added.

"Right," Felipe turned to him, "but in truth they never went away. I've even heard more than one suggestion that a reconquest by Mexico is underway."

Aurélia stifled a yawn. "I hate to bow out, but I'm fading."

"Don Felipe, thank you for all the work you've done." Gar rose to shake the professor's hand. "One way or another, I intend to find out what happened to the rancho and see if it's possible to reclaim it."

"So you should. But don't get your hopes up. It'll be involved and expensive—not to mention anything of the enemies you'll make."

"I'll be mindful of all that, Professor."

"Keep that grant document in a safe place," he said.

23

Meeting Hernán's political circle was giving Gar second thoughts. When Hernán picked him up the following Sunday, he let those thoughts be known.

"You trust this Enrique Torres, Don Hernán?"

"Absolutely. He goes by Hank Towers, the English translation of his name. He's a lawyer turned talk-show host, very popular. He can be a sonuvabitch when people get in his way. At the moment he wants to be the mayor of Los Angeles."

"What are his chances?"

"He's got great name recognition, a good reputation as an attorney, and he's a home boy out of East L.A. The law firm, TV station, and weekly show have made him wealthy. Whether all that's enough..."

"Any real support? Money?"

"That's the rub. He'd be a spoiler running against other Latinos, as well as the incumbent, who's also a Democrat. In the last election the winner was backed by a coalition of liberal Anglos, Asians, most of the Jewish vote, and African Americans who deserted the Anglo incumbent."

"Sounds complicated."

"It is."

"Why doesn't he just back the Democratic incumbent?"

"Two reasons: ambition and fear. If the incumbent is re-elected we'll continue to have the status quo, which hasn't turned out to be all we hoped for."

"Is that what you alluded to the other day at lunch?"

"As I implied, he's in the debt of his Anglo backers."

"So, you see him as a sellout? A puppet?"

Hernán left the question hanging.

"What have you told him about me?" Gar finally asked.

"That you're a journalist new in town. Nothing about your status. Also mentioned your land grant. Hope you don't mind."

"Why did you think he'd be interested?"

"Hank has descended from a *Califórnio* family that also lost land in the U.S.-Mexico war."

"Did he ever make an effort to reclaim it?"

"Not that I know of."

As a lawyer with a successful firm, he did nothing to reclaim valuable property? Hardly credible, Gar reasoned.

"We're late." The monthly Sunday get-togethers were informal, but Hernán still liked to be on time.

Mar Vista, an upscale neighborhood, offered no view of the ocean, though Gar smelled salt on the breeze.

A high masonry wall with glass shards embedded along the top enclosed Hank's compound. The late afternoon sun momentarily painted the off-white stucco a light orange-pink. A heavy wrought-iron gate broke the plane of the thick wall. A small plaque next to it read CASA TORRES.

Hernán pressed a button and spoke into an intercom. A buzzer sounded, allowing them to enter. A stone walkway led through a lush patio garden profuse with the blossoms of birds of paradise and succulents. The pathway divided around a splashing fountain of sculpted stone before rejoining and leading to a shaded arcade along the front of the single-story stucco.

"Not bad." Gar admired the ornate iron grillwork on each of the large front windows. "Even the *rejas* look authentic."

"Enrique imported a lot of stuff from Mexico when he built this place," Hernán explained.

A maid guided them through two large tile-floored living spaces to a broad low-ceilinged chamber. A pool table lit by three low-hung pendulum lamps dominated the room. Three men, each holding a pool cue, turned to look as Gar and Hernán walked in. A fourth, bent over the table, concentrated on his aim.

"Six in the side pocket," he announced. He struck. The six ball with a resounding *clack* disappeared, the cue ball backing up a few inches. "Seven in the corner pocket." Same result.

"Shit, Enrique's run the table again," one of the men grunted, leaving the table for a beer.

Two men and a woman talked quietly at a small wet-bar in a corner of the room. A third man behind the counter prepared a drink. The bar stood by sliding glass doors opening onto another patio and a swimming pool. The woman fell silent when she saw the visitors.

"*Órale*, Hernán, Gar, come on over." Professor Villareal waved.

"*Buenas*, Don Hernán," one of the players said as they passed the pool table. The other two nodded. The fourth, ignoring them, stuck to his game.

"What can I fix you, *señores?*" The man behind the bar asked.

"You forget I'm on the wagon, Esteban?" Hernán said.

"There are juice and soft drinks here, too."

"Thanks, anyway. I'll pass."

"How about your friend?"

"A beer, please. Negra Modelo, if you've got it." Gar turned to the older man. "Good to see you again, Don Felipe."

"*Igualmente,* Gar."

Hernán was about to introduce Gar to the others, when one of the pool players walked up to them. He was soon dominating the group.

"This the friend you told me about, Don Hernán?"

"My associate, Gar Montalvo. Gar's a journalist from Texas, with a lot of experience in Mexico. I thought he might find our work interesting."

"*Bienvenidos*, Gar. *Mi casa es su casa*." Hank extended his hand. "Have you met the rest of us?"

Gar looked at the others expectantly.

"Let's all go out to the pool area," Hank suggested. "I'm sure there are enough seats to go around." To the small wiry man at his side, he said, "Joe, remind Marta not to forget the wine when she brings the buffet cart."

The balmy air, redolent of flowers and the nearby ocean, had shifted inland, cooling as the afternoon wore on. Deck chairs, arranged in a large irregular circle, each had a small folding table next to it.

As conversations were struck up or resumed, Gar looked over the group. He could only guess at all the motives drawing them together. Greed? Ego? Insecurity? Revenge? And what were they willing to risk to get what they wanted? More importantly, did they really trust each other?

A few chairs away, Hank quietly spoke to the woman next to him. Gar studied his chiseled profile and full wavy head of meticulously styled gray hair. His silk shirt was probably tailor-made. Like his cream-colored linen slacks. The sandals looked handmade, too.

"Your first time in Los Angeles?" Hank spoke to Gar.

"My first time in this part of the southwest."

"You covered politics in Mexico?"

"Among other things."

"Do you find it interesting that Mexico's moving to a multi-party, if not a two-party system?"

Gar waited a beat or two, meeting Hank's intense stare with a smile.

"My interest amuses you?"

"In a way. Americans are proud of our so-called two-party system, but they're unanimous in keeping Latinos down. In that respect, there's just one party."

"You'd compare this to Mexico's Institutional Revolutionary Party?"

"There's little difference. For more than seventy years the PRI perpetuated itself for power and greed. Here, it's more a *them* against *us* thing, with the power to achieve social, economic, and political agendas reserved for elite groups."

"Hmm. I see how the argument could be made. We must talk some more."

24

"We should get Danilo Gómez involved." Hank's voice rose above the others.

"What could he do for us?" someone asked.

Hernán told Gar the man asking was Esteban Reverte, a former migrant worker who'd made his way up under César Chavez to become a farm labor leader.

"You kidding? Dan's an L.A. insider," another man next to Hank snapped.

"That's Joe Reyes, Hank's right hand." Hernán whispered. "Former lightweight champ. Tiger Joe, they used to call him. Now he's a short-tempered agitator."

Esteban reminded Gar of Rodin's sculpture of the *Mask of the Man with the Broken Nose.*

"Meaning what?" Esteban glared.

Hank put up a restraining hand. "Esteban, Danilo's been one of L.A.'s most influential players, a top advisor and campaign rainmaker during a number of city administrations. I'm surprised you don't know of him."

"So he plays both sides of the fence. He a *tío taco?*"

The discussion soon became a three-way argument as Esteban clearly wanted to keep pretenders and opportunists out of the group. The other two, including Clara the lone woman, had personal agendas, which Esteban disliked.

Hank listened to the contesting positions, but kept a firm grip on both the people and the meeting. In the end, Esteban lost the argument and the person proposed for membership accepted.

"*Señores,* I want to talk campaign strategy. Your thoughts,

Don Felipe?"

"You'll have to appeal to the general electorate," Felipe said.

"You may be willing to overlook the way we've been treated, Professor, but I'm not!" Joe Reyes waved a finger in the air. "Let's elect Hank with our own people."

"That's the opposing view," Hank said. "Let's pursue it. Most of you know Rodolfo Tamayo of Soto & Soto Associates. Rudy, please tell us what we're dealing with."

"As we all know numbers win elections," Rodolfo began. "So it's critical to understand the breakdown of gender, ethnic, and socio-economic status of voters. But what's of immediate interest," he paused and looked around at the others, "is that Latinos are now a majority in both the city and county. Moreover, projections indicate that Latinos will constitute well over fifty percent of L.A.'s population in just five years. In other words, we've got the numbers."

"Questions for Rudy at this point?" Hank glanced around the circle of faces. "Anything else, Rudy?" Rodolfo raised his hands. He was finished.

"There you have it," Hank said. "We're a majority and still not in control. Comments?"

"You're saying we should have had Latinos in power long ago." Felipe broke in.

"So what's wrong with that picture, Professor?"

"Our miserable history as voters and office seekers is well known. Even so, our people have made great strides in the last few elections. Nearly thirty percent of the lawmakers in Sacramento are Latinos, which, incidentally, relates to our growing presence in the country's population."

"You're making my point, Professor." Joe Reyes said. "It didn't take the Cubans 150-plus years to take control in south Florida, did it?" Other heads nodded.

"If I may," another man spoke up.

"That's Raimundo Maldonado, of the Southwest Voter Education and Registration Project," Hernán told Gar.

"Joe, I disagree. Here's why. Our numbers sound really impressive until you break them down. Latinos here are a disparate group from all over Latin America, and then there's the fact that much of L.A.'s population is transient."

"Yeah, yeah, we know all that." Joe interrupted.

"Let Ray finish," Hank said.

"A transient population means weak political machines and even weaker parties." Raimundo looked around at the others. "That makes media politics very expensive. The population has exploded and so has the cost to manipulate it. Media campaigning costs megabucks."

"Ray," Esteban Reverte broke in, "I don't think Latino diversity here is that big a problem. Money's a major concern, but money isn't the only way to manipulate a constituency. If we can arouse people with a cause or an event to make them rally, the press will cover it and we'll get our message out. The voters will follow."

"You have something in mind, Esteban?" Hank asked.

"Maybe you remember the janitors' strike against ISS, the big Danish-owned corporation, back in the '90s? Latino janitors working in Century City struck for a union contract and better pay. Those immigrants were not only new, but there were so many others around that the strikers could easily be replaced. They scared shoppers away from businesses by gathering on the sidewalks and staring at the customers inside shops. They got their message across just by being there."

"Could you please get to the point and wrap it up?" Joe urged.

Hank raised a hand. "Let him finish."

"Two weeks into the strike," Esteban continued, "the unions rallied 400 strikers. The police attacked. The strikers made great action TV for a week, and finally got what they wanted."

"Nice story, Esteban," Joe broke in, "but striking is a lot different than getting people to vote."

"You're missing the point, Joe." Felipe said. "Esteban has shown that, if organized, even the powerless can press their demands and do it on a shoe string." He looked at Hank. "Here perhaps is a tactic for your overall strategy."

"It's true that we have a common language and feel the effects of discrimination," Rodolfo Tamayo said, "but there's more common ground on which to base a campaign."

"What's that, Rudy?" Hank asked.

"The gulf between the haves and have-nots is getting wider and has never been more visible than it is here. Workers are falling behind, while the top twenty percent prosper and withdraw from public society."

"You including me, Rudy?" Hank chuckled.

"Not at all. Clara can tell you how the rich have resisted spreading their taxes outside their own communities, the need for better schools and teachers notwithstanding."

"Good point," Joe spoke up. "This is serious stuff we can exploit."

"This has been worthwhile." Hank said. "Esteban, I ask that you get others together to consider tactics of the type you recounted. We'll meet again, next month. Meanwhile, please enjoy the food and drink." Turning to Gar, he asked, "You shoot pool?"

"Not my game, I'm afraid."

"Damn, it's hard to find any real competition in this bunch," Hank chuckled.

"You mind losing to a woman?" Clara asked from behind him.

"Can't turn down a challenge like that." Arm in arm, the two walked towards the game room.

A few in the group talked with Gar as he and Hernán prepared to leave. Esteban stepped forward.

"Hernán's already on board. I could use a new pair of eyes and a fresh mind on my tactics group."

"I'd like that," Gar said, meaning it.

"Felipe's working on how we might finance researching

what happened to the Rancho Santa Anita," Hernán said, on the drive back to Culver City,

"That's great. Has he come up with anything?"

25

It was noon when Felipe Villareal checked his watch at the entrance of El Cholo. Though the retired professor often dined there, he always winced at the name. *Cholo* could mean *mestizo*, or mixed blood, and was probably the intended meaning. But it also translated to mean a low-life, an unwelcome reminder of the professor's youth as a gang member.

The restaurant was one of L.A.'s oldest and most renowned Mexican eateries. In an aging building a few streets south of Wilshire Boulevard, it boasted an authentic menu and a history as a place for making business deals, proposing marriage, and planning political strategy.

"Yes sir, how many?"

"You have a reservation under the name of Gárza?"

"They're here. This way, please." She led him to a large dining area.

Their table was hidden behind the stone fountain at the room's center. The professor had to look around for his companions. Hernán and Gar rose to greet him. Their mutual back slaps resounded in the room.

As they took their seats, Felipe patted his briefcase and set it on the floor.

"I have the translations of the letters and the diary as well as the originals. I hope you've brought your appetite. This place is famous for its exceptional margaritas and tamales."

"Don Hernán warned me they won't measure up to those in Mexico. But I'm no gourmet. I eat to survive."

"It's good you feel that way. Everything here gets Americanized—the food and the people."

"Is that so bad?" Gar asked.

"Only if you're a purist. It's not all bad and not always good." Smiling at Hernán he said, "*Viejo*, we're seeing more of each other since Gar arrived. I could get used to that."

"Same here. I'm too old to make new friends, much less one like you."

"Now, about your legacy." Felipe clasped his hands and leaned on the table. "After our strategy meeting with Hank Towers last weekend, he called to discuss ideas for his weekly show that could support his run for mayor."

"I've yet to watch it," Gar admitted. "My landlady has the only TV in the house. You think he has a chance?"

"No doubt about it. He'd do a better job than any of the mayors we've ever had in this town. He knows what it means to be poor and Latino in a city that has long despised both. As an attorney and businessman he's a winner. His talk show has set him up with great name and face recognition."

"As I told him." Hernán sat back in his chair.

"You've brought this up for a reason." Gar said.

Felipe's eyes widened. "You recall at the meeting we discussed ways to rally Latinos?"

"I remember."

"Your land grant could be one. I'm not sure how it would be used, but Hank's PR people can sort that out. Later it might help you in court."

"I do want my day in court. Given my status, though, how can I get it?" Gar looked at each of his companions.

Felipe left the question hanging, and changed direction. "You've been learning more about the old land grants?"

"It ought to be taught in the schools."

Felipe nodded. "Most Americans know next to nothing about their country's history, not to mention this part of it. What's taught is mostly propaganda." Felipe asked what he'd learned.

"For one thing, acquiring a grant wasn't easy."

"A bureaucracy even then?" Hernán said.

"More ceremonial than bureaucratic. The grantee—always a male—had to be of *la gente de razón,* the right people, Mexican, and a Catholic. That meant a foreigner had to become a Mexican citizen, embrace Catholicism, and marry a Mexican woman—*una hija del país,* a native daughter, as they called her."

"So the government locked a grantee into the culture?"

Gar nodded. "There's more. The grantee submitted a map of the land he wanted. When the governor approved it, surveyors plotted the land using measuring chains graded in *varas*, a *vara* being a little less than a meter. Markers were placed."

"About the size of our yard," Hernan said.

"Then an official, with other landowners present," Gar added, "performed a ritual called an Act of Possession."

"Remarkable. What did that involve?" Felipe asked.

"Before the assembled group, the official would say to each of the four compass points, *In the name of the Mexican Nation, I put you in possession of these lands.* The new owner then had a year to make improvements."

"You mean like building a home and cultivating the property?" Hernán said.

"Precisely."

"I like the openness, their respect for the land and the community," Felipe said.

Gar nodded. "Simple, but profound."

A commotion from the bar caught Gar's attention. "Who's that?" he asked.

Craning for a look, Hernán told him it was Weegan Rollem, the Republican candidate for mayor, and his entourage. "Looks like he's glad-handing the wait staff as if that were enough to capture the Latino vote."

The restaurant's hostess guided Rollem's group to a reserved booth.

"He's not going to get many Latino votes, based on the speech he gave to city businessmen a couple of weeks ago," Felipe said.

"Here you are, gentlemen." The waitress set two brimming margaritas on the table and a glass of water for Hernán. "Ready to order?"

"Tamales and chiles rellenos all around." Felipe decided for them. Raising his salt-rimmed glass he said, *"Salúd.* To friendship." Felipe and Gar toasted each other.

"For the sake of discussion, how would Hank use Gar's land grant case?"

"He said his law firm would pay for researching the grant and, maybe, the filing."

"That's quite a commitment, Gar." Hernán was impressed. "That expense was one of the reasons I couldn't pursue the grant for your parents."

"In exchange for those services," Felipe continued, "you'd appear on the show. We'd maybe have an historian, a state legislator, and me as panelists."

"At some point Hank will have to know about your status. Don't worry about it for now."

Hernán suggested appearing as his attorney so the issue could be aired to their advantage.

"Could work. Can't say if Hank'll buy it," Felipe said as he was thinking that the important thing was to make it real, show the grant document along with a map of the area, expose the sordid way those lands were taken. "He wants to create excitement, shake people up."

"Right, it's like this," Hernán said. "Hank wants to show that this land was ours. It is ours."

Felipe picked up the theme. "Show how the U.S. stole the land by goading Mexico into war and forced her to sign an unfair treaty."

"Reconquest would mean coercion, force." Concern seeped into Gar's voice. "You don't want violence, do you?"

Felipe shook his head. "Our numbers are growing

without any help from us. No, we will do what can be done within the law, play the political game."

"The same way Anglos have played it all these years," Hernán said.

"And this time we'll beat them." Felipe banged the table with his fist.

"If you succeed? What then?" Gar asked.

His companions both sat back in their chairs.

"First of all," Felipe said, "it's not *if*, but *when*. Second, the goal is a more fair society."

"Something it's never been here, for us or any other minority," Hernán added.

"Hah! You shoulda' seen the look on their faces." Weegan Rollem's voice suddenly boomed throughout the restaurant.

"Sounds like he's had too many margaritas." Hernán shook his head.

Weegan's loud voice took over the room. The whole place was listening to him, while his waitress tried to calm him. She scurried off to get what he'd demanded, and laughter from his table erupted again, with Weegan's voice still rising above the rest.

"What a jerk," Felipe said. "He must be drunk."

A moment later the hostess confronted the noisy table.

"Come on, honey," Weegan slurred. "We're just having a good time. Now, how 'bout you get someone over here who speaks English! Don't you have any decent waiters in this place? I can imagine where you're getting your help."

"Honey, please don't," the woman next to him pleaded.

"Everybody here is legal, sir," the hostess replied calmly, "and Lídia knows her business."

"Yeah, well, get me somebody competent!"

"Careful, Felipe," Hernán warned, as his old friend stood up. "Not our fight."

"Honey, please calm down," the woman begged again.

The room had fallen silent. With everyone staring at

him, the big man shut up. He raised his palms to the hostess.

"Forget it. Look, I got carried away, OK? No harm." His companions stared at their plates of cooling food as Weegan smiled sheepishly at the woman next to him.

"That hostess has got a major pair of *cojones*," Hernán chuckled.

"Yeah, but it was all I could do to stand by while that asshole abused her." Felipe stared in Weegan's direction.

Hernán looked at Gar. "Despite his size, my old friend here still thinks he can take on the world."

"I'll tell you this," Gar said, "knowing that *pendejo* over there is running for mayor settled it for me. Tell Hank to go ahead. We'll deal with my status later."

"Good. We'll get started."

"Ah, food at last."

26

Since his lunch with Hernán and Dr. Villareal, Gar had wanted to explore the Santa Anita area himself. There were the police and *la migra* to think about, though. Plus, he had no way of knowing if Salinas's agents were looking for him. The uncertainty couldn't stop him, however. Meanwhile, he wanted to learn more about the political history between the United States and Mexico.

Like most Mexican schoolboys, Gar had grown up hearing about the treaty of Guadalupe Hidalgo without knowing much about it. He'd never read the treaty or even contemplated Mexico's loss of a half-million square miles. So he turned to the Internet to find the text of the treaty.

What struck him first was the irony of its title. *A Treaty of Peace and Friendship*? Anything but. The title remained at odds with Mexico's anthem, still sung each September 15th, the eve of Independence Day: *War, war without truce against those who would blemish the honor of the fatherland! War! War! The patriotic banners drenched in waves of blood.*

"Now I see why I was never pushed to read the treaty in school," he muttered.

"Really?" Hernán surprised him.

"I didn't see you standing there."

"What was it you didn't read?"

"This treaty." Gar pointed at the computer monitor.

"Weren't you told to read it in school?"

"It makes Mexico's utter defeat so clear, I guess we were spared the humiliation."

"Doesn't the winner always dictate terms?"

"Kicking a man when he's down doesn't bother you?"

"Best time to kick him."

Gar stared deadpan at Hernán.

"Bad joke. I suppose it would bother any thoughtful person," he continued, "but from the standpoint of the United States, it gained land and kept down a potential adversary."

"You're Mexican, aren't you?"

Hernán sipped his coffee and studied Gar. "I may be Mexican by birth, but I cast my lot with this country long ago. Far as I'm concerned, the treaty, unfair as it may be, is about another time, water under the bridge."

"What about the racial hatred that continues?"

"Despicable, I agree."

"Then how...?"

"Let me finish. As a people we've tried, with notable success, to create a better country. It's a work in progress. I grew up here and have gained much. You share your country's loss. I understand your resentment."

Gar could only turn back to the computer monitor. He took a deep breath and tried to calm himself. After a few moments, he added, "Anyway, it's this that applies to my case."

"What's it say?" Hernán moved to look over Gar's shoulder.

"*That Mexicans in the lost territories may continue to live where they resided, or return to Mexico,*" he read aloud.

"Isn't there something there about citizenship?"

"People choosing to remain became U.S. citizens." Gar traced a finger across the screen. "It's this part that sets up the betrayal."

"How so?"

"*In the said territories, property of every kind, now belonging to Mexicans, shall be inviolably respected,*" Gar read. "*The present owners, the heirs of these, and all Mexicans who may hereafter acquire said property by contract, shall enjoy with respect to it guarantees equally ample as if the same belonged to citizens of the United States.*"

"Plain enough, despite the legalese. But things didn't always turn out that way."

Gar went on. "According to my ancestors' letters and the diary, those citizenship rights were given lip service. The rancheros' claims were disregarded on technical grounds, or just taken by outright theft."

"I won't argue any of that."

Gar watched Hernán depart. He'd been wrong to assume that Hernán shared his feelings. Water under the bridge? Yet he and his group wanted political power returned to Latino hands. Wasn't that a contradiction? Gar wondered about Hernán's motives, his true feelings about the *Califórnios* and their lands. He couldn't let it go.

Bonita's face told him something was up.

A woman stood inside the office, staring out the barred window. She remained facing the street as Gar entered the front room.

"You look fascinated by something."

She turned, and he was surprised by her attractiveness. "The graffiti on the walls out there. If it were painted on canvas, I'd want to own it."

Her green eyes complemented her pale olive complexion. She seemed unaware of her immense beauty, which made Gar instantly want to like her.

"Yes, some of those artists have real talent. Are you here for Hernán Gárza?"

"I'm here to see you, Mr. Montalvo."

Gar smiled. "Have I forgotten an appointment?" They shook hands.

"I'm Eva Muñoz, a paralegal at Mr. Torres's law firm." Her dimples danced as she spoke.

"You're here about researching the land grant?"

She released his hand. "It looks like a can of worms."

"What do you mean?"

"This kind of thing can be very complicated."

"Please sit down." He pointed to the small sofa across from his desk. "I re-read the Treaty of Guadalupe Hidalgo, yesterday. Are you familiar with it?"

"Sure. I have a copy here." She patted her briefcase. "What's more important is the Act of March 3, 1851."

"I've not heard of it."

"It's what the U.S. Congress passed to settle land claims after the war. I'll leave you a copy."

"Thanks. You've done some research?"

"Yes, but what I have won't take long. Native Americans have made a lot of claims in California." She looked up from her folder. "A few were successful. I've found no such claims by Spanish or Mexican heirs that were ever brought to court here, and the land commission closed in the 1850s."

"You've exhausted the record?"

"Not at all," Eva smiled. "I've searched the Internet, which is just a starting place. The legal databases are so voluminous they haven't been posted and they may never be. I'm talking about old land records and civil-court proceedings. They go back a long way."

"What do you need to get started?"

"Your guidance."

"The main thing is to discover how the Rancho Santa Anita was lost."

"For that I may have to go to Sacramento. I'll check in, maybe once a week?"

"No," he said. "Just let me know if you find something of interest."

"Do you have anything that might be helpful?"

"Come with me."

She followed him into the adjacent office to the map of Los Angeles behind Hernán's desk.

"The rancho included about 20,000 acres. Hernán thinks it's in this area here, where Sierra Madre and Arcadia are now."

THE LAST CALIFÓRNIO

"So I'll start at the L.A. County office of land records. You have some documentation?"

He gave her copies of the translated letters, diary, and the grant document. "Take them with you."

She glanced through the topmost papers. "Except for the grant document itself, the rest would only be considered anecdotal." She put them into her briefcase, anyway. "One last question. Will this be a civil suit?"

"Eventually. First we need to know what the grant boundaries are. Also, I want to see the land itself, so it won't be such an abstraction."

"Good idea. Maybe I'll go with you when you do."

"Let's plan on it." Eva finished the notes she'd been writing and moved to leave.

Gar studied her for a moment. "Muñoz is a fne Spanish name. May I ask, is your background Mexican?"

"Yes, but..." she hesitated. "One side of my family comes from a long line of Egyptian merchants. They emigrated to Mexico more than a century ago."

"Muñoz is hardly an Egyptian name."

"That side of my family assimilated into Mexican life and culture. Those who came here in more recent generations consider themselves Latino, as I do. That's a long answer to a short question."

After she left, Gar turned to the folder she gave him.

27

Two restless days of waiting passed before Eva returned. When he saw her again, her smile erased his impatience.

"I've done a little research," she said, "and I think we should add Monrovia to the areas of Sierra Madre and Arcadia. I'm pretty sure the Rancho Santa Anita included parts of all three."

On their way, they stopped the car now and then to walk in the crowded suburbs, which did little to give Gar any sense of connection with the land. Only the San Gabriel Mountains, the towering backdrop to the rancho, provided a vague link. Beyond that stood the timeless silence of history and a hazy knowledge of long-dead ancestors.

On the return trip, Eva suggested they take Las Tunas Drive, a more scenic route than the freeway. The scenery didn't impress him much, but a sign for the San Gabriel Mission caught their eye. Eva was sure the Rancho Santa Anita had once been part of the mission's lands.

"You think there's much left of it?" he asked.

"If the U.S. Park Service maintains it, there'll be something to see."

Surrounded by busy highways and modern buildings, the mission's 300 year-old architecture was out of place and time. The adobe construction, in surprisingly good condition, suggested much of it had been restored. Exploring the overgrown gardens, they came upon an elderly priest emerging from one of the buildings.

"Are you newcomers to the mission, my children?" The old man asked.

"We are, Father." Eva said.

"You've just missed the ranger's tour, but perhaps I can show you around."

"That would be wonderful," Eva said. Gar nodded.

They followed him.

"The Franciscans established La misión San Diego de Alcalá, the first of the twenty-one California missions, in the San Diego River valley in 1769," the priest began. "The good friars built this one, La Misión San Gábriel Arkángel, two years later in the shadow of the mountains you see there, which they also named for their saint."

He led them through arched passageways into a cluster of thick-walled adobe rooms.

In the semi-darkness, Gar imagined he was face-to-face with something his ancestors had known.

"In the mission's heyday," the priest said, "these rooms were workshops, storerooms, and dormitories."

They passed into a high-ceilinged sanctuary and stood in silence for a few minutes. A rack of votive candles, the only illumination, cast a pale glow on the rough-hewn benches and kneelers. Faded frescoes of the *Stations of the Cross* adorned the walls, and the sanctuary itself was redolent of incense and a history of countless Masses. The priest began to talk again.

"Mass hasn't been said here in over a century, but Catholics from all over the world still come here to pray. The paintings date from the late eighteenth century," he said with a sad pride. "Holy treasures. Like those gold-embroidered vestments and illuminated books." The priest noted the relics locked in glass cases mounted high on the walls, out of reach.

In what sounded like a memorized monologue, the priest recited the story of the mission's rise to prosperity, the great herds of cattle that roamed its lands, the barrels of wine its vineyards produced. He told about the work the mission did among the Indians, though failing to mention that the Indians were kept in virtual slavery. He bordered on anger when describing Mexico's secularization and ultimate breakup of the mission system.

"They can't eradicate it," he whispered behind them. "Mankind holds onto its past. First in trying to abolish it, then, treasuring it, wanting to dig it up again."

Eva and Gar observed the artifacts for a few moments longer. When Gar turned to thank him, the priest had gone.

"Didn't get much from it," Eva said when they were back in the car and on the road again.

"Except for the mountains," Gar said, "it was impossible to visualize the land as it might have been. Driving around the area was worth the trip."

"How about the mission?"

"You got a sense of the past in the garden. I think the old priest was trying to tell us something."

"About digging up the past?"

"I wanted to think he knew why we were there."

"He disappeared, almost as if I'd imagined him."

They drove in silence for a few minutes.

"He was bitter in talking about the breakup of the mission system," Gar said, "as if the Church should have been entitled to remain independent."

"I could understand his regret," she said. "Didn't you find him a bit melodramatic?"

"That's the Church for you." Gar shook his head.

Bonita's voice came through the intercom. "Eva Muñoz on line two, Mr. Montalvo."

"I'm just leaving the hall of records," Eva told him. "I've been through thousands of microfiches, most of them irrelevant."

"You found something?"

"I'd rather show you. I think you'll want to see what I've found."

In his office a short while later, she handed him a sheet of paper.

"It's the layout of the rancho." The perimeter made the shape of a rhomboid.

"The *diseño*!"

"Complete with boundary markers." Finding it was astonishing." The landmarks are a little crude, but they may yet be discernible on the ground. See here?" She pointed to the small hill on the western extremity. "This river down the middle of the tract is bound to exist in some form. Even if it were dry now the old riverbed would be hard to eradicate. I'm sure it would still show up in an aerial photo."

"And these three mountain tops on the east side must be there." He pointed. "What about the other boundary lines?"

"You can't tell from this drawing. It's just a sketch," Eva reminded him. "A surveyor can shoot the other points. Who knows what might still exist on the ground. Anyway, we've only started digging."

"Is this enough to define the grant area?"

"We'll find that out soon enough. It's a good start."

"It's a big start. Did you make copies?" He held up the sheet of paper.

"Ten. You owe me a dollar."

"Happy to pay it." Gar wanted to hug her, and maybe it showed. She turned away.

"Nothin' to it."

"You have time for a drink, something to eat?"

She was good for that.

28

Gar and Eva chose a table on the patio at El Tepeyác, where Hernán had taken Gar the day the two men first met.

Over cold bottles of Negra Modelo and a basket of tortilla chips with salsa, Eva began to ask questions. "What newspaper did you work for in Laredo, Mr. Montalvo?"

Her question caught him off guard. He knew more would follow. As they worked on the rancho project together he'd begun to feel a comfortable rapport with her. Now, he liked the way she referred to them as "we."

"I worked as a stringer," he said, "a freelance reporter." He searched her eyes trying not to sound strained. "Please—call me Gar." The feeling of unease persisted in the silence that followed. What's the matter with me, he thought, I'm here with this beautiful woman and tongue-tied? "I hope you're not uncomfortable being here with me," he said.

"Not at all. Though I have to admit I've been treating you as a client. I'm enjoying this project. Until I found the rancho's layout, I thought I was letting you and Mr. Torres down." After a pause, she added, "You're right. *Ms. Muñoz* is a bit too formal. I also answer to Eva." She was smiling when she went on to ask, "Is Gar a nickname or a shortened version of a longer given name?"

He shook his head. "That's the whole thing, and it doesn't have anything to do with the fish of the same name."

She laughed. "I guess you've had that suggested before."

"Then I wasn't entirely wrong about the formality?"

"Not entirely. It had more to do with our professional situation, than with you."

"I'll accept that."

"When I asked about your work, I wasn't just making conversation. I really am interested. I know you're a journalist, but I have the impression that you're not working as one."

"I now do similar work, in a way. I do research and write for Hernán Gárza's organization. At the moment, it suits me and pays a livable salary."

"You're lucky to find a job so soon. This is a tough town to start in, especially if you're alone."

After a pause he asked, "Is that your situation?"

"Yes, but it's not that bad. I do have a social life."

Many of the documents Eva found were in Spanish. On those, they worked together, still searching through court records and transcripts. But even the dry leads meant more time with her. Gar valued the work she was doing on his behalf and soon realized that his appreciation of her intelligence and diligence had grown. He admired her now as a very competent woman.

Her story wasn't all that complicated, she told him on the evening of the second day. They were in a small café, wine glasses in hand, having just eaten. At twenty-nine, she was still single, though she'd once come close to getting married.

"He and I were in the fashion design program at UCLA. We moved in together, mainly for economic reasons. One thing led to another and soon we were talking a partnership, then marriage."

"That explains your unique wardrobe, which by the way I like very much."

"An eye for clothes shopping is about all that remains of that would-be career of mine."

"What moved you to jump from art to the law?"

"I'm not sure I've really made the jump. Mr. Torres has offered to finance law school, but I still can't decide if lawyering is how I want to spend the rest of my life."

"How does your family feel about it?"

She briefly eyed Gar, as if deciding how much to reveal.

"My mother would like the idea if she were alive. When my parents emigrated, they settled in East L.A. My father left us when I was eleven. Then my mother found a job working for Mr. Torres, and she got us out of the barrio but died while I was in high school. That's when I began to work weekends for Mr. Torres myself. I did the same in the summers and all through college."

"My condolences about your mother. You owe a lot to Mr. Torres?"

"More than you can imagine. Let me show you something." She extended her hand and pointed to a fleshy web between the thumb and forefinger."

"The scar?"

"It's what's left of the tattoo that marked my membership in a girls' barrio gang."

"You belonged to a gang?"

"Yep, for a while. That's why mother got us out of East L.A. But I'm not giving you a chance to tell me about you. You haven't told me very much."

"I'm more used to asking questions than answering them."

"Your family is also from Mexico, right?"

Gar looked away.

"Sorry. Did I hit a sore spot?"

He was silent for a few moments before answering. "More like a wound. My parents were murdered."

"My God." Eva put a hand to her mouth. "I'm so sorry. I had no idea."

"There's no way you could know."

"Really, I'm very sorry. That's so awful."

"I probably shouldn't have told you."

"No, I'm glad you did. It explains a lot." She paused a beat. "Was the killer caught?"

THE LAST CALIFÓRNIO

"Not yet."

It took an effort of will to push the thoughts from his mind. In the following silence he thought she was waiting to see if he'd divulge more. He wanted to tell her about Salinas and his own illegal crossing. Now wasn't the time. She changed the subject.

"I've really enjoyed being with you tonight," she said. "Thanks for dinner."

"*De nada.* It's been a pleasure for me, too. I hope we can do this again."

"I don't see why not, or why it only has to be about our research. Do you?" A faint smile lifted the corners of her mouth.

"Not at all."

She put her hand on his arm. "Should I tell you something else?"

"Please do."

"Mr. Torres is planning a TV special about land grants in the southwest and wants it to feature the Rancho Santa Anita. He didn't want you to get too excited about it."

"Has he set a date?"

"Maybe in late August or early September. Anyway, we might have to wrap up our investigation."

"But we're not finished."

"No, but I'm pretty sure we've exhausted the possibilities here in L.A. We've found the rancho's design, which gives us a solid start, but we need more. Something to give the program punch. Assuming something like that exists."

"You know I'll do whatever I can to help."

"Are you ready to go to Sacramento?"

29

He knew something had happened as soon as Eva picked him up. The easy comfort of their previous evening had vanished.

Sporadic conversation made the seven-hour drive to Sacramento seem far longer. He'd been looking forward to the prospect of being together in a place strange to them both and even allowed himself the fantasy of sleeping with her. The trip should have had the effect of drawing them closer. Instead she was acting like a stranger.

For most of the drive he said nothing about it, but as they approached Sacramento he had to clear the air.

"You're angry? Am I the reason?"

"I've never been here before," she said, "but Map Quest makes it easy. We're looking for a Travelodge. It would have a big orange sign."

Whatever Eva's problem, she wasn't discussing it. He depended on her cooperation to get the research done. This was no time to get involved in personal differences.

"With any luck we can get our work done with just one or two night's stay," she said. "I've reserved a room for each of us. The federal building where we'll be working is on the next street over."

The room arrangement was a bit of a let down, but fine with Gar. Still, he couldn't let the strain between them continue.

"Why don't we freshen up and then meet in the bar for a drink before dinner?" He looked at his watch. "Shall we say in an hour, about seven?"

Eva walked into the bar at the agreed time. Every man in the place stared at her, as did their annoyed companions. Eva's outfit, exquisitely tailored, deserved applause. She moved toward him with a dancer's grace.

Diós mio, she's beautiful. He rose as she reached the table. Taking one of her hands, he brought it to his lips.

"What's that for?" she asked, her face cracking a smile.

"With every man in the room admiring you, I wanted to show my appreciation too."

They sat.

"What will you have?"

"Wine, I guess."

He signaled the waitress. "Red or white?"

"Look," she said, "I'm sorry about the way I acted on the drive up here. It's not about you."

"Well, I'm glad of that. What is it, then?"

She hesitated for a moment. "Last night, I had a visitor."

"Someone you didn't want to see?"

"Yes. I told you about my partner in grad school, my former boyfriend?"

Gar nodded.

"To cut to the chase, he seemed to think we should pick up where we left off. I disagreed, but he wouldn't take no for an answer. He can't accept that it's over. I had a hard time getting him out the door. It left me tired and upset."

"You should have called me."

"Wasn't your problem. Anyway, enough about that, it's finished." She shook her head as if to clear it.

"I'm glad of that."

After a pause she brightened. "Hey, just because I'm on the firm's tab doesn't mean we can't enjoy ourselves. Do you dance?"

"Do I dance? I've been known to salsa with the best of them."

"We'll see about that."

"Are you up for it?"

"Sure am. I need to loosen up. There's a place here called Harlow's with a salsa band of some renown," she told him. "Food's supposed to be excellent. It's close enough to walk to—and it's a beautiful evening out."

They danced well together, their movements so fast and smooth that other dancers often stopped to watch them. After midnight, they walked back to the hotel, arms around each other's waists.

"I had a wonderful time tonight," she said. "You are one hell of a dancer."

"You made me look good."

In the hallway's semi-darkness they came to her door.

"I think we've both been wondering about this moment," she said, looking up at him. "The courthouse opens at nine tomorrow and, until I see you at breakfast at around 7:30..."

She reached up and kissed him full on the mouth, and her lips lingered; he took her into his arms. She put a hand on the back of his neck. Then as quickly as she'd come to him, she pulled away and unlocked the door.

"Goodnight, Gar," she said, locking the door.

Back in his own room, he found sleeping impossible. The evening with Eva had stoked pent-up desires and stirred memories. His mind leaped from the present to the past, with thoughts of his youth washing over him. With an effort, he forced his mind to the reason they were in Sacramento. Recalling the urgency of what they had to accomplish ended his erotic inventions but threatened to keep him awake the rest of the night.

30

The next day, Eva was all business. At a few minutes before nine, she and Gar fell in step with the swarm of others hurrying into the modern federal building. They began their research on the tenth floor.

It was late morning before they found anything that mattered.

"Finally. Pay dirt!" Eva said, sitting back in her chair and letting out a sigh of relief.

"What is it?" He tried to read the writing on the microfiche but the angle was wrong.

"Transcript of a local court hearing in January 1855."

"Is it significant?"

"What it means is the U.S. Land Commission didn't hear the case." She read on. "It goes pretty much as your ancestor Enriqueta described it, though it's clear she didn't understand what was happening."

"What do you mean?"

"In one of her letters she wrote about the hearing in which the judge disallowed the description of the property."

"I recall she wasn't happy about that. What about it?"

"According to this there was nothing wrong with the boundaries, as she claimed."

"The man who represented her was the same one who wanted the land. He didn't want her to understand."

"You mean Don Perfecto, the one she thought had José murdered?"

"That's right." Gar grimaced. "It wouldn't surprise me if the bastard deliberately misinformed her."

"Nothing here says she gave up any rights to the rancho, though she left it in his hands."

"His, meaning Don Perfecto's?"

"Yes, but the name given here is Hiram Rollem."

"You think they're the same person?"

"Can't say for sure, but I'd think so from her letters and description." Eva looked up at him.

"Wait a minute. Rollem... I've heard that name before."

"Of course you have," she said. "That's the surname of the man running for mayor of L.A."

"Might be coincidence. Even if it is his ancestor, could you still hold Weegan Rollem accountable?"

"Maybe not, but Towers will use it if it works for his campaign."

"Then I don't see how this leaves us any farther along," he said.

"Hey, we aren't finished here by a long shot."

Near closing time, they found what they'd been looking for on another microfiche.

"Look at this." Eva leaned away from the monitor. "It's a land patent from 1856, granted to our friend Rollem. He claimed Enriqueta Montalvo sold him the land she left in his care."

"Not possible!"

"Take it easy." Eva put a hand on his arm.

"We know from her letters that she never sold the rancho to anyone," Gar insisted.

"The letter isn't identified as a bill of sale, but..."

"Then how...?"

"Maybe the judge and lawyers couldn't read Spanish, her signature could have been forged, or she sent a bill of sale later."

"I'm sure there was no sale of any kind. Anything dealing with the land was too important not to be included in her letters. Remember, she sent her son to reclaim it and others tried later."

Eva sat down. "I don't disagree, but there's something else our friend Rollem could have used."

"What's that?"

"After the '48 gold rush, hundreds of separate property jurisdictions came into being, claims staked out by miners, each authority with its own records and rules established by local consensus."

"Local consensus?"

"Those were associations formed by immigrants and squatters with claims in the same general area. They made and agreed upon their own set of laws and elected their own officers."

"And I suppose if you were Mexican, those associations could ignore your grant and issue patents as they pleased."

"I'm no expert, but in my opinion that's most likely the way our friend Rollem acquired the Montalvo property."

"You mean stole it!"

"Yes." Eva put a hand on his arm again. "What makes it questionable is that the hearing took place before the U.S. government passed the preemption statutes."

"Preemption," he repeated. "Another of those damned legal terms. Meaning what?"

"The government's prior right to something—in this case, land. Those laws did away with the informal property rules in California and other places in the country. Until that then, people like your Don Perfecto, and maybe Hiram Róllem, could lay claim to the Rancho Santa Anita."

"Wouldn't a later hearing by the U.S. Land Commission override claims like that?"

"Supposedly. Who knows what deals were struck, who got paid off, or how many claims slipped through? We've gone as far as we can. You'll need a lawsuit to clear it up."

Anticipating an early start the next morning for their return to L.A., Gar and Eva ate dinner in the hotel restaurant. Gar hardly touched his food.

"Sorry," he said, "I'm not very good company."

"I'd have been surprised if you'd reacted to our findings any other way."

His eyes rested on the single black pearl dangling from a silver chain just above her cleavage. She was stunning, even in jeans and a simple blouse.

"I know that what we found today wasn't quite what you'd hoped for, but it's still important," she said.

"I hope you're right. But will it be useful to my case or to Hank Torres?"

"Oh yeah. If the land was transferred illegally, there's a case. Winning it is another matter. As for using it as a campaign issue, believe me, Towers will take full advantage. If we confirm a family connection to Weegan Rollem, there's no telling how much damage it could do to him. Take heart."

They lapsed into silence. She sipped her wine and looked away.

After their trip to the Mission San Gabriel, he'd wanted to tell her the truth about himself. He'd almost shown her the *Los Angeles Times* clipping about the death of the border patrol agent, Fausto Vásquez. Gar knew that if he didn't risk squaring things with Eva, they couldn't go on.

31

"There's something I want to tell you," Gar said.

"I'm all ears." Eva said, turning to face him.

"I haven't been entirely honest with you."

"You mean about what happened to your parents?"

"No, that part's true." He hesitated.

"Like the rest of the story about your coming here?"

"You suspected something?"

"I wondered about things, like your accent. Tell me."

Gar began telling her the truth—why and how he'd left Mexico, about the odyssey to Los Angeles, his family tie to Hernán Gárza.

He took the *Los Angeles Times* clipping about Fausto Vásquez from his shirt pocket and handed it to her.

"This is part of it, too."

When finished reading, Eva said, "That's quite a story. Is that all of it?"

"Not quite." He told her about buying a set of forged documents and getting a driver's license.

She stared at the clipping again. "I'd say that being driven out under threat of death in effect makes you a refugee rather than an illegal."

"That's what Hernán said."

"I agree with him. And it's an important distinction."

"Maybe. What difference does it make? I'm still just another illegal."

"That's not necessarily true," she said. "Hernán could petition the immigration authorities to grant you refugee status. It's been done for others—Cubans who arrive by boat, thousands of Salvadorans."

"Yes, he could do that and I'm sure he would. In the meantime I'd be jailed. I used Fausto's name for a while. It wouldn't take much to connect me to his death. Then I'd be charged. Maybe with his murder. Apart from that, the people responsible for my parents' deaths are hunting me. They may even know I'm in L.A."

Eva gazed at him for a long moment.

"I'm glad you've told me all this," she said softly. Then in a different tone, she added, "but why did you decide to tell me now?"

"Because I can't live a lie with you. I care about you."

"Now you're going to tell me we can't see each other when we get back to L.A. Isn't that what you're really saying?"

He understood why she might think so.

"I hadn't thought of it that way," he said, "but it makes sense to be careful when we get back. Not because I want it that way, *querida*." Reaching across the table, he took her hands in his.

"But what?"

"There's no but," he whispered. "If I'm picked up, you could be jailed for consorting with an illegal. That could jeopardize your job, not to mention your future."

"I don't care!" She freed her hands from his grasp and shook her head. "You can't be blind to how I feel about you."

He reached across and captured a tear from her cheek with a fingertip and brought it to his lips. He rose, pulled her up into his arms and with a hand holding her head, gently pressed her face into the hollow of his shoulder. Ignoring the patrons staring at them, he lifted her chin with a hand, kissed her forehead and then her lips. A line had been crossed, a bond formed.

Seconds later, she pulled herself free and sat, dabbing at her eyes with a napkin.

"I'm sorry. I've embarrassed you and everyone else," she

said, making a sweeping motion with her hand.

"Forget people, *querida*, and don't apologize. Your reaction was more than I could have hoped for. I had no idea how you felt."

"Yes, you can be dense." Her smile, different this time, made his heart leap.

"*Querida*," he said, "I want us to be together tonight."

She stared at their entwined hands. When she looked back up at him, he saw vulnerability, her brow conveying a struggle between uncertainty and desire. He raised her hand to his lips.

Gar signaled the waiter for the check.

"Come on," Gar said.

They left the restaurant. As they walked to her room, he could feel her excited trembling, which matched his own.

As the door clicked softly, locking them in the room's dim interior, she pressed herself into him, arms holding fast, face upturned, her breath on his lips. They fumbled with their clothes, undressing each other. She pressed her face against his bared chest. Her touch on his skin sent sensations shuddering through him. He caressed her naked back with his fingers and after a moment, she lifted her arms and arched her torso, an invitation to carry her to bed.

Time seemed to lose meaning. Propelled by pent-up mutual need, their lovemaking evolved into an overwhelming smorgasbord of sensual delight. Eva's energy and appetite thrilled him. Not long after their first frenzied coupling, they again gave free reign to desire. They stopped only when their energy was finally spent. Eyes closed and nestled into each other, they stayed that way for some time as if absorbing through their pores and intermingling breath the miraculous discovery of each other.

For some time neither spoke, and he wondered if she was asleep. But then she questioned him with surprising directness.

"Gar? Is there someone, a woman waiting for you in

Mexico?"

He should have expected the question. He raised himself on an elbow and with a hand turned her face to his.

"No," he answered, and kissed her. In the dim light he saw her smile as he lay down again.

Even as he watched the smile on her face, Gar's thoughts flashed to Teresa, his last *novia*. She'd asked him to leave as soon as she learned he was being pursued by narco-agents. Gar couldn't blame her for wanting to avoid what was clearly a dangerous situation.

"If you hadn't been forced to leave Mexico, would you ever have tried to find out about the rancho?"

"I've wondered about that myself. My father left me no information, no instructions. And I'd only met Hernán once before, when I was just a child. He'd put the files in storage. If I hadn't shown up here, I suspect he would've eventually destroyed them."

"Now that you may have a crack at getting some kind of restitution...?"

Her question trailed off, but he knew the rest of it. "I still want to bring my family's murderers to justice."

"Won't you have to return to Mexico for that?"

"Right now all I want to think about is the two of us. I don't know what the future holds, but I want to be in yours."

She nestled closer to him. Their lovemaking this time was unhurried, lasting until dawn, when they fnally collapsed into sleep.

32

On the long trip back to L.A., Gar thought Eva might be too exhausted to drive the whole way. They'd agreed he shouldn't drive in case they were stopped. He wanted to lean back and close his eyes but, if he couldn't share the driving, he could at least help her stay awake.

They said little, and he wondered if she were thinking about their newfound relationship. When he placed a hand on her shoulder, she flashed the kind of smile that answered that question and more. Whatever thoughts and feelings she might be having she kept to herself.

At times during the drive, she pressed him for details about life in Mexico, his childhood, and his experiences as a journalist.

"If I'm being too nosy, just let me know," she said.

"Don't worry, I will." He did his best to answer what she asked, for once not clamming up at what he might have regarded as prying. "Remember, I'll have my turn with you. Now that you know all the mundane details about me, I suppose you'll lose interest."

"Yeah, you're just a run-of-the-mill sort of guy," she said, laughing.

They headed into a range of wooded mountains. "The Santa Susanas," she told him. Then she asked, "What's next for you?" as if she were afraid of the answer.

"You mean for us?" In reality, he hadn't thought it through. Discovering the rancho and his involvement with Hank Towers had been his only focus in recent weeks. And avenging his family's deaths would always be with him.

When she figured out that their time together hinged on his quest for vengeance, she'd want to know if they had any future together at all. The question troubled him, too, but first he needed to sort things out for himself.

"What's next is to get what we discovered about the rancho to Hernán so he can put the lawsuits together. When you report to Hank Towers, we'll find out how he plans to use it."

"Already know that," she said. "He's been itching to get the show organized. He'll get moving. He has the gist of our report and I'm bringing details. His advisors are already exploring how to use it."

He wished she'd say something about their night together. Had it not really meant that much to her?

They began a descent into a broad plain. The setting sun could hardly penetrate a vast, gray-brown blanket of pollution hanging over the valley.

He glanced at his watch. "Any idea where we are?"

"San Fernando Valley, the northern part of L.A. County." She looked over at him. "Not far from where I live. Maybe we could go there, unless you're in a rush."

"I'd like that." He wanted to see what Eva called home. "Where's your apartment?"

"Actually, it's a bungalow. In Van Nuys, a little farther south off the 405. The turn-off is just up ahead."

Both sides of her street were lined with cars, some parked in driveways. The neighborhood's stuccoed houses sat close together, back from the road. Gar relaxed. The area's middle-class ordinariness meant it was unlikely that anyone would come looking for him here.

As he carried in their luggage, Eva had already opened a pair of windows.

"Evita," he went to her and opened his arms as she turned, "I don't know what you're feeling, but I'm..." Her kiss stopped him.

She smiled up at him when their lips parted.

"It's a little scary?"

She nodded. "But not too scary." She kissed him again. "So now I'm Little Eva?" she said, as he released her.

He managed a nervous laugh. "I didn't mean anything. It just came out."

"That's what my father called me. I like being your beloved better." She was smiling now.

"You're artistic," he said, glad to change the subject and his arm sweeping the room. "I like your taste. The Tamayo, especially." He pointed to a framed print hanging on the wall behind a sofa.

"My favorite Mexican painter. It's just a poster, but it still took a bite out of my savings."

"Worth it. The prints are scarce and the originals are a fortune, especially at auction. I've never seen a poster for sale. You're lucky to have one."

"I know. I got it at a major retrospective of his at the L.A. County Museum of Art. We should go one day."

He nodded. "Rufino could make even a monstrous red dog look mysterious and iconic." He walked to the picture for a closer look.

"Relax and get comfortable," Eva told him. "There's beer in the fridge, or wine if you prefer. I'm going to shower and change. If you like, you can do the same, while I see what there is to eat."

As they finished the light supper she prepared, Gar turned and pointed at the bookcase against the wall.

"Hernán has a collection of pre-Columbian art, too, one of the largest I've seen in private hands."

"I've seen it," Eva said. "He's the one who got me started. I've been with him to the auctions and galleries. He invites me along to special exhibitions. The whole antiquities thing is fascinating, though some of the people I've met who deal with them are a little strange. I've bought a few pieces on eBay, even though Hernán advises against it because there are so many fakes out there."

"Hernán must have been at it a long time to have put together such an extensive collection," he said.

"Actually, he got started after winning a big case. He took part of the client's collection as his fee. He's been at it for years since then."

That cleared up how Hernán had been able to afford some of the more valuable pieces. Gar wanted to ask Eva more about that but didn't.

"My father collected," he told her.

"Is that what the, um, the killers, were after?"

"Hard to say. He traded so much, so I couldn't tell if pieces were missing. I gave his entire collection to the National Archeological Museum." Gar looked away.

"I'm sorry, I didn't mean to put a damper on things."

He shook his head. "Sometimes it's unavoidable." He changed the subject. "How did you happen to pick this place to live?"

She looked relieved. "UCLA's a quick drive down the 405 from here and the rents are cheaper."

"Did you share?"

Eva hesitated. "With my ex-boyfriend. I kept it after he moved out. He took half the furnishings with him. That's why the rooms are on the spare side."

"I didn't mean to pry."

"No problem, though I wouldn't mind if you were a little jealous." She rose to clear the dishes.

"Let me help you with those." He surprised himself. He'd never think of making an offer like that in Mexico.

Standing behind him, Eva put her hands on his shoulders to stop him. She bent to kiss his neck and then leaned around and kissed him on the mouth, holding his bearded chin in her cupped hand. She pulled back and looked into his eyes.

"The dishes can wait. Follow me."

Gar and Eva lay spooned into each other in her dark

bedroom. He listened to her even breathing as she slept. Shards of light sneaked through partings in the curtains, streaking the ceiling and walls. He recalled the graceful way she moved across the dining room in Sacramento. Her remarkable physical beauty fascinated him. He eased away, afraid his prodding might wake her.

Gar wondered what it would be like living together. He'd often spent the night with a woman but never allowed it to go far beyond that. Was this time different? Was this love, or just a more complicated lust?

Eva turned onto her back. "What else are you thinking about?" she asked him.

"You, us," he said, pulling her to him. "That I've never felt more comfortable with a woman."

She stretched against him. "You're definitely saying all the things a girl likes to hear."

"You don't think I'm serious?"

"I think you're quite sincere. I feel the same." The ambient light reflected on the whites of her eyes.

"Then why the skepticism?"

"It's just that I don't know how long you're going to be around, and I don't want either of us to get hurt."

"You're right." He waited a beat. "Last night when you asked about my return to Mexico I didn't answer. You were correct to ask because I will have to go back. As of now, I can't say when that will be. Even so, I'd hate to think that having found each other, we can't continue in spite of that uncertainty." Seven months had passed since he left Mexico, and maybe the situation there had cooled enough so he could return and try to bring his family's killers to justice. But those thoughts weren't where he wanted to be just then.

"Who said anything about not continuing?" She reached under the covers and ran her hand down his lower abdomen. As he turned to her a knock at the front door startled them.

"Who the hell is that at this hour?" he asked.

Eva rose on an elbow to look at the clock on the nightstand. "It's after ten." The rapid series of knocks came again, this time louder.

"I'll go." Gar pulled on trousers and a shirt as the knocking repeated.

"No, better let me." She went to the closet and put on a robe. Gar followed her to the front door and waited to one side as she looked through the peephole.

"Damn it," she whispered, looking at him. "He's back." She sighed. "I'll tell him to leave," she said, opening the door before Gar could stop her.

"You again. Rafe, I told you it's over," she said to the man at the doorstep.

"I don't think so. Let's talk about it." He started to push his way in. As he did so, Gar pulled Eva aside and stepped between them.

"You heard what she said," Gar told him evenly. "Now leave." Gar stood with hands loose at his sides.

"Who the hell are you?" Rafe blurted. Rafe looked Gar up and down, for a moment staring at Gar's bare feet. After a few beats, he backed away and turned to leave.

Gar watched until the man reached his car, then Gar closed Eva's front door. He felt her trembling when he took her in his arms. "You think it's over, but he doesn't. And, more importantly, I can see that he still upsets you. Are you all right?"

She nodded, resting her head on his chest and wrapping her arms around him. "I'm sorry that happened while you were here."

"I'm not." He lifted her chin to kiss her. "He knows you're not alone now. He won't bother you again."

"I hope you're right. You can't tell with him."

Later as they sat on the sofa drinking coffee, she said, "Where were we before the interruption?"

"I was saying that I'd like to spend as much time together as we can."

"The same for me." Eva paused before adding, "Do you really like renting a room in a group house?"

"I'd rather not, but it'll have to do for awhile. Besides, I see now that it isn't all that far from you."

"If you say so. I wish you were closer." She put down her coffee and gazed up at him, a smile on her face. "I think we left something unfinished in the bedroom."

After she fell asleep, Gar lay awake thinking that living together could be dangerous—people were still searching for him.

33

"Eva Muñoz, Mr. Montalvo," the secretary announced over the intercom.

Mental telepathy? Gar had just been thinking about Eva. For the first time since crossing the Rio Grande, he felt as though he had something to get up for in the morning.

"I can only reach you at your office," Eva said. "Hope I'm not interrupting anything important."

"Nothing that can't wait. We have another assignment?"

"Nothing like that. I have a few days' breather before Hank's land grant program. Thought we could spend some time together."

"I'd like that. Something particular in mind?"

"The L.A. County Museum of Art. I meant it when I said I wanted to take you. An exhibit of pre-Columbian artifacts opens on Saturday."

While Gar hadn't shared his father's fascination with the ancient art, being with Eva mattered more than his disinterest in pre-Columbian artifacts.

"Sounds good."

"Pick you up at your place at nine? We can have lunch and head for the beach afterwards, or whatever. You can buy a bathing suit there."

Even before he hung up the phone, anxiety set in for Gar. If they were stopped by the police... And then there were Mexican agents out there someplace. He debated about calling Eva and backing out of the date, reminding her of his unresolved troubles. He decided to brush off the worry and take his chances.

"Hernán was surprised when I told him we were going to the exhibit together," Gar told Eva as they headed into the museum. "For a minute, I thought he might invite himself along."

"Would've been fine," Eva said. "He knows a lot about the artifacts and could have given us a private lecture tour."

"That prospect could be why he didn't ask to come," Gar chuckled.

The main exhibit hall was crowded with people craning for a better view of the art. Somehow, the monumental Toltec heads and towering Mayan and Aztec steles didn't seem out of place in the high-ceilinged space.

They arrived in time to hear a welcoming address by a cultural attaché from the Mexican Embassy, who had made a big deal of flying all the way from Washington, D.C. to open the exhibit. Eva seemed interested in his remarks. Put off by the black suits watching the crowd, Gar heard little of what the attaché had to say. Not wanting to spoil Eva's enjoyment, he remained silent, telling himself his fears about being followed were unfounded.

As they toured the exhibit, Gar became more drawn to it. He pointed out pieces similar to those his father had owned. He wondered aloud if some hadn't been in the collection. Time passed quickly.

"Well, you seemed to enjoy the exhibit," Eva said on the drive to Venice Beach.

"It was more extensive than I imagined. Moving the larger pieces must've been tricky. It amazes me how the ancients carved the pieces without metal tools and moved them with nothing but manpower."

They drove in silence for a few minutes. Then Eva looked at him sidelong.

"Come on, admit it. You were as nervous as a..."

"Nothing gets by you, does it?" Gar smiled.

"Didn't you think I'd know you'd be anxious? Being out in public? Don't worry, the beach crowd isn't likely to have immigration, or whatever, out on the hunt."

Eva treated him to lunch at the Rose Café, one of Venice's famous eateries. Afterwards they shopped for a bathing suit for him. When they made it to the beach, they were disappointed by a sign warning them of water pollution.

"One day, I want to take you to some of Mexico's beaches." He didn't spell out a comparison with Venice.

Since they couldn't swim, Gar and Eva contented themselves with watching the circus of scantily clad rollerbladers, bronzed beauties in thong bikinis, and sweating body builders working out. On blankets in a nearby area, clusters of old hippies toked openly and entertained each other with pointless talk and song.

"You see this kind of thing on Mexico's beaches?" Eva wondered.

"What you see mostly are a lot of overweight Americans and Europeans. But not even the topless beaches are as amusing as this."

"I'll bet," she said.

He could feel her studying him behind her sunglasses.

Later, sunburned and relaxed, they were slowed to a stop by a backup on the Santa Monica Freeway.

"Can you make out what's holding things up ahead?" Gar asked.

"Could be anything. Most likely an accident. Maybe I can get around it."

Eva tried to work toward an exit once traffic started moving again, but she was repeatedly blocked by other drivers with the same idea. The starting-stopping continued until they reached a police checkpoint.

"Looks like they're checking for drunks, licenses, and registrations. Some drivers are being asked to get out of their cars." Eva craned to verify her assessment.

"We're hardly drunk," Gar offered. "Think I'll have to show mine?"

"Doubt it. But you never know what these guys may be up to." She paused. "They do this for a while after there's been a horrific crash involving drinking. They seem to be flagging vehicles at random."

Her last comment left Gar unnerved.

A motorcycle cop waved them to the shoulder, where a pair of policemen approached the car, one to each side. The cop on Eva's side tapped the window and motioned for her to lower it. Gar took a quick glance at the one next to him and looked away. He watched Eva show her license and hand over the registration.

"You folks been drinking?" the cop asked.

"I'd hardly call a glass of wine with lunch drinking. One glass each," she told him.

"Please step out of the vehicle, m'am."

Gar resisted the impulse to protest. He'd have to sweat it out.

Eva stood on the roadway. The policeman put her through the drill of touching her nose, counting backwards, and walking the white line. As she answered his innocuous questions, Gar rolled down his window.

"Is all that really necessary? She's obviously not drunk," he said to the other policeman.

The cop stared at him for a few seconds.

"Please step out of the vehicle, sir."

"What? I wasn't driving."

"Please step out the vehicle, sir," the demand more forceful. "Let's see some ID."

As Gar was opening the door, the sound of a crash and shouting came from behind. Both cops turned and started moving in the direction of the commotion.

"We're done, get them out of here," the cop with Eva yelled to his partner.

They were underway again.

"That was a surprise," Eva said, shaking her head. "They usually only throw up those roadblocks on holiday weekends."

"Got started a little early this time," Gar said. "Glad you were driving. He told me to get out and asked for my ID, anyway."

"Oh my God. I didn't know that." She glanced at him. "Well, you did warn me."

"Nothing like a little excitement to end the day."

"Let's not push our luck. We'll have dinner at my place. I think we can entertain ourselves there."

34

In the days before Hank's show devoted to land grants aired, Gar got caught up in the excitement of seeing the rancho featured. His fears about being followed also resurfaced. On the night of the show, Hernán's qualms didn't help either.

"I have an aversion to this kind of exposure," Hernán told him. He looked distinguished in his dark blue suit, the tie and pocket square matching his silver hair.

"I'm surprised you agreed to go on," Gar said. He was glad the old attorney would take his place on the show.

"Hank wanted you on the panel, too." Hernán glanced at him. "He got angry when I told him why you couldn't. He ranted about how he couldn't afford to be associated with illegal immigrants."

"So, what happened?" Gar had a growing feeling the evening would end badly.

"I told him you're a de facto refugee hunted by Mexican agents. He still didn't like it. But what could he do? Things had moved on so far that he couldn't cancel the program. He even suggested you be on camera in another studio as though talking from Mexico via satellite."

Gar could have done that. Before he could say so, Hernán shook his head.

"Talked him out of that. In the end, we agreed that I'd appear as the attorney representing the Montalvo claim."

"The land grant must be important for his campaign."

"You bet. More so after you and Eva discovered that his likely opponent's ancestors may have stolen the rancho. That had him rubbing his hands together. It won't win an election, but'll make it a helluva lot more interesting."

They rode in silence for a few minutes, with Hernán watching the street signs.

"Will anyone else be on with you?" Gar asked.

"Three, maybe four other people. Hank likes roundtable discussions."

"Do you know who they are?"

"So far, only our friend Felipe. He'll talk about the treaty and answer call-ins."

"Yes, Mr. Gárza, we're expecting you." A voice sounded from the call box as they pulled up to the studio parking lot. A steel arm lifted in front of them.

They walked into a plush, carpeted lobby with walls covered by photographs of media stars.

The receptionist gave them each a clip-on pass as they signed in.

"Please take a seat." She pointed in the direction of the sofas against the far wall.

A pair of Latino-appearing men in black suits sat in the waiting area. At Hernán's and Gar's approach, they turned as if to hide their faces. Before Gar could wonder further about them, a young woman arrived.

"This way, gentlemen. You'll be in Studio C, down the hall on the right. Another of the on-air guests has already arrived," she told them.

"Would that be Professor Villareal?" Hernán asked.

"No, sir, it's Señor Salinas, the Mexican Consul General here in Los Angeles."

Gar felt as if his scalp were expanding. Being illegal, he'd never considered getting any help from him.

"Uh, miss, I'd like to use the men's room."

"No problem," she said, "it's at the end, on the left." She pointed. "I'll wait in here for you."

Gar led Hernán down the hallway.

"He's the *pinche* minister who ordered my parent's

murders," Gar told him in the men's room.

"You sure?"

"It's got to be. I should go in there and strangle the *cabrón* right now. I'd like to get him alone."

"Whoa, take it easy." Hernán held him. "Not the time or place for anything like that."

"I know, I know." Gar stared at the floor.

"I understand. You have to control yourself. OK?"

Gar took a deep breath and nodded.

"Who would've dreamed he'd show up here?"

"It's not unusual for Mexico to fill diplomatic posts with hot politicians," Gar told him. "Gets them out of the way for awhile. They can be sent anywhere, but the U.S. is preferred. They call it the Golden Exile. His friends must have arranged it after I exposed him. And if that's true, I'm responsible for his being here. How's that for irony? Maybe I should leave. I don't want to create a scene. I can come back for you later."

"You're right. No point putting yourself in harm's way."

"Wait," Gar said. "On second thought, I could be jumping to conclusions. Salinas is a common surname. We should make sure who it is."

"Good idea. You ever meet Salinas face-to-face?"

"No."

"You've seen him or his picture before? You'd recognize him?"

"I'd never forget that face."

"I'll bet. If the consulate were alerted, the advisory may or may not have included a photo. Even if it did, I doubt he'd recognize you with that full beard." He paused. "What's your mother's maiden name?"

"Romero."

"I'll use that when I introduce you. Let's go in there and meet this guy. I'll introduce you as my associate. If he's the right one, give me a nod."

Gar felt pulled into a potentially dangerous meeting.

"Gentlemen," the intern said, "let me introduce *Señor* Salinas, the Mexican Consul General here in Los Angeles."

Short and bald, his jet-black mustache neatly trimmed, the Consul rose from his seat at the mirrored dressing table and turned to greet them, a hand extended. His face shone with a light film of sweat.

"Hernán Gárza," Hernán said, grasping the Consul's hand. "And this is my associate Ben Romero."

Gar forced himself to do the same, trying to keep his face a blank.

"The pleasure is mine, *señores*." A broad smile transformed the Consul's face, its practiced sincerity only painted on. "This evening's discussion should be interesting."

"Yes, the issue is sensitive."

Gar stared at the man. If the Consul sensed his fury, he didn't show it. Seconds later when Hernán looked at Gar, he made a slight nod. The man was indeed the right Salinas.

"Quite so. Talk of stolen lands raises latent antagonisms, don't you think?" The Consul studied their faces for reactions.

"Possibly," Hernán said. "The issue has been raised repeatedly since the war of 1846."

"Of that I'm well aware, but not by Mexico. Do you gentlemen ever travel to my country?"

"I emigrated from Mexico as a child. I've not been back in many years," Hernán told him.

"It's been some time for me, too." Gar said.

"I recall your being in the news." Hernán said.

"Relative to what, may I ask?"

"Something about Mexican immigrants being the vanguard for the reconquest of California, if not the whole southwest."

The Consul nodded and pursed his lips. "That was a comment made in jest by my predecessor. He was misunderstood."

"How unfortunate. It exploded like a bomb here."

THE LAST CALIFÓRNIO

The Consul's discomfort clouded his smooth façade.

Salinas studied Gar, observing him like a collector in front of a painting he might buy.

"Have we met before, Mr. Romero? You seem familiar. Perhaps at a reception at the consulate, or...?"

Before the Consul could finish, the intern led Professor Villareal and another man into the room, and they were followed by two women in white smocks.

"*Órale*, Hernán," Felipe said, smiling as he turned to greet Gar. Hernán interrupted.

"You remember my associate, Ben Romero?"

The professor was quick to understand. "Yes, of course. Good to see you again," the professor said.

As the on-air guests were asked to sit for make-up, the Consul looked at Gar's reflection in the mirror, focusing on Gar as if he were the only other person in the room.

Then Hank Towers entered the room, and Gar held his breath.

"Gentlemen, welcome. I wanted you to meet each other before airtime and to thank you for coming. I look forward to an interesting discussion. I'll see you on stage in a few minutes."

Hank motioned for a relieved Gar to follow.

"Thanks for the time and effort you put in working with Eva," he said. "You both did a great job. You gave us the punch we need. I think you'll enjoy watching."

The panelists fled out of the make-up studio. Gar watched from the control room as Salinas took his place on the sound stage with the others.

35

From the control booth, an assistant counted down the remaining seconds to airtime and then pointed at Hank.

"Good evening, I'm Hank Towers. Welcome to Towers Forum Live." He sat in front of a panoramic, smog-free view of the city.

"Tonight on the Forum, an issue that reaches back into American history, one of great consequences for the people of Los Angeles and for Latinos throughout the southwest." He paused. "Earlier today, in unprecedented actions, suits to seek justice for lands allegedly stolen from their former owners here in California were filed in both the U.S. Ninth Circuit Court and the Claims Court of the Superior Court in Los Angeles."

A map of Mexico and the western United States flashed on the screen. Highlighted in pale gold was a large portion labeled *FORMER MEXICAN TERRITORIES*.

"Most Americans know that Mexico and the United States fought a three-year war beginning in 1846, in which Mexico lost about half of its former lands." He paused again. "Less well known is that, according to the terms of the instrument that ended the war, the Treaty of Guadalupe Hidalgo, Mexicans who stayed in those former territories automatically became U.S. citizens and were guaranteed the ownership of their property.

"Tonight, we'll talk about what happened to those lands. In the opinion of most historians, the prelude to the war as well as the war itself and its aftermath were not proud periods in American history.

THE LAST CALIFÓRNIO

"With us to provide four perspectives are," a camera focused on each panelist as he was named, "Dr. Felipe Villareal, Professor Emeritus of Ethnic Studies at UCLA; Señor Armando Salinas Gutiérrez, the Mexican Consul General in Los Angeles; California State Senator George Harrix; and Mr. Hernán Gárza, Esquire, representing the Montalvo family, whose granted lands are the subject of the suits filed earlier today.

"Welcome, gentlemen. *Señor* Salinas, please give our viewers some background on the land grant system employed by the Spanish Crown and the Government of Mexico before the 1846 war."

"Certainly." He began to tell how, in the last half of the eighteenth century, Spanish priests and *conquistadores* established a chain of twenty-one missions along the Pacific seaboard to settle and control the California territory. When Mexico gained its independence from Spain in 1821, the Church lost its holdings in the lands then known as Tejas, Nuevo Méjico, and Alta Califórnia. To encourage settlement in these regions, some mission lands were turned into *ranchos* and granted by the regional governors to aristocratic Mexicans to settle and farm. Some *ranchos* in Tejas and Nuevo Méjico—which included what are now part of the states of Arizona, Colorado, Kansas, New Mexico, Nevada, Oklahoma, and Utah—were held for common use. For nearly the next twenty-five years in the Alta Califórnia region, and until the United States conquest of Mexico, wealthy *rancheros*, calling themselves *Califórnios*, dominated this area Americans have since called California.

"Professor Villareal, would you care to comment?"

"Yes, but first, I must say that I doubt most Americans know a war was fought between Mexico and the United States in the late 1840s, much less about what was at issue. I'd like to expand upon what happened to the lands *Señor* Salinas mentioned."

"Go right ahead."

"In 1849, and in the years following, there wasn't only a gold rush in California, there was also a rush to strip the land from its Mexican-American owners, sometimes by force, in other cases by judges deciding that deeds were insufficient proof of ownership. Still others were taken for unpaid taxes the owners were unaware had been levied on the property. And if none of those tactics worked, the legislatures of the states, as each was formed, passed laws to deny ownership of disputed lands to their Mexican- American owners."

"Senator Harrix, would you agree with those characterizations?" The camera shifted to the senator's solemn face.

"There's no doubt that confusion reigned in the aftermath of the U.S.-Mexico War, with ownership of the lands constantly in flux. As *Señor* Salinas has outlined, the land was taken from Native Americans by the Spanish, later by Mexico from Spain, then from the Catholic Church, and so on.

"Now as to the Professor's characterizations, while some of the practices he mentioned may have been used in a few instances, it's also true that our government went to some lengths to resolve land ownership disputes, eventually settling all of them. Americans need not be ashamed about the history of this period. Mexico lost the war and all this about land claims just sounds like the complaints of the losers."

"If I may?" Felipe broke in.

Hank nodded.

"The senator is incorrect. The land wasn't in the hands of losers, but in those of newly made American citizens, whose continued ownership the United States Government guaranteed by treaty. It is precisely the abrogation of that guarantee that makes the theft of the lands so egregious."

Senator Harrix shook his head.

"Second," Felipe continued, "even a cursory reading of court records, of scholarly writings on this period—not to mention personal accounts by both American land agents, squatters, and the *Califórnios* themselves—show that if anything, my characterizations are generous."

"Senator Harrix?" Hank turned to the senator.

"Well, all I'm saying is non-Hispanics don't know or care about this matter."

"Don't know or care, Professor?"

"I agree that many Americans may not know," Felipe replied, "but being a fair-minded people, I disagree that Americans don't or won't care. If they don't know, it's because this history has been suppressed. It is indeed a shameful period, which like so many others involving minorities, must be aired to be rectified."

"Well, that might be..."

"Excuse me, Senator, in a moment," Hank said, "but first, Mr. Gárza, please outline, if you will, the substance of the suits you filed today."

"The suit filed with the Ninth Circuit charges that the Federal Government failed to live up to and enforce the provisions of the Treaty of Guadalupe Hidalgo, the one Professor Villareal just mentioned. It asks for monetary restitution to the heirs of the Montalvo family."

Senator Harrix interrupted. "Determining the value of the land would be next to impossible."

"On the contrary," Hernán responded. "That's something well within the court's ability to determine. As for the other..."

"Pardon the interruption," Hank said, "but before you continue, can you tell us where those heirs reside?"

"They all reside in Mexico at the present time. But that fact has no bearing on the legitimacy of their claim."

"Thank you. And the other brief?" Hank asked.

"The suit filed in the superior court charges that the lands belonging to my clients were taken illegally. It asks for return of the lands and for punitive damages."

"Senator Harrix?"

"That's preposterous!" He was shaking his head. "You

can't expect properties that have been sold and resold in good faith during the past 150-plus years to be summarily returned to owners, not only long-since departed, but whose claims and boundaries were imprecise and often lacked written documentation of ownership."

"On the contrary," Hernán continued in a calm voice. "In our legal system, stolen property of whatever sort may not be lawfully disposed of and the owner is entitled to be made whole. There's plenty of precedent to bring these kinds of suits to the courts and with a reasonable expectation of success for the plaintiffs."

"Senator?" Hank nodded at him.

"Do you realize what a firestorm this would start? And not only here in California."

"Yes, I do," Hernán replied. "As we speak, a number of such claims are before the courts in Colorado, Texas, and New Mexico. Some have also been brought by Native American tribes."

"Before we give our viewers a chance to join the discussion," Hank said, "I ask you, *Señor* Salinas, whether Mexico has made, or plans to make, any claims to lands it lost as a result of the 1846 war."

"There was one such claim, The Chamizal Convention, for a strip of land that lies along what you Americans call the Rio Grande. It adjusted the boundary between our two countries, resolved 100 year-old boundary problems, and transferred some 400 acres to Mexico."

The Consul's remarks came as news to Gar.

"Thank you. Mr. Gárza, what can you tell us about the physical size of the claim?"

"The land in question is roughly 20,000 acres. We're re-surveying to be sure where the boundaries lie, but generally they extend south of the San Gabriel Mountains in the vicinity of Mt. Wilson, between and including parts of what are now the Cities of Pasadena and Arcadia."

"Hank, this is really farfetched!" Senator Harrix shook

his head. "That area would include land on which are situated institutions like, uh, the Jet Propulsion Laboratory, prestigious universities, museums, businesses, and some of the area's most affluent private homes."

"On that you are quite right." Hernán agreed.

"Well, now," the Senator continued, "a ruling in your favor would create a huge uproar and open the door for others to file similar claims, real or imagined. Such claims couldn't be allowed to go forward."

"Which is why we have courts," Hernán reminded him.

"Our switchboards are alive with calls from our viewers," Hank said, "The first comes from here in Los Angeles. Please go ahead, Bill."

"Yeah, I agree with the senator that all this is so much hokum. When you have a war, the winner takes all."

"Do you have a question, caller?"

"Nah, you people are already taking over L.A."

"If I may." Felipe said. "The caller should know that these lands weren't lost during the war, but in the years, in some cases many years, afterwards."

"Yes, Alicia in Albuquerque, you're on the air."

"Mr. Gárza, my ancestors also lost their land here in New Mexico. Will your law suits open the way for me and others to bring similar suits?"

"There! That's just what I mean," Senator Harrix cut in. "Copycat suits!"

"Please, Senator," Hank said. "Allow Mr. Gárza to respond."

"Each case would have to be made on its own merits," Hernán said. "I can't make judgments on any case other than the one I've prepared."

"Dr. Villareal, have there been other suits like this one in California?" Hank asked.

"Not in California. In the 1960s, Hispanos in northern New Mexico seized land they claimed had been granted to their ancestors."

"Was that the effort led by Réies López Tijerina?" Hank asked.

"Yes, the minister who founded the Federal Alliance of Land Grants. His group occupied part of a national forest and a piece of an old land grant. When they later arrested two forest rangers for trespassing on the so-called new state, López Tijerina was himself arrested and tried."

"That's exactly my point," Senator Harrix said, calmer now. "These claims fail because they're without merit."

"Not entirely true," Felipe countered. "Some Native American tribes have had successes. Until just recently, all efforts by Mexican-Americans to regain ancestral lands have been stalled by the established powers through legal restrictions, questionable judicial procedures, and even threats of terrorism. But in *Lobato v. Taylor*, the Colorado Supreme Court vindicated Mexican-Americans' claims to the Sangre de Cristo Land Grant, proving that this and similar cases do have merit. They're very much alive. In a recent subsequent ruling, a district judge reinstated the rights of the descendants of Mexican settlers to a 77,000-acre ranch, which is part of that land grant."

"Yes, Fred in Colorado, go ahead," Hank said.

"Is the Colorado case the only time anyone has tried to reclaim granted lands?"

"No," Felipe said. "One of the most recent is by a group in Texas, the Asociación de Reclamantes, which is seeking redress from Mexico."

When the Consul's face came up on the screen, he was shaking his head.

"George in Roswell, New Mexico. Go ahead."

"Say, Professor, didn't former Republican U.S. Representative Gingrich promise to bring up land-grant claims when he was campaigning in 1998?"

"Yes. A sop to Latino voters. But he did nothing and is long gone from Congress."

"Elizabeth in San Jose, please go ahead."

"As I understand it, the State of California courts were within their rights to require proof of land ownership determined by survey measurements, the system brought over from England. Isn't that true?"

"Yes, measurements of that type weren't necessary under Mexican law, though some were so delineated," Hernán said. "Knowing that, state legislators passed laws requiring all lands to be re-measured and claims to be filed with the government. To the detriment of Mexican-Americans, that put the burden of proving claims on the landowners, and many lost because they couldn't show proof of exact boundaries. Other landowners lost territory because they couldn't show written proof of grants made to their families centuries before by the Spanish Crown."

"That hardly seems fair," the caller said.

"So it may seem, caller," Senator Harrix's voice was eager, "but can you imagine buying the property your house sits on today, whose boundaries are only described in terms of land marks?"

"I see what you mean," the caller said.

"Your response, Mr. Gárza?" Hank asked.

"My clients have both written evidence of the granted lands and the boundaries properly delineated," Hernán responded.

"I believe these are the documents you're referring to, are they not?" Hank said. The image of the Montalvo land grant document and next to it the *diseño* of the Rancho Santa Anita boundaries flashed on the screen.

"There are others, such as the letter granting the lands to my client's ancestors from the regional governor, as well as anecdotal evidence in a contemporaneous diary and letters," Hernán said.

"Rubén in East Los Angeles. Please go ahead."

"*Señor* Gárza, sounds to me like many of those new Mexican-American citizens had their lands stolen." The caller spoke in accented English. "Could the Montalvo claim be an issue during an election?"

Hank broke in. "That's an interesting thought, Rubén, but Mr. Gárza is an attorney representing a valid claim, he's not a politician. Thank you, caller. I'm afraid we're out of time." To each panelist, Hank said, "Gentlemen, thank you all for being here tonight. I suspect this will not be the last we'll hear about the issues raised. I hope you'll agree to return to continue the discussion."

As the credits rolled, Gar had the first real sense that reclaiming his birthright might be possible.

It dawned on him that the black-suited Latinos he'd seen in the lobby were likely Salinas's bodyguards. He rushed to the studio entrance, just in time to see Salinas leaving. If the Consul had recognized him, his bodyguards would now know what he looked like.

36

The unexpected meeting with the Consul stunned Gar, whose earlier anxieties flared up at knowing that his nemesis was in the city yet impossible to get to.

Two days later, Gar was still thinking about the Consul while sitting in a traffic standstill on the way to the office. A radio DJ blamed the upcoming Labor Day weekend for the morning's snares. Not even Charlie Parker's "Don't Blame Me" served as a comforting enough distraction from the blare of horns honking.

Ever watchful when driving on the freeways, Gar checked out the other drivers when stuck in traffic. Usually, most of them returned only a bored glance. On this morning, however, a pair of swarthy Latinos stared back from inside a black Mercedes Benz. The instant Gar made eye contact, he noticed a flicker in the driver's deadpan gaze and began to realize that the two men were familiar. *Mierda*, Gar thought. Who the hell are they? Could they be working for Salinas? The Mercedes moved ahead, then drifted back beside him. Gar sped up and then held back, trying to inch into the next lane. The other driver matched him move for move. If they were Salinas's men, had they followed him from Gisela's house? How would that even be possible?

The Mercedes jockeyed to keep even with Gar, and he started to sweat. Could one of them be lining up a shot? *¡Jesucristo!*

A sudden gap in the lane to Gar's left opened. He darted into it. The car behind him filled the vacated space, blocking the Benz. Gar maneuvered three car lengths behind it, then five.

He forced his way in front of cars, forcing drivers to slam on their brakes. After edging to an exit lane, he spotted a last hazy glimpse of the Mercedes in the rearview mirror.

On a side street, Gar doubled back three or four blocks and found a gas station with a pay phone. He sat for a few minutes before trying to use it.

"Eva, it's Gar."

"What is it? Are you all right?"

"I've just been stalked on the freeway."

"What? Who would be after you?"

"When I met the Mexican Consul and two of his bodyguards at Hank's TV studio, he must have recognized me. I think the two men in the car were his. They must have found out where I live, and they may even know who my associates are."

"That's awful. How can you be sure? Maybe they were just guys angry because you cut them off, you know, road rage. Happens a lot."

"Listen. They may come after you, too."

"Why would they be interested in me?"

"To get me."

"You mean like hold me hostage? This is sounding like a plot for a bad movie."

"Eva, this is serious. These men are killers. You should get out of town for awhile, at least until I see that there's nothing going on."

Eva sighed. "I hope you're wrong, but I can't really argue. What are you going to do now?"

"I'm going to the office. They may be watching the house. I can't go back there tonight. Maybe Hernán can help me figure out what to do. Let him know where you'll be and I'll be in touch with you later through him."

"Be careful."

"Yeah, they could've been the Consul's people." Hernán

looked up as Gar entered the office. "I noticed the way he watched you at the TV studio. Think you were followed here?"

"I don't know. I parked a few streets away."

Hernán looked troubled, but said nothing.

"I don't understand how Salinas would know how to find me."

"The guest register? On his way out he could have checked it to see if the name you wrote was the same as the one I used to introduce you."

"That wouldn't have told him anything. I only signed in as *visitor*."

"No shit. Man, you are wary."

"It's possible that one of the Latinos we saw in the studio waiting room followed us when you drove me home after the show."

"Maybe." Hernán nodded and raised a hand, as if he'd just thought of something. "There's a more likely explanation. Having recognized you, the Consul could've had an aide contact the DMV to see if your vehicle was registered."

"Isn't that privileged information?"

"Yes, but they could claim a family emergency in Mexico and an urgent need to contact you."

"That would give them everything."

"We're still not sure. At any rate, you think it was more than road rage?"

"The way they looked and acted?"

"Who else would track you like that?"

"I haven't been here long enough to know anyone like that. Can't think of anyone."

"There's something strange about it."

"What do you mean?"

"If they were tailing you, they would have been following you instead of driving alongside you, where you'd see and lose them, as you did."

"Go on."

"The encounter could have been pure chance. I don't think they were tailing you."

"Unless one of them was preparing to shoot me."

"It still seems remote. The way you described things and with traffic often at a standstill, there were plenty of chances to fire and get away."

"Salinas could have ordered them to bring me in alive to be deported. That would be neater."

"Ah, now you may have something," Hernán said. "I'm still skeptical, but you've raised enough doubt that it's only prudent to take precautions."

"What about Eva? She's sitting out there..."

"Yeah, there's her situation, too. Can she go out of town for a few days?"

"I've suggested that but she can't stay away long. Her disappearing for too long might raise questions at her office."

"That'll buy some time. In the meantime, you can hide out with one of my colleagues. Esteban Reverte might take you in. He was illegal when he got here. He'll understand. Take the laptop with you so you can continue work on the grant. We can stay in touch by email."

"Uh, that's going to be a problem. In the rush to get going this morning I grabbed my backpack instead of the computer, which holds all my notes."

"A lot of my other stuff, too." Hernán muttered.

"I'm sorry." Gar didn't mention that the backpack contained Fausto Vásquez's pistol.

"Nothing to do about that now." Hernán moved on. "Load the proposal criteria onto a CD and take another laptop."

While Hernán called Esteban, Gar busied himself installing what he needed for work.

37

Esteban didn't press him for details, but soon after Gar moved into the labor leader's central L.A. home, he knew Hernán had told the man all about him. Gar discovered that he and Esteban thought a lot alike.

Originally from Durango, Esteban had farmed a few family hectares and owned a small trucking firm. Life turned sour for him after being falsely accused of a crime. He'd refused to pay a large "fee" to stay in business and out of prison, and a local crime boss sent in his goons. With no other choice, Esteban crossed illegally to *El Norte*, where he eventually decided to stay and make a new life.

In California, the former migrant worker showed himself to be a natural labor leader. A strong wily idealist, he had an overriding sense of purpose for getting what his farm workers needed.

"Reminds me what it was like trying to work in Mexico under the PRI," he told Gar on their first evening together. "What I hated was politicians allowing developers to cheat *campesinos* out of land for resorts and other government projects. It's not that different here. Labor contractors supply workers to growers, make migrants toil, and often cheat them out of their meager pay." Esteban talked from the kitchen, where he was busy heaping *arroz con pollo* on a plate for Gar. "Politicians here are no different. Can't trust them, either."

"That doesn't surprise me," Gar said. His mouth watered from the mixed aroma of rice, tomatoes, onions, and cilantro. Living alone obviously didn't mean that Esteban couldn't eat well.

"My toughest job is forcing the growers here to make even the barest concessions to our pickers." He re-filled their glasses with Dos Equis. "The governor and many assemblymen are so dependent on the growers for campaign money, it's been rough to get their backing."

"How've you managed?" Gar chewed and talked at the same time.

"Any way possible."

Gar admired the man's determination, and his culinary ability. Despite their shared disgust with politicians, Gar sensed a gulf between them, one he suspected had to do with the respective classes each of them came from in Mexico. That probably explained Esteban's apparent lack of interest in reminiscing about life there. If life in Mexico had been any good, he likely would have moved to another state, rather than leave the country. Though Esteban had risen to a position of relative power in California, he nevertheless retained a modesty that Gar guessed came from starting life penniless in a *barrio bajo*.

Gar cleaned his plate for a second time. When it came to cooking, Esteban knew what he was doing.

"That was delicious," Gar complimented him. Where'd you learn your way around the kitchen?"

"If you can believe it, I managed to marry a woman who not only *couldn't* but *wouldn't* cook for me. We didn't last long and after we split, I had to eat out or learn to feed myself. The secret to success is marinating the chicken overnight in beer, something my mother taught me."

Before going to bed, Gar called Gisela.

"Hey, good thing you called, you didn't tell me you weren't legal."

"I thought it would be better if you didn't know. Keep you out of trouble."

"Well, that was thoughtful. Legal or not, you're still a sweet guy, Gar."

"I hope you aren't in any trouble over this."

"Nah. When the immigration types showed me their badges, I just told the truth. Told them that you always paid on time, that you were friendly and got along. They kept pressing me, but I insisted I didn't know much about you, where you worked, or where you came from. Listen, I wouldn't have told them where you were, even if I'd known."

"Thanks for that. It may be a while before I'm back. I'll keep up my rent so you can hold the room for me. And there's one other thing. There's a laptop in my room that belongs to my boss. I'd appreciate it if you'd hold on to it until I can pick it up."

"Consider it done. You take care. We miss you."

So immigration authorities were now on his trail, too.

"Something on your mind?" Gar asked Esteban the next morning. "I'm in your way here, I know."

"It's not that. Stay as long as you need to." He lit and drew on a cigarette, holding the smoke for a moment. "I hate to see any man on the run. It's bad enough you have to dodge the immigration people, though at least with them there's no personal motive. The *Mejicanos* hunting you, on the other hand, are out to do you harm, not just get you deported."

"I know, but what I can do about it?"

Esteban contemplated Gar's question.

"You know, our late great labor leader, César Chavez, preached Gandhi's methods of non-violence and used them to great effect." He paused. "In my experience, a more direct approach is sometimes necessary."

"Yes?"

"Last night I told you we used any way possible to get concessions from the growers: strikes at harvest time, market boycotts, and even a little selective machinery destruction, anything to make the *pendejos* give an inch."

Gar didn't respond, but Esteban hadn't finished.

"A man's first responsibility is to look out for his own

life. There must be something you can do. If you do nothing, it'll fester and maybe kill you."

Gar understood. He anticipated another attack. Should he turn the tables and go after Salinas? Meeting Salinas in person changed the game, and Gar wondered what Esteban thought he should do. Kill him? *¡Ay, Jesucristo!*

Gar had considered going after Salinas with his father's pistol before leaving Mexico. Then he realized how woefully ill-equipped he was to be a killer. Except in self-defense, he'd never understood how anyone could kill another person.

His father had always said the world was made up of those who make things happen and those who let things happen to them. Even if that wasn't entirely true, it was true often enough. He'd made something happen when he exposed the Consul, and that had brought him to this place and time. Was going after Salinas next? Wasn't it his duty to do so? Did he have any choice?

Later, as they walked up Wilshire Boulevard, Gar felt more exposed than ever.

"Hey, relax," Esteban told him on the way to meet Hank's cabal. "Unless you're picking crops or working in a hotel kitchen or some other place that Latinos congregate, immigration isn't likely to be looking for you."

"Why are we meeting in this part of town?" Gar asked.

"Hank owns the building and isn't likely to be hounded by media types here."

"Do you think this'll take long?"

"Hard to say. Sometimes these meetings run on. Look, I know you've got other things on your mind. But stick around for some of the discussion. Then you're welcome to take the pickup and do whatever it is you're doing."

38

Sunlight spilled from a row of high windows into the conference room. Whatever the meeting agenda, Gar's mind drifted elsewhere.

Hernán and Felipe stood around with others snacking on danishes and waiting for Hank, who burst through the door with Joe Reyes moments later.

"*Buenos días, señores,* please, let's get to it." He shuffled through papers while the others took seats.

"First, a welcome to Danilo Gómez, who's joined our cause." They all nodded, smiling.

"Did you read the letters to the editor in the *Times* this morning?" Dr. Felipe Villareal unfolded a newspaper. "Most of them are about your show."

"What's the gist?"

"Two writers worry that Latinos will try for a land grab. Listen to this one:

> **Take Back the Land**
> It's time the public learned the truth about how land was stolen from the Califórnios. Thursday's "Towers Forum" pulled back the veil of suppression that has surrounded this subject. A great injustice was done by our government and must be rectified. We need a full-scale investigation into how each of these grants found their way into the hands of their present owners. If that investigation shows that lands were transferred through purchase, or other legal means, then well and good. But if it shows they

> were in effect stolen, they must be returned to the heirs of the grantees. This latter effort should begin with the return of Rancho Santa Anita.

That wasn't even written by a Latino."

"Yeah, I liked that one, too." Joe Reyes spoke up. "We should keep this land grant thing going."

"Do what, Joe? Complain?" Felipe slapped the table.

"Hell, I'm drop-dead serious, Professor. No, investigate. Send out press releases. Give interviews. Keep it on the front burner while Hank campaigns. Force others to take a position."

"Let's run with it for a while." Hank nodded with others around the table.

"Rally Latinos," Joe continued. "Get them off their asses. Got any problem with that, Gar?"

"Not unless Don Hernán does."

Heads turned to the old attorney.

"I'll have to give that some thought. Keep in mind, not all Latinos are of the same origin."

"Yeah, but they've all got Latino blood."

"I won't argue that," Esteban broke in, "but that still doesn't involve all Latinos. You have to appeal to something more, like their common sense of justice."

"Hold on," Hernán raised a hand. "Don't get carried away. Isn't this all a bit high-minded?"

The old lawyer ignored the hands raised in the room.

"In the past, we've been too bitter, too defensive. Our demonstrations and stale slogans don't hold up. All your press releases, op-ed pieces, and letters to the editor might just add up to nothing more than a hill of *frijoles*."

"What are you suggesting?" Hank asked.

"I'm saying, substance is important but it's style that plays in political movements."

Joe told him, "Please get to the point."

"We need a slogan, or a bunch of them, to draw in

Latinos—and not just Mexican-Americans. We need songs by Latinos, Anglo, and Black celebrities. Some new banners paired with the *Stars and Stripes*."

Hernán knew he was stepping on toes, but he wanted to get and hold their attention.

"Think of past demonstrations." Hernán looked around at the others. "Too much disorganized flag-waving. People chanting mindless slogans in Spanish. Provincial, right?"

There he goes, like he's addressing a jury, Gar thought.

"It made them feel good," Hernán continued, "but they looked ridiculous, even frightening, on the eleven o'clock news. Made them look impotent and unconvincing." He was challenging anyone to contradict him.

"I agree with him." Felipe said. "But I still think we've got a good idea working here. We just need to do it the way Hernán says."

"OK, he's got a point," Joe conceded, "though every country south of the Rio Grande has a bone to pick with the good ol' U. S. of A. If they weren't invaded, they've been exploited or under the thumb of an installed dictator. Even in standoffish Argentina's case, the U.S. supported the British in the war over the Malvinas. We Latinos all have plenty in common. Use the land grant thing and build on it."

"*Sangre y Tierra!*"

"What was that?" Hank asked.

"Blood and Land," someone said. "That could be one of our slogans. Might sound melodramatic here but in context, blazoned on blood-spattered banners fluttering in the wind, along with stirring music, it could be real theater and very inspiring."

Hank nodded. "Joe?"

"I'm already writing it down."

Hank looked around at the group. "OK, not a bad start this morning. Let's move on. What's next, Joe?"

"Getting the message out. Hank's TV station isn't enough. We have to create a commotion, get other media involved."

"He's right." Esteban said. "Hank's opponents are perceived as sticking to the rules. But voters sitting around the dinner table will be talking about Hank's slogans, actions, and the street theater. You want to get people to talk about your product."

Joe Reyes gave him a thumbs-up.

"I get that our strategy will be to make a lot of noise and position me as a rebel in the campaign and the Democratic Party," Hank said. "Sooner or later, though, we must get to the real issues. So please, in the time left this morning, let me hear from some of the rest of you on that."

"There's little new in the way of issues, Hank," Danilo, the newcomer, spoke for the first time. He went on to mention education—schools, teachers, and security in the schools. Others added toxic waste sites in minority areas and the lack of affordable housing as issues.

"None of this is dramatic stuff, but it hits our constituencies where they live," Danilo concluded.

Gar, only half listening to the discussion, jotted a note and motioned to Hernán to pass it to Esteban, who took a spare key from his shirt pocket and indicated it should be passed to Gar.

"I hoped you'd stay for the tactical discussion," Hank said to Gar, who rose to leave as Joe began passing out what appeared to be the draft of a speech.

"My contributions are included with Esteban's."

While he didn't want to pressure Gar into jeopardy, Hernán needed his laptop—and the information on it.

"Why don't I just call Gisela?" Gar had suggested. "If no one's been asking about me, and if she hasn't seen anyone suspicious in the neighborhood, I'll pick it up."

"Not a good idea," Hernán told him. "Lord knows who's watching her place, waiting for you to show up."

"Maybe she could take it to her office and I could pick it

up there."

"I don't want to implicate her any more than she already is. Leave it for the moment."

Late the next morning, Gar decided to forgo Hernán's caution and go after the laptop anyway.

39

Should be simple enough to check out Gisela's house from across the street, Gar thought. If all was clear he'd make a dash for the house, grab the laptop, and run.

He parked Esteban's pickup a couple blocks away and entered the alley behind the row of bungalows opposite from Gisela's. Dogs barked at him as he passed their yards.

Gar approached the back yard to the house directly across from Gisela's, hoping no one was home. The high wooden gate closing off the backyard was locked. A good shove popped loose the screws fastening the hasp.

Once inside the gate, Gar snaked his way to the front lawn and ducked behind a hedge, where he had a clear view of Gisela's house. He crouched and waited.

He hadn't been waiting long before a black Mercedes with two men inside it rolled by. Once the car was out of sight, he stood to make a dash for the house but stopped, the sound of footfalls behind him. A burly man with the scarred look of a washed-up wrestler was coming at Gar.

"*Venga con migo,*" the man ordered Gar to come along.

Gar whirled and leaped to one side, then backed away to keep a distance between them. Advancing and motioning with his hands, the man repeated his demand and charged. Gar quickly sidestepped and pushed the man, sending him crashing headlong into the hedge. Gar back-pedaled, but fell as he stepped on a hockey ball. He landed on a hockey stick. Gar leaped to his feet and threw the ball as the man came at him again. He swung the hockey stick, striking the man's rib cage. Stick in hand, Gar worked toward the back of the yard, heading for the gate.

As the man closed in, Gar struck him again. This time the man parried the blow with an arm and narrowed the gap between them. If Gar couldn't get to the gate, he'd be trapped in a corner of the fenced-in yard.

The man lunged forward, arms spread wide. Instead of trying to dodge the man's grasp, Gar dipped a shoulder and barreled into the man's chest with all the force he could muster, the impact shooting sharp pains through his shoulder. The man grunted as he stumbled backwards, and he struggled to regain balance.

Surprised to be on his feet and still gripping the hockey stick, Gar swung, catching the man on the temple and causing him to collapse with a thud. Gar took a quick look around, hoping no one had seen the struggle. Blood ran from the man's temple. Gar felt for and found a pulse.

"*Pendejo*," Gar muttered. "Let's see who you are." He emptied the man's pockets of car keys, a wallet, and a cigarette lighter engraved with a crown of thorns encircling a bleeding heart—the logo of a Mexico City crime ring. A California driver's license named him Marco Sandale of Long Beach. Another ID showed the man to be an employee of the Mexican Consulate. He slipped both cards into his shirt pocket, wiped the wallet on his trousers and dropped it. He threw the keys over the fence into the adjacent yard and kept the lighter to show Hernán.

Gar bent over to catch his breath, when behind him an angry voice suddenly mumbled something in Spanish. With no time to aim, he spun and lashed out with the hockey stick, hitting a knee. The man dropped to the ground, writhing in pain.

Gar leapt over the hedge and dashed across the street to Gisela's house and let himself in. Gisela's room was open but the laptop was nowhere in sight. Where would she hide it? Under the bed? In the closet? He checked both, and then he looked under and in her chest of drawers.

A noise in the hall made Gar freeze.

"Oh, you've come back." Annie watched him from the doorway.

"I can't explain anything right now, Annie. Do you know where Gisela might have put my laptop?"

"She told me to keep it. I'll get it, if you want."

"Please. I have to get going."

Moments later, as she handed it over, Gar thanked her, and said he'd be in touch. Retreating to the alley, he ran to the pickup.

Gar knew it was only a matter of time before either of the men caught up with him. He also now understood that it wasn't immigration chasing after him—they had bigger game. He was being tracked by the Mexican Consul's henchmen. The encounter confirmed something else, little consolation as it was: Salinas wanted him taken alive. Back safely at Esteban's, Gar checked in with Hernán.

"You were right," Hernán said. "The bastards mean business. We had a little excitement here, too, with a break-in last night."

"Salinas again?"

"Thought so at first. But there's nothing here he'd want. The police dusted for fingerprints and asked the usual questions. Doubt anything will come of it."

"They got through all that steel you have on the windows and doors?"

"I need better locks."

"What's missing?"

"They wrecked the place. Files were strewn everywhere, but so far the computers and almost all the disks seem to be here. They only took the photocopy of the land grant document and the CD with the court briefs."

"Those wouldn't interest Salinas."

"My guess is that Weegan Rollem sent in his people. Hank Torres has leaked word that he's getting ready to sling a little mud and finger his forebears as those who stole the

Rancho Santa Anita."

"Would that hurt his campaign?"

"It must matter some. The Rollem camp is busy denying the candidate's culpability. All we care about is that it rallies Latinos."

"Was that your only copy of the grant document?"

"Felipe had made others. The original sits in the safe deposit. The briefs are still on the computer, and Hank's office has copies of them as well as the material you and Eva brought back from Sacramento. As Felipe Villareal predicted, the original grant has become an important piece of paper."

"Now we both have to watch our backs," Gar said.

"They won't be back."

"What I mean is, the Consul will try to come after me through my associates. That means you."

"Don't worry, I can take care of myself."

"I'm also concerned about Eva."

"You tell her what happened?"

"She's finally convinced she should go into hiding. But she can't do that forever."

"She could work outside the office and telecommute. Though that would mean bringing Hank into this. I'll see what I can do."

"We'll both appreciate it."

"We need to get the Consul off your back. Right now I don't see any way to do that."

Gar hung up the phone. The distressing thought that he'd have to eliminate the Consul troubled him. He couldn't deny that fear made him reluctant. Yet, if he followed through, avenging his family would be a matter of honor. An eye for an eye.

40

Mexico Independence Day to Be Observed
Los Angeles—(AP). According to the Mexican Consul General in Los Angeles, Armando Salinas Gutiérrez, the start of Mexico's 1810 struggle for independence from Spain, usually commemorated on September 16, will be a major event here. Consul Salinas stated that Mexican Ambassador to the U.S., His Excellency Juan Arévalo Seguín, would host the Independence Day observance this year. There is some speculation the change signals the possible visit of Mexico's president. Consul General Salinas has declined further comment at this time.

Each year in cities across the U.S., Latinos celebrate Cinco de Mayo, the date associated with Mexico's 1862 defeat of the French. In recent years, observance of Mexico's Independence Day has taken on greater significance in the U.S. as the Mexican and Mexican-American population continues to burgeon.

Gar set down the newspaper. A schoolbook image of Father Hidalgo, the heroic priest, came to mind. The priest's *Grito de Dolores* inspired the largely Indian and Mestizo uprising in 1810, in the university city of Guanajuato.

It seemed unlikely that the Mexican president would make an appearance at the Los Angeles celebrations, as the *Times* had suggested. Gar couldn't recall any Mexican president not showing at the Zócalo, the prominent square in the nation's capital. On the eve of every Independence Day, presidents traditionally led a triple cheer of "*Viva México!*" The national fiesta demanded his presence.

"It would be unprecedented," Hernán agreed, when Gar called with his doubts about a Mexican presidential appearance in LA. "Hank thinks it's a big deal. He plans to make the most of it. He'll interview the ambassador on-air, be involved in festivities."

"At the Consulate?"

"The Westin Bonaventure, a big hotel over on Figueroa, near the Civic Center."

"If Salinas is going to be there, that would be my chance to..."

"What're you talking about? Are you crazy?"

"I could check in under another name."

"No, forget it."

"Salinas is a killer."

"He should be tried in court."

"The man's a diplomat. He has immunity."

"I'm talking about a Mexican court."

"I say this with respect, Don Hernán, but you're dreaming. In Mexico, the powerful always get off. When I became a threat, he sent his agents after me. They're vicious people. They'd follow someone into a hospital to finish the job. I've been lucky. Salinas would just buy the judge—or threaten to kidnap his family." Gar was surprised to be explaining how the system worked in Mexico. As an attorney, didn't Hernán know how it worked? "I didn't ask to be the avenging angel. If not me, who?"

"I understand how you feel. But you're being irrational. Let me put it this way: I won't be party to assassination. If you persist, you're on your own."

Anger and a sense of betrayal burned through Gar as he hung up. Hernán was the one person in L.A. he thought he could count on and now the attorney had abandoned him. Hernán had one thing right: killing Salinas had possessed Gar. He'd do it on his own, if it had to be that way.

Killing Salinas necessitated getting the Consul in Gar's sight. And then he'd need a shoulder holster and a silencer for the Beretta. He pushed aside thoughts about being caught and going to prison. Shooting Salinas near the Consulate would be unrealistic, but Gar could start tracking his comings and goings, watch the building for a day or so.

The Consulate was on West Sixth Street. Gar located a coffee shop directly across from the building. From there he could watch everyone entering and leaving during standard business hours. Later in the day, he could watch the rear parking lot.

Gar's shoulder-length hair fell to the barbershop floor, along with his beard. Without all that hair, Gar looked much younger and he hardly recognized himself. After the haircut, Gar bought a hat and sunglasses. Those and his now visible gold earring helped in the transformation.

The following morning at the coffee shop, Gar sat at a table by the window, giving him a full view of the Consulate. At mid-morning, the swarthy man Gar encountered on the freeway came into the coffee shop for cigarettes. The man never gave him a second glance. Still, being in the same room with him put Gar on edge. Three times that day, Salinas passed by in his chauffeured Mercedes, always accompanied by two bodyguards.

From her perch near the cash register, the Asian proprietor kept a close eye on Gar, who continuously ordered coffee and snacks. Near the end of the day, curiosity finally got to her. "You write book, yes?" From then on, she referred to him as "the writer."

When he next talked to Hernán, it was clear to Gar that his friend still worried about his anger and impulsiveness. Hernán told him to lie low and stay out of Salinas's way. "Eventually he'll return to Mexico and be off your back."

"I don't doubt that you're right, but it'll be later than

sooner. He's been here less than a year and who knows how much longer he'll be on this assignment. Meanwhile, my life is on hold here and that'll be true in Mexico, too, when he returns."

If Hernán agreed, he didn't say so. He'd washed his hands of anything Gar might have in mind to do about the Consul.

Gar wasn't sure what to tell Eva—or whether he should tell her anything at all.

41

During their two-week separation, Gar and Eva talked on the phone every day. On the second weekend, they enjoyed a feverish reunion at Hank Torres's beachfront home in Malibu.

"You can't imagine how I've missed you," he told her.

She pressed into him. "Who's this beardless guy lying next to me?" she asked. "I liked the long-haired guy better. Suppose I'll have to get used to the earring, too. You sure you have it on the correct ear?"

"Meaning what?"

"I'm told that wearing it on the left ear can mean one thing, and on the other something else."

"Never mind, we'll both have to get used to the new me. How'd you explain using this place to Torres?"

"Just told him I needed a few days off. I also told him we're an item." She turned to face him.

"How'd he take that?"

"Very well, actually. He said he wasn't surprised, even though he thinks he's my guardian and can get overbearing about it. Anyway, the partners use this place for entertaining clients. I guess you're one of them. My request wasn't that unusual."

Gar pulled her to him, cupped a breast, and kissed her. She returned and held it, his response immediate.

"You have an electric effect on me."

"I don't need you to tell me that. You telegraph it quite well." She turned onto her back and kicked off the sheets.

An hour later, Gar got up and pulled on a pair of shorts.

THE LAST CALIFÓRNIO

Opening and stepping through the sliding glass doors onto the deck, he raised his arms to the warm breeze and wondered about what it must be like to afford the luxury of a place like this. Wearing a terrycloth robe, Eva settled herself on a deck chaise, joining him for the sunset. His preoccupation interrupted her relaxation.

"You seem a little different," she told him.

"A shave and a good haircut will do that."

"I don't mean that, it's something else."

"Maybe that's because I've decided to stop running away from my situation."

"What does that mean?"

"Sooner or later all this has to come to some kind of resolution."

"All of what?"

"I'm talking about the Consul and his people coming after me. And now the immigration authorities. Things can't go on like this."

"Can we talk about it?"

"I've tried to think of a way out, but always end at the same place."

"You mean, feeling trapped?"

"Trapped and with no control."

"Isn't it just a matter of waiting? Getting help from Hernán and his friends?"

"He's done all he can. I don't think they can help me change this situation. I have to take things into my own hands."

"I don't like the sound of that. You're not thinking of killing someone."

"Can you think of another way? The police here can't help me and if I return to Mexico I'll be thrown into prison or, more likely, killed."

"Come on. There must be other ways."

"It's not that I want to do it. Maybe this contest between Salinas and me was predestined. It has to be resolved."

Eva took everything in. "You mean a lot to me," she said slowly. "You know that. I see you as strong, sensitive, and caring. That's what makes it so hard to understand how you could consider killing another human being. I can't believe we're having this conversation." She paused, her voice becoming almost a whisper. "Growing up, I lived in a place where killing was commonplace. Often the first thing people resorted to. I couldn't have anything to do with a killer."

Gar started to speak but held his tongue for a moment. "*Querida,* that sounds like an ultimatum. I had hoped for more understanding." He turned toward the railing and watched a few cycles of surf crash against the beach, the white patterns of froth appear and dissolve. "You're right, I feel trapped, and the fact is I am. Those who're after me have already made two attempts and may be closing in. Now the two people I care most about are deserting me."

"Look at me. I don't know about Hernán, but I'm not deserting you. I'm saying we can find another way."

"You mean wait until Salinas returns to Mexico? None of us knows when that might be. Even if he went back tomorrow, it wouldn't solve anything. He'd still be after me and I'd still be here illegally. I'm stuck. I can't go on this way."

"We can start a new life. You with a new name and maybe even a new face."

"I'm happy with the one I've got."

"All I'm saying is, this is a big country and hiding in it isn't that difficult. The FBI hides hundreds of people in its witness protection program. If others can do it, so can we. It's not that hard."

"Hiding is not as easy as you might think," he said. "Everywhere you turn here there's a surveillance camera. If I were stopped, the police could get instant feedback on me. Even if hiding somewhere else were possible, it wouldn't change things. I'd still be illegal and hunted by Salinas. I can't spend the rest of my life looking over my shoulder."

THE LAST CALIFÓRNIO

"You're making this out to be much worse than it is."

"You're forgetting I have a duty to avenge my family."

"I haven't forgotten." She rose and turned her back to him. "Killing Salinas won't bring back your loved ones. It would make restitution for the rancho pointless."

Ay, the rancho! She was right. He watched his toe trace a meaningless pattern on the deck.

The sound of the surf grew louder. Finally, he spoke.

"You've never had to see the bodies of your loved ones lying in their own blood. It's with me all the time."

"I'm sorry you're haunted like that. But you'd only be adding another to your nightmares. Please wait. Don't do anything right away."

He struggled with the realization that going ahead would mean losing her. She came to him and he enclosed her in his arms.

"We'll figure a way out of this together," she murmured in his ear.

42

Gar regretted giving in to Eva. He realized that delay only heightened the anxiety for a face-off with Salinas.

He sat in the darkened kitchen nursing a coffee, wondering what there was about the Consul's habits he might be overlooking.

Gar suspected that the Consul probably had a mistress somewhere in the city. He might visit her without security, or maybe he might be dropped off by the bodyguards. If Salinas went to her from his home, he could be followed. It was worth a try.

The Consul's home sat in a quiet, upscale area a few miles from the consulate. It was a white stucco bungalow, with a neatly trimmed lawn and shrubs.

He'd no sooner parked than the old pickup began to attract looks from passersby. Even if one didn't call the police, a cruiser on routine patrol could come by at any time.

Twenty minutes into the hour, a black Mercedes arrived. From the house, Salinas emerged and slithered into the back seat. Gar trailed the sedan for a short distance and soon saw it was headed for the consulate. He realized his plan was going nowhere, as trailing could go on for days.

While eating lunch at a fast-food joint, Gar reconsidered exploring what had upset Hernán: attacking the Consul at the Hotel Bonaventure. The idea quickened his pulse and revived his enthusiasm.

Once Gar fgured out the pattern of the one-way streets, he found the hotel and parked the pickup a couple blocks south of it. With no plan yet in mind, he hoped to find inspiration once he entered the hotel.

A cloverleaf-shaped atrium joined the hotel's five gleaming towers. The atrium, therefore, gave entry to hundreds of rooms and suites by means of circular walkways at each level. The meeting and banquet spaces, exhibit halls, and conference rooms off the atrium offered hiding places but could as easily become traps. Nothing inspired a plan.

On one of the mid-level floors, Gar spotted elevated pedestrian walkways arching over the streets below and leading from the Bonaventure to adjacent buildings. For a moment, he thought he might be able to enter and escape the hotel from one of the adjoining structures. Yet the reconnaissance only confirmed that getting to Salinas would be as unlikely as Hernán said. Out of ideas, Gar left the hotel feeling dejected.

Gar found an article in the next day's *Times* electrifying.

Trade Pact to Highlight Heritage Festivities

Los Angeles (AP)—At a press conference last night, Mexican Consul General, Armando Salinas Gutiérrez, confirmed that the Mexico Independence Day celebration scheduled for September 16, will be hosted by Mexican Ambassador to the U.S., Juan Arévalo Seguín. Mexican Trade and Economics Minister, Rigo Quiroja Baeza, will also be in attendance.

The festivities will kick off with a motorcade from City Hall to the El Pueblo de Los Ángeles Historic National Monument, the original site of Old Los Angeles. Mayor Mano Izquierda, Governor Alfred Headlong and Ambassador Arévalo will speak at the monument before moving on to the Westin Bonaventure Hotel & Suites, where the minister and the governor will ink a trade pact between Mexico and the State of California. A lavish reception and luncheon will follow. The

> dual observances are planned to coincide with the start of Hispanic Heritage Month, and involve a variety of political and entertainment personalities. A sponsor group headed by local media giant Towers Communications is underwriting the festivities at the Bonaventure.

"Hank said it would be a big deal," Hernán later reminded Gar when they talked about the article. "Hank's the major sponsor of the event and he'll get plenty of visibility. Immediately afterwards, he intends to announce his own candidacy for mayor."

"Sounds like good timing for him, and undoubtedly there will be a big turnout of local Latinos," Gar said.

"Anybody who's anybody."

"Why the extravagant publicity and the governor's involvement? Trade pacts like this aren't new."

"This one's really about votes. Trade means jobs, and that translates. The governor's chair is open next year and the incumbent mayor's administration is on shaky ground. With Latinos making up a solid majority here, Hank and the governor want to take maximum advantage of the event. The other runners are complaining about being shut out."

"*Comprendo*. Tell me, what's this so-called Hispanic Heritage Month all about? It sounds rather patronizing."

"You're right, it's condescending. The public couldn't care less. Our own organizations and institutions are perfectly capable of honoring Latino culture and achievements, as other ethnic and racial groups here do."

"*Claro*."

By the time Gar hung up the phone, the idea of killing Salinas overtook him. The Heritage festivities would give him the needed cover.

A map accompanying the *Times* article detailed the motorcade route from City Hall to the Bonaventure. Somewhere along that route there had to be a point where he'd have a clear shot at the Consul. According to the *Times*, the procession would travel north on Main Street to the Old Pueblo monument, where the dignitaries would speak. From there, the motorcade would proceed north to and left on César Chavez Avenue, then to and down Grand Avenue, where the bulk of the presumed cheering throngs should be. The motorcade would then continue south to Fifth Street before turning right and ending at the hotel's entrance.

Local, national, and international media would cover the entire series of events—the parade, speeches, trade-pact signing. As Mexico's local man on the ground, Salinas would be in the middle of it all.

¡Jesucristo! Gar could be caught on live TV! Worse, in the process of killing Salinas, he might wound or kill innocent bystanders.

Hernán branded the idea as crazy, and Gar was beginning to see how right he was to label it as such. Gar's father had often reminded him that our biggest mistakes are those we make fully conscious. Gar was completely aware of what he was doing when he tried to expose Salinas. Look where that got him. Now, he was about to make a grave mistake all over again. Yet, he resolved to play out the final act of this life-or-death drama.

The following day, Gar drove the publicized route from City Hall to the monument, hoping a plan would pop into mind. He had just five days until the event, and he didn't want the opportunity to slip by. He searched for a firing position that also offered an escape. After three tours of the route, he hadn't found one.

43

Calle Olvera, known to tourists simply as Olvera Street, ran north from the circular plaza of the El Pueblo de Los Ángeles monument and was an attempt at recreating the flavor of an original Mexican village.

It had been months since Gar first saw the plaza and the narrow bustling street of stalls catering to sightseers. The place still reminded him of a gringo's theme park. How he could use the setting to get at Salinas remained obscure for the time being.

He left the street for another circling of the motorcade route, at times stopping to explore likely spots. Continuing along the route, Gar was convinced the plaza offered the only realistic firing site. There, the target would be close enough and stationary. If he were successful, disappearing into the Olvera Street crowd on foot might be easier than trying to cut through a clog of traffic by vehicle.

Judging from the placement of the bleachers being erected at the plaza's center, the mayor and invited guests would address the horde of tourists from the bandstand. Hiding among the crowd should be simple enough. But that was the easy part.

The notables would have to mount the steps on its east side and face west to Main Street. The plaza could handle a standing-only crowd of a few hundred. Some could also find space atop the large brick planters situated around the plaza's periphery. A larger crowd on Main Street would listen to the speeches over loudspeakers. He thought of firing from one of the planters but he'd be too open there. He'd never be able to escape.

As Gar watched construction workers set up the bleachers, someone spoke from behind him.

"Hi there. Haven't I seen you around here before?" Gar turned to see the same pale-faced man with yellow teeth he had seen by the museum. There was no mistaking him, not with that greasy ponytail.

"Isn't this exciting?" The man feigned enthusiasm.

Gar said nothing, backing away.

The man moved closer. "I mean all this." He swept his arm over the site.

Gar imagined a shoulder holster under his suit coat. What did the man want with him? He continued to back away, leaving the man looking confused and dejected.

Gar went to one of the outdoor cafés along Olvera Street and sipped a coffee, hoping the strange man would go away. But he saw the man wandering down the street, pretending to window shop. From time to time, he looked back at Gar and smiled.

The man didn't drift out of sight until nearly an hour had passed, and as soon as he did, Gar returned to the plaza. He spent the afternoon finding and rejecting one location after another.

As Gar was about to leave, he spotted the Grin staring at him from a short a distance away. The man's smile broadened, and he took a few halting steps in Gar's direction. He was convinced that the grinning fool saw him as a possible pick-up. He fingered his earring, knowing the time had come to remove it.

During the drive back to Esteban's home, Gar realized how little he knew about the crowd and how it would affect his ability to shoot and escape. He'd have to develop an attack as the opportunity presented itself.

That evening Gar called Eva and told her how much he missed her. They talked about the September 16 celebration.

He said nothing about his reconnaissance of the parade route and plaza site.

"The event will be televised," she said. "Why don't we watch it together?"

"I'd like that, *querida*, but with police and security forces out in greater numbers I don't think it's a good idea for me to go anywhere." He didn't have to mention the unexpected freeway checkpoint they'd run into earlier. "I don't feel like watching, anyway."

"Why not?"

"Why would I want to see Salinas out there enjoying himself and basking in glory, while we can't even show our faces in public?"

"Will I see you on the weekend?" she asked him.

"Count on it."

44

September 15, Thursday evening

Esteban had just returned from negotiations with growers in the central valley, and the success of the talks put him in the mood to celebrate. Lounging in what he called his media room, he raised a shot of tequila and touched his glass to Gar's beer bottle in a toast. A second round followed.

"*¡Viva Méjico!*" Esteban shouted the traditional *grito*. "Come on, join me." Flushed with alcohol and national pride, they yelled it the requisite three times. Downing a shot in one swallow, Esteban looked slightly put out when Gar failed to drain his beer.

Gar watched Esteban down one drink after another. He remembered his father once telling him that a man was most likely to reveal his soul when drunk. Esteban appeared well on the way to revealing his.

"What would you be doing tonight if you were back in *Méjico*?" he asked Gar.

"If my family hadn't been murdered, I'd be with them for dinner, and then I'd be out dancing for the rest of the night with a girlfriend. How about you?"

"I'm not much for dancing, so I'd probably have fun with friends—and I'd be drinking too much."

As the evening wore on, Gar couldn't ignore that Esteban's drinking tradition was destined to continue. The drinking clearly made him want to talk.

"The *pendejos* finally came around," he said, meaning the growers. His frown turned to satisfaction. He chased another tequila shot with a long pull of Tecate beer.

"Tough to deal with?" Gar said, still working his way through the first beer.

"Believe it or not, I appreciate their position." The labor leader held up his bottle, admiring the golden liquid. "I understand that they've got to make a profit or go out of business. We'd be in trouble if that happened. But there's plenty of margin there to make a few concessions." He drained the bottle and let out a sigh.

"Like what?"

"Nothing really big," Esteban burped and waved a hand, his eyelids half open. "I'm talking about the bare essentials—livable wages, housing, decent quarters for the families, school transportation, and some basic medical care." He paused, frowning. "Those *pinches* use insecticides on everything. Do the *cabrónes* really believe the pickers are immune to them? They're all the same fuckin' things the United Farm Workers've been fighting for since César Chávez founded it."

"You managed to get all that?"

"Yeah." He stared wistfully at the empty bottle still in his hand. "It sounds better than it really is."

"What do you mean?"

"Growers'll agree to your face and then behind your back ignore what they've promised. All the while they're lobbying the legislature to return things to their advantage. At least we're lucky to have the union, some sort of power to stand up for the pickers. Latinos in construction have no one. If the poor bastards get hurt, they're kicked out to get what care they can in an emergency room. Besides, contractors think nothing of cheating them. Kitchen help and waiters can stage impromptu strikes to force management to get help for injured co-workers."

Esteban poured another shot and tossed it back. He stared blankly at the empty glass, and Gar waited to see if he had more to say. He was drunk.

"*Mire*, Esteban," Gar said. "I'm grateful for your letting

me stay here. I don't know what..."

"*Mano, es nada.* I'm gone mos' uh the time, anyway."

"You think it's nothing, but for me it's been a lifesaver."

"Glad to help." He waved a hand, trying to stay focused on Gar. "Tell me, how's life bein' the hunter, 'stead uh the hunted?"

"Hasn't made life any easier, but you were right about my self-respect."

"Hey, tha's better. Mind tellin' me what you plan to do?"

"Shoot him."

"'*Mano,*" Esteban sobered. "When? How?"

"Tomorrow morning, at the celebration in the *placita.*"

"¡*Ay!* In public?" He snapped a bit more awake.

"¡*Absolutamente!*"

"They'll catch you for sure."

"Not if things go right. What matters is killing him."

"Does it have to be in public? Couldn't you get him in an alley, some place like that?"

"He goes nowhere without his bodyguards. Anyway, maybe the world should see it. You should know about that."

"*Sí,* I do." Esteban sat pensively for a second or two. "Any way I could change your mind?"

Gar shook his head.

"It's your business. Keep this in mind: As soon as you raise the pistol, some hero in the crowd will be all over you."

Gar listened, wide-eyed.

"Even if you shot Salinas, he'd never know who did him. If I were doing this..." he paused to burp. "If I were doing this, I'd want to be sure the *cabrón* knew I it. That would be as important as killing him. If the *pendejo* doesn't know who shot him, what's the point?" He looked at Gar for a long moment, tapping his chest repeatedly.

Esteban was right on both counts. To the first point, Gar had been in denial. He'd given no thought at all about the second point. For vengeance to have meaning it couldn't be ambiguous or anonymous.

"We never had this conversation. *¿Me entiendes?*"

Gar nodded.

"Eh?" Esteban waited.

"Understood," Gar said.

"Come on, then, let's get something to eat before I pass out." Esteban patted Gar on the shoulder.

They chose a Mexican restaurant, where Gar could only pick at his food and Esteban ate with gusto. In a bar afterwards, Esteban bought a round of drinks for the house and led a few choruses of "Cielito Lindo," a song about human contraband.

Shortly after midnight, Gar drove them home. Getting Esteban's rubbery form out of the pickup and into the house was a chore. Gar left him passed out on his bed fully clothed.

Later, unable to sleep, Gar sat in his room feeling utterly alone. If he killed Salinas he could forget about his day in court for the rancho.

Gar stretched out in bed, hoping to sleep but his mind churned. He finally dozed off, dreaming of his parents' and Alma's deaths and his flight from Mexico. Now before dying himself, he was re-playing his life, drifting in and out of sleep, moaning in the darkness.

At one point when he woke and couldn't return to sleep, Gar sat on the edge of the bed in darkness. He'd had that schooldays dream again of nearly killing his classmate. The feelings of childhood vengeance were still there, waiting to come out in the man. Yet, even if in his rational mind killing still horrified him, what was the point of being alive, if not to fulfill his duty?

His thoughts returned to what Esteban had said. How could he kill Salinas so he'd know who'd done it? What about police or his own safety? Despite the unanswered questions, Gar believed it was still worth doing.

Gar closed his eyes and envisioned a cordon of police facing the crowd, holding it back as the procession of dignitaries arrived. The mayor, the governor, and their Mexican entourage formed the inner ring, and were surrounded by security as they moved to the bandstand.

And then what?

Up to that point, the scene presented itself as if projected on one of the room's walls. A sudden revelation brought him upright. Of course! He could see it clearly now. He lay back staring at the ceiling, his thoughts racing with the newfound insight.

He knew exactly what to do.

45

Well before the alarm went off Gar gave up trying to sleep. While shaving he listened to a newscaster give background on the dignitaries, schedule of events, and parade festivities. Following a weather update, the traffic reporter warned of street closures along the motorcade route and disruptions in rush-hour connections.

Despite the early hour Gar dressed, putting on a pair of Esteban's suit trousers. They were a bit short, but they'd have to do. The jacket fit better.

With time to spare, he sat on the bed staring at the Beretta and silencer glistening in the light of the bedside lamp. From a box on the nightstand, he took out a bullet and weighed it in his hand. So small and so lethal, he mused. He loaded only five rounds, set the safety, shoved the clip into the grip, and released the slide. The muted thunk of a chambering round signaled the readiness of his weapon. Was he ready?

He slipped into the shoulder holster and suit jacket. He'd carry the silencer in a pocket and install it later from a public toilet at the plaza. Studying his appearance in the mirror hanging inside the closet door, Gar hoped that with the black suit, dark glasses, and wire from Esteban's recorder in an ear, he'd either pass for a member of the visiting Mexicans or the Consulate's security detail. Each contingent might take him for part of the other. If not... He slipped the sunglasses into the suit's breast pocket, along with the Consular ID card he'd taken from Salinas's man. Esteban, he noted, was still sleeping off the previous night's binge.

THE LAST CALIFÓRNIO

In the early morning fog the city was already wide awake, with traffic zooming along the freeway. Keeping within the speed limit, Gar drove east on the 10, then north on the 110 before taking the Santa Monica Freeway east. Exiting at Temple Street, he headed north on Hill to east on Ord, getting by just before barricades were put in place. He cut across north of the Old Pueblo monument to Alameda Street and parked beyond the blockaded streets a few blocks north of the plaza.

Still too early to put himself into position, Gar ducked into a café for some breakfast. The minute hand of his watch barely seemed to move. The Seiko. Fausto Vásquez. The border patrol agent who died in the crash in Texas. The events of his odyssey now struck him as distant and shadowy as a dream.

Before leaving the café, he visited the men's room and adjusted the holstered pistol. He joined the flow of people headed toward the monument, barely aware of the traffic noise or the babble of those moving with him.

It was after nine o'clock when he arrived at the plaza. The fog had lifted. Over on Main Street the TV trucks had arrived. At the bandstand, musicians wearing oversized sombreros and black *Charro* outfits, had arranged themselves against one of the planters. The silver-studded costumes sparkled in the morning sunlight. The group's mariachi music blared from the public address speakers.

Attendants wearing CITY OF LOS ANGELES badges handed out miniature flags of the U.S., Mexico, and California. Street vendors hawked balloons, souvenirs, candy, and soft drinks. A troupe of clown-faced jugglers entertained children and their families.

The crowd grew. More policemen arrived in alarming force, forming an audience-facing circle around the bandstand. With arms outstretched, they began to push back the crowd.

Gar saw now that the moment to fire would be when

Salinas waited to mount the stairs between the mariachis and the bandstand. He would move up close behind him and fire point blank. With the silencer, the music would muffle the gunshot. A familiar voice from behind jolted Gar from his thoughts.

"Hello again."

Mierda, the weird grinning man! The pest recognized him even with his disguise.

"Back for the main event, are you? I thought you'd be here." The leer never left his face.

"Get away from me!" Gar made a move toward him.

"Hey! No need to get angry."

"I told you, get away. I won't tell you again." He put a finger just under the man's nose.

"OK, OK." The man raised his hands, backing away.

"*Pendejo*," Gar muttered. The blood pulsed in his temples as he moved into the crowd on *Calle Olvera*, still aware of the grinning idiot. As the crowd between them expanded, the man dropped from sight.

Just before ten o'clock, Gar pushed through the crowd to the portable toilets on Main Street. He stepped into one, screwed the silencer onto the Beretta and slid it into his waistband. He donned the sunglasses and sidled toward Our Lady Queen of the Angels Church. Inside the entrance he had a full view of the area cleared for the dignitaries' cars.

The plan as he visualized it was coming together. With the wire in his ear, he took a deep breath, cleared his throat, and approached the nearest police officer.

"Mexican Consulate security." He showed the Consular ID card.

"Hey, glad you guys're here, we can use the help." He motioned Gar past him, barely glancing at the ID. Once inside the police cordon and with a hand to his earpiece, Gar scanned the crowd as if on duty.

Promptly at ten o'clock, the arrival of the motorcade brought a collective murmur from the crowd. The mayor, the governor, their wives, and staffs emerged from the two leading vehicles.

The prospect of confronting the Mexican entourage made his pulse race. He fought a powerful urge to walk away. He was fully committed.

Police cleared a path, allowing the mayor and his wife to make their way to the bandstand, with the governor and his wife trailing closely behind. The foursome smiled and waved as they passed the whistling and cheering crowd. Led by an aide, they made their way to the east side of the bandstand and waited at the base of the steps.

Gar turned to see the Mexican ambassador and minister arrive and stand beside their guarded vehicles. Salinas was speaking with an aide.

The newly arrived group began to move. The Consul passed him and Gar fell in step with the other security men. One of guards, acting as if in charge, beckoned to him, then motioned again. Gar nodded and then raised his hand, pretending to speak into a supposed microphone on his lapel. The guard stepped toward him. Desperate now, Gar flashed the ID card. It, too, failed to allay suspicion. Gar pointed with his other hand and warned in Spanish, "Look, they're going." Glancing at the Mexicans now moving away, the man nodded and turned to catch up, and Gar fell in step again at the rear of the security detail. The entourage joined the mayor's group near the bandstand.

The least important of the VIPs, Salinas stood in the back of the entourage. Gar stayed a short distance behind him, mimicking the other police and security guards. More than once he had to wipe his sweaty palms on his jacket.

The tumult from the crowd nearly drowned out the mariachis' rousing, "Yo Soy Mejicano." For a while, the media and camera crews elbowing one another for advantage engaged the VIPs. Gar had to keep pushing to stay close to Salinas.

The mayor's aide signaled for the dignitaries to ascend

the steps to the chairs waiting for them on the bandstand. The mayor and his wife led the way, and Salinas would begin the climb in a matter of seconds.

Time seemed to slow for Gar, who had the sensation of being outside his body. He reached into his jacket for the pistol, loosened it in the waistband, and released the safety. Steady, he ordered himself. He removed his sunglasses, stepped up behind Salinas's right shoulder and bent to his ear and said, "Armando," speaking the Consul's given name.

The Consul turned his head, eyes wide in shock. He opened his mouth but no sound came.

46

"Hank's putting on quite a show, *mi amor*." Hernán, reclined in an armchair with his feet up on the matching ottoman, called his wife's attention to the television screen. "The motorcade has just finished unloading."

"If Hank's anything, he's a showman." Aurélia moved to a seat on the adjacent sofa. "What a spectacle. Any sign of Hank?"

"I doubt he'd be on the scene, or involved in this part of the festivities. But the mayor and governor are already on the stand. See those two men on the bandstand steps? One is the Mexican Ambassador and the other the Trade Minister. This is the Ambassador's first visit to L.A."

"The one on the steps now?"

"Yeah, the shorter of the two in the black suits. The taller one is the Trade Minister. The short one behind them there is Armando Salinas, the Mexican Consul General in L.A. He was on Hank's show with Felipe Villareal and me."

"I suppose we're in for the usual platitudes."

"Of course. It's what they do."

"I'm making coffee. Want some?"

Hernán nodded, thinking that Gar, if he were watching, would surely be seething.

Eva, barefoot and wearing nothing but panties and a t-shirt, sipped her coffee and looked out at the ocean. From inside, she could just make out the announcer's commentary on the events taking place at Old Pueblo. She tried to visualize Gar at Esteban's home, listening and watching the day's events on

TV. He would never really try to assassinate the Consul, she believed, certain that leaving Los Angeles for another part of the country was their best hope.

A few minutes past nine, she went to the kitchen for a refill. On the way back to the deck, she reached for the living room telephone and paused to watch the TV. Her eyes followed the TV cameras panning the crowds. She lifted the receiver and froze.

"Oh, my god! Please don't let that be Gar!"

She set the phone back on the receiver and leaned toward the TV, straining to catch another glimpse of the face she thought she recognized as Gar's. A moment later, the face reappeared and she knew it was Gar pushing his way through the mass of people. She also knew why he was dressed in a black suit.

A lie she could swallow, but killing was another matter altogether. Maybe she could stop him.

She dashed to the bedroom, tugged on jeans and sneakers, grabbed and pulled on a sweatshirt. Forgetting makeup, she shook out her hair and, with her purse slung on a shoulder, raced to the highway below, scanning for a taxi among the vehicles streaming past. Dangerously, she brought one to stop by stepping in front of it.

"Olvera Street! Hurry!"

"Yes, yes, I am knowing this Olvera Street," answered the cabbie. "I am getting you there fast."

Traffic on the coastal highway was unusually light for that time of day. In her desperation Eva barely heard the driver's steady accented chatter, though she had to tell him repeatedly to quit turning to look at her as he rattled on about himself. Once on the Santa Monica Freeway, they slowed to a bumper-to-bumper crawl.

The morning rush hour was still at full-tilt when they switched to the 110 heading toward the Civic Center. The closer they got to the downtown area, the more congested the traffic.

"There's an extra twenty dollars for you if we make it to Olvera Street before ten o'clock," she shouted. Initially insisting he could, the driver finally told her he would be dishonest if he continued to promise they'd make it that quickly. With every passing minute Eva's mission seemed all the more impossible. She surveyed the sea of vehicles barely creeping along and began to lose hope.

Because of the roadblocks, the cabbie had to drop her a fair distance from the plaza site, on César Chávez Avenue. Eva leaped from the taxi, dodged through and around people and cars in her sprint to Olvera Street.

"Let me through, please, let me through." People made way for her. At the outer edge of the plaza, Eva shouldered her way through the throng around the bandstand, with no idea what she'd say or do when she got there.

Shouting his name might be enough, though it could probably get him arrested. As he'd told her, arrest would sooner or later mean his certain death. Such a reckless plan, she concluded, was not workable. Fretting was not an option, either.

Standing for a moment at the edge of the crowd, she spotted Gar. He was still yards away, between the mariachis and the dignitaries, aides, media, and security guards. She scanned the clutch of dignitaries figuring Gar would end up somewhere nearby.

She spotted Salinas, and with Gar in sight, too, she began to push toward the mariachis. The police repeatedly forced her back into the spectators. Maybe just seeing her would be enough to stop him. The staccato blaring of trumpets and percussive thumping of the *gitarrón* accentuated the beat of her racing heart.

Right as policemen ordered her back again, the mariachis had begun their next tune. She stopped where she stood as if frozen in place, but not to listen to the lively music. Astonished, she watched Gar moving toward the short man she recognized as the Consul. She watched Gar remove his sunglasses and sneak up and say something in the Consul's ear. Desperate to stop what she knew would happen next, she screamed. Her cry drowned in a crescendo from the mariachi band and the powerful high-pitched voice of its singer. Eva's last glimpse was of Salinas turning to look at Gar. Salinas seemed to smile, but in an instant, shock overtook his expression.

47

Salinas knew who the man behind him was and what he intended. The Consul stiffened at the feel of something hard pressing into his lower back.

The mariachis played at full volume and had just reached the refrain of their signature piece, "Jalisco No Te Rajes." The singer's potent voice, the sawing whine of the violins, the rhythmic strumming of guitars, the resonant thumping of the *gitarrón,* and the ear-piercing trumpet blasts tore a whooping roar from the crowd like a communal orgasm, all but swallowing the sharp crack of the first shot splitting the air.

Gar flinched as the zing of a bullet snapped past his head. In rapid succession, a second bullet forced the Consul to spin around and the third bullet exploded his head, spraying Gar and others nearby with blood and tissue. Salinas crumpled and lay sprawled on the plaza pavement.

With gunfire reverberating in the air, a collective scream of horror rose from the crowd. Terrified bystanders, police, security guards, and even Gar, who had no clue where the shooting had come from, threw themselves to the pavement as if suddenly slapped down by a great-unseen hand. Only the mariachis, deafened by their music, remained oblivious for a few moments longer, before looking about dumbfounded at the figures on the ground. The plaza erupted into a pandemonium.

Security guards stationed on the bandstand flung themselves over dignitaries to shield them, while down on the pavement the police waded into the fleeing crowd in a chaotic search for the gunman. They shouted commands and barked for control. People scattered everywhere.

"Holy shit!" Hernán shouted from the den." Aurélia, come here and look at this. Oh, my ever lovin' God!"

"What is it?" She ran into the room. Hernán was on his feet, pointing at the TV, as they listened to the confused announcer trying to make sense of the incoherent scene.

"That young fool." Hernán slapped his forehead with a palm. "Godammit, I told him it was crazy. Now look what he's done." He shook his pointing finger at the screen. "Damn, damn, damn, I can't believe he did it. Right there in plain sight!"

"What's happened? What are you talking about?"

"He's been shot. Salinas, the Mexican Consul is down." Hands pressed to his temples, he sputtered, "My ever lovin' God. I can't believe he did it. Right there at the speaker's stand and with the fucking cameras rolling."

"Hernán, please! You mean that young man who works for you, the one who came here for lunch? Are you sure?"

Hernán nodded. "The same."

"I can't believe he'd do something like that. Did you actually see it?"

"Look for yourself. The Consul is down. He must've done it. I know he intended to. Terrible, awful."

"Hernán, what you're telling me isn't making any sense." Aurélia dropped to sit on the sofa.

"Of course you don't know, how could you? Sorry, *mi amor*." He took a moment to catch his breath. "A year or so ago, when he was finance minister in the Mexican government, Salinas had Gar's parents murdered. Gar exposed his involvement in a money-laundering scheme for narco-traffickers thinking that would at least get him jailed. It didn't happen. Instead, Salinas sent his goons after Gar. That's why Gar left Mexico. He's here illegally."

"Why didn't you tell me?"

"It was better you didn't know. In case of trouble with immigration. I didn't know how you'd feel about his being illegal."

Aurélia shook her head. "It wouldn't have mattered, especially if I'd known his story."

"Thought I'd convinced him to find another way. Seems I failed him."

"He's a grown man. You didn't pull the trigger."

Gar sprung to his feet, mingling with the fleeing throngs heading up Olvera Street. He passed a knot of people staring at an unmoving body on the pavement. That first shot had struck someone in the crowd! He forced his way in for a better look.

At first glance he thought it was the body of a man. On closer inspection, he could see it was a woman lying on her back with her face turned away. The sight of auburn hair partially covering the woman's face stunned Gar. Please, not Eva! His mind raced, recoiling at the possibility. *Mierda.* What have I done?

He dropped to his knees beside the body and could see she'd been hit in the shoulder and blood oozed onto the pavement from under her. "Call an ambulance!" he demanded to no one in particular.

"Already done, buddy," someone behind him said.

Eva's eyes opened as he brushed the hair away from her pale face. She flashed a look of fierce anger at Gar.

"*Querida,* I'm so terribly sorry this has happened," he whispered to her.

She slipped into unconsciousness, her head lolling to one side. A policeman approached and knelt beside Gar, checking Eva's neck for a pulse. "You know her? She your wife, sir?"

Gar shook his head no.

"Lucky she's alive," he told Gar and rose to push back the gawkers.

The sound of an ambulance siren echoed from Main Street. The crowd of curious bystanders straining to get a look at Eva's still form barely registered with Gar. He wanted to slip a hand under her back and draw her to him, but a repeated tap on his shoulder chased the thought. The police were clearing a space to make room for the medical team and their gurney. He touched Eva's cheek one last time before standing to watch them lift Eva's body into the ambulance.

"Where will you take her?" he asked one of the medics, who handed him a card.

"Good Samaritan Hospital on Wilshire. You coming with her?"

Gar shook his head. Going with her would inevitably require him to speak with the police. He forced his mind to his own tenuous situation. He had a pistol in his waistband, and police were still swarming the area. He hoped they'd think he was part of the Mexican security detail or a good samaritan who witnessed the shooting.

He took a quick look around. At the bandstand more police and remnants of the Mexican security detail surrounded the medical team picking up Salinas's body. When the ambulance sped off, the security detail stayed behind to talk to the police. Eventually the remaining group, which likely included some of Salinas's people, broke up and drifted away. None of them had given so much as a glance in Gar's direction.

Most of the media covering the event had also departed. One TV crew member, held at bay by the police, was busy interviewing bystanders. Gar kept his back to them. If they got around to him he'd probably show up on the evening news. With the ambulance carrying Eva gone, the last of the media and lingering onlookers drifted away too.

Or so he thought. Suddenly, Gar was forced to answer a policeman's questions about Eva. He denied knowing her and claimed ignorance about who she was or what she was doing at the plaza. The officer let him go and he wasted no time leaving the plaza area, brushing off an interview request by a lingering reporter.

He walked to the far end of *Calle Olvera* for a last look at where Eva had been shot. Fewer tourists occupied the street now. One or two gawkers were climbing on the bandstand, though for the most part a quiet had settled over the place. Gar shuddered at his flashback of the shooting. It didn't make sense or even seem possible that he could have been a target. Yet, he'd been scant inches from the Consul's head.

With wobbly legs, Gar retreated in sadness to the pickup. I must look like a mess, he thought, as people stepped aside to avoid him. He still wore the blood-spattered jacket so as to cover the pistol, and made only a halfhearted attempt to wipe the blood from his face.

He leaned against the pickup and vomited. He stood there trembling for a few minutes before climbing in. Unable to drive away, Gar sat at the steering wheel, staring vacantly through the windshield. He couldn't shake the image of Salinas's head exploding.

Gradually, other thoughts crowded into Gar's mind. Had the actual shooter been caught? Who was the shooter? Someone else had beaten him to Salinas. Justice was served, and even though it was done without his intervention, Gar appreciated the satisfaction of knowing that his was the last face Salinas saw. Unfortunately, something terrible had happened to Eva. And there was no getting the image of her angry stare out of his mind.

48

Gar returned to an empty house. For the moment at least, he was grateful not to recount to Esteban what he'd been through at the plaza. What he couldn't avoid was his mind replaying the awful events that took place there.

A long, steaming shower washed away the blood but not the memory of what it represented. A change into clean clothes helped clear his head. How would he explain himself to Eva, make things right with her? And then there was Hernán. Gar would give as little detail as possible about his actions at the *placita*.

He dialed the Gárza's number late that afternoon. No one answered. Hank Towers would also have to be told what had happened to Eva. Hank had not yet returned to his production office, but news of Eva's shooting had reached it. A shaken secretary told Gar what he already knew.

"Did you hear?" she asked, breathless. "Ms. Muñoz and a man were shot at the *placita*. Ms. Muñoz is in the hospital, but the man died right there. Can you imagine? I'll tell Mr. Torres you called. Where can he reach you?"

Gar gave the number and hung up.

Later, he dialed the Gárza's number again. There was still no answer. He sat staring out of the kitchen window, sorting through his changed circumstances. After a time, he tried the number again. Aurélia finally answered.

"I'm so glad you called," she said. "Hernán has been taken into custody."

"What! Because of me?"

"For what I've feared about for years—those artifacts of

his. The L.A. police and the FBI are involved, I think."

"Is there anything I can do?"

"Thank you. Hank Towers has one of his people representing Hernán. He should be released by tonight."

"I'm glad of that. How did they find out about his collection?"

"He wasn't taken in for his collection, but for his association with an antiquities dealer. There was a shooting at the plaza. Have you heard about it?"

"Yes, that's why I was calling. Eva and I were there. She was struck by a stray bullet and taken to the hospital. The injury is serious but not life-threatening."

"My goodness. The poor girl. Which hospital?"

"She's at Good Samaritan on Wilshire Boulevard."

"I'll call to see when I can visit her. I must tell you that the man in police custody is the same one who used to come here to sell Hernán antiquities."

"That must also have been a shock. Have the police given a motive?"

"I haven't heard about one. We were watching the celebration on TV and saw the Mexican Consul get shot. Apparently, the police caught the killer right away. But until we heard about it—and please forgive us—Hernán believed you had shot him. We owe you an apology."

"No apology needed. Let me give you a phone number where you can reach me. I want to talk with Don Hernán when he's available." As he spoke, the image of Eva lying on the pavement reared to mind again.

"I appreciate your concern," she said. "I'll let him know. And thank you for telling me about Eva."

Hernán got arrested? Gar recalled the times he'd questioned the legitimacy of the attorney's collection. Now he wondered if Hernán's careful documentation would be sufficient to keep him out of jail.

With his lover injured and alienated and his mentor and employer in custody, Gar felt completely adrift. The Consul was dead and no longer a threat, but Gar still needed help. The phone rang.

"Gar, it's Hank Towers."

"Thanks for calling. I'm sitting here stunned about Eva and I've just learned about Don Hernán."

"It has not been a good day."

With some trepidation Gar asked, "Have you gotten a report on Eva's condition? How serious is Don Hernán's situation?"

"Eva is resting comfortably, but her left arm will be in a cast and sling for at least six weeks and she'll have to go through physical therapy. As for Hernán, it's too soon to tell, but he'll get our best legal representation."

"I feel terrible about not being able to accompany Eva to the hospital."

"I understand. You can visit her in a day or two." After a pause, Hank continued, "I'm calling because Hernán was concerned about your return to Mexico. You'll be thinking about that now, will you not?"

"Yes, I will."

"Getting you squared away with immigration is better done sooner rather than later. I'll have someone at the office in the morning to help you out. Do you need directions?"

Hoping to speak to Eva, Gar called the number at the Good Samaritan Hospital. The depth of her anger was only too clear, however, when a nurse informed him that Eva had requested that his calls not be put through.

The next morning, Gar sat reading the *Times*. The front page depicted someone named Barney Spokes, Salinas's alleged killer. Gar nearly dropped his coffee cup: This Barney Spokes was the same man who had pestered him on Olvera Street. "*Chingow!*" he blurted, then read the article outlining the motive: Spokes sought revenge on Salinas for reducing his take on antiquities deals. "Revenge? We were both there for the same reason!"

THE LAST CALIFÓRNIO

Hank and Gar met in Hank's office over the weekend. Gar braced himself for an interrogation about why he and Eva had been at the *placita*. Instead, Hank began by confirming what Gar had learned from Aurélia. He barely listened as Hank spelled out Spokes's connection to the Consul.

"It appears that Salinas had a major smuggling operation going on in L.A. He avoided customs inspections here and in Mexico by shipping antiquities in diplomatic pouches."

"Sounds like a foolproof scheme," Gar said.

"You'd think. What went wrong was the usual: No honor among thieves. Barney thought he was Salinas's principal contact on this end. He took all the risk for disposing the loot while receiving what he perceived was a declining share in the profits. The breaking point came when he discovered the Consul was diverting the richer contraband to another dealer. I guess that's when he decided he'd had enough."

"I don't understand Don Hernán's role in all of this."

"That remains to be seen. For now, it seems to be simply guilt by association."

Gar still sensed that Hernán's situation wasn't good.

Hank broke into his thoughts. "Right now, we've got work to do. I'm informed that you must leave the country in two days."

Within days of Salinas's assassination, Gar contacted his newspaper in Mexico City. Through diplomatic channels, the publisher asked that Gar be allowed to remain in Los Angeles to cover the murder and the trafficking of looted pre-Columbian artifacts. Despite the best efforts of the Acting Mexican Consul, U.S. immigration authorities insisted that Gar leave the country and re-enter with proper documentation. He suffered a few anxious moments when it appeared that he might be taken into custody before his departure. Thanks to Hank and the intercession of the Mexican Ambassador, Gar was allowed to leave the country on his own as long as he met Immigration's deadline.

Back in his room at Gisela's house, he tried calling Eva. His call was refused once again. Struggling to control his ire, he drove to the hospital, determined to see her. He only got as far as Reception before being turned away. With his impending departure in mind, he took the only course left. The letter he wrote didn't outline new arguments justifying his actions. Rather, he reminded her about his family obligation and love for her. Maybe being apart for a month or so would allow her see that he had no choice but to carry out what he now believed he had been fated to do.

49

Mexico City

Self-reproach weighed on Gar. Earnest efforts to reclaim the broken strands of his life in the city could not push it aside. He had alienated Eva. Thoughts of trying to get her back were with him in every waking hour.

With the perspective of time and distance, he saw how dangerously obsessed he'd been with taking a vengeance on Salinas. He could only be grateful that events turned out differently, though with their own steep price.

The deaths of people he loved would always overshadow whatever he felt about Mexico City. He'd left less than a year ago, and the return should have been easy. Yet he didn't feel at home. Despite welcoming his return, his colleagues sensed it too. Some even regarded his escape as betrayal. Gar didn't bother wondering whether any of them might have done differently. He would soon leave again.

Gar struggled to find a plausible explanation for his family's deaths and Eva's injury. He'd never accepted the notion that events in one's life happen for a reason. Yet, over the past year, circumstances challenged his beliefs on that.

He remembered his first meeting with Hernán. The old attorney had lightly joked that Gar's father had made a covenant with the devil. At the time, the notion was so preposterous he'd brushed it off. In hindsight, how else could he account for his surviving repeated brushes with death? The illegals he crossed the Rio Grande with, who'd beaten and robbed him, could have easily murdered him. It was Fausto who died when rednecks forced them off the road. He walked away from the Old Pueblo plaza unharmed. Had the Devil exacted his due after all, sparing his life at the cost of losing Eva?

Within the first few days of his return to Mexico City, Gar started working on a cathartic article about Salinas's role in his family's murders. He now understood that because Salinas had needed to realize how much Gar knew and whether he'd left instructions for release of information in the event of his death, Salinas had ordered him captured rather killed.

The phone rang, interrupting Gar's writing and giving him a burst of hope.

"Eva?" The moment vanished with the male voice on the other end.

"Sorry, it's Hernán. Wanted to let you know that I've been cleared of any involvement in the smuggling ring."

"Great! Have you seen or talked to Eva?"

"I have. She's doing very well."

"I'm glad. I've tried to call her repeatedly, first at the hospital and then at her home. I could never connect. I wonder if you'd do me a favor."

"Sure."

"Please tell her I'm trying to reach her, that I'll be back."

"I'm not cut out to play cupid, but I'll do what I can."

"Thanks. I should be back in about a month. I'll let you know when."

With Salinas gone, Gar's editor and publisher were rediscovering their backbones. They let him publish, under his own byline, all the damning information he'd collected. As he'd expected, the piece caused a sensation. This time, there could be no cover-up. A number of Salinas' associates were rounded up and imprisoned.

In the following weeks, Hernán regularly updated Gar.

"Hank's mayoral campaign had gotten off to a good start," Hernán told him. "As for events surrounding the late

Consul's assassination, no blame has been laid on Towers Communications for sponsoring the Independence Day activities."

"Any developments regarding the *rancho*?"

"In a way. The Rollem campaign is in turmoil over the possible theft of the Rancho Santa Anita. After first denying a connection with his ancestor, his people now are trying to shift the focus and play up the idea of a so-called Latino Reconquest as a scare tactic."

"How about the lawsuits?"

"Preliminary hearings will begin within six months, which will be good timing for Hank's campaign."

"I should be back in plenty of time to hear your arguments. Anything else?"

"You bet. Lots of other things are happening here. Some of Esteban's tactics have gone over well, like the sit-ins by working-class Latinos in Beverly Hills and Hollywood. They really shook things up, showing that Latinos have power to use. A number of similar mass demonstrations are scheduled for the coming spring, complete with banners and performances by a variety of celebrities."

After three weeks of work, Gar's preparations for his return to L.A. forced his mind beyond Eva. He focused on what might await him in *el norte*. Absent any threat to life or freedom, he imagined the return trip would be anti-climactic. A new passport and visa, together with his press credentials, would give him entrée as correspondent for *El Observador Diario*. The city's concentration of Latinos, mostly of Mexican origin and many of them able to vote in Mexico's elections, made Los Angeles important; his role as a correspondent there was essential for the newspaper. Of course, participating in Hank Tower's mayoral campaign would be out. Having been on the inside of his cabal would nevertheless make Gar's reporting on it more insightful and interesting for his readers.

Gar had no idea whether Fausto's death would ever resurface or be tied to him, so he did his best to forget it.

"Good thing you're leaving town." Gar's editor had called. "Even though some of Salinas's associates have been captured, others may be out gunning for you."

"Thanks for the warning. My new passport arrived two days ago. My flight leaves later today."

"What time should I send a car for you?"

Cleared for takeoff, the plane trundled down the runway, picked up speed, and climbed into the overcast sky. Gar sighed as he watched Mexico City disappear below the smog. He wondered when he'd be back—he still had real estate and other interests there that would eventually need attention.

Gazing out of the plane's window, Gar realized he was trading one perennial blanket of gray-brown hydrocarbon for another. What mattered to him now was winning back Eva and the Rancho Santa Anita. Even if the civil suits failed, he'd at the least have made a good-faith try to reclaim it, meeting an obligation to his ancestors.

Gar could only guess where his return to California would lead. Life had been rather ordinary before his family was gunned down. Ironically, their deaths opened a world that would otherwise have remained unknown to him.

The uncertainties his ancestors faced in California were far greater than his own. Even with their world crumbling around them, Enriqueta had done her best to hold onto the land and charged her descendents with reclaiming it. That knowledge made Gar's belief that his ancestors had wanted him to reclaim the Rancho Santa Anita stronger than ever. He didn't believe in a supernatural ordering of events. Yet he couldn't shake wondering whether his coming to California was more than coincidence. That his ancestors had opted to become American citizens loomed large for him. Becoming one himself would be his personal reconquest. As the last in the family line, he was the sole person capable of carrying on the Montalvo saga.

The aircraft began its descent, and Gar pondered what awaited him upon landing. He'd asked Hernán to intercede for him with Eva, but he'd never gotten an explicit agreement that he'd do so. He could only hope that Eva would be there to meet him at the airport.

Hernán greeted Gar at the international arrivals gate. He mentioned nothing about Eva.

"Welcome back!" he said. "Began to wonder if the narcos would let you leave the country." He wasn't joking.

"So did my editor," Gar said. "Thanks for meeting me. I'm glad to be back."

"Go get your luggage and meet me outside at the taxi line."

As he walked to the baggage claim, Gar searched the forms and faces of the women he passed and saw no sign of the one he longed for. Then, as he left the terminal, his heart skipped. Was that Eva with her back to him, waiting at the taxi line? It had to be. How many women were likely to be at this airport with a left arm in a sling?